FORSYTHIA'S RIDE

Matt Fitzpatrick

Forsythia's Ride Copyright © 2023
by Matt Fitzpatrick

Ordering Information:
Special discounts available for **book clubs, corporations,
associations,** and others.
For details, contact the publisher at director@vanvelzerpress.com.

The characters and events in this book are fictitious. Any similarity to real
persons, living or dead, is coincidental and not intended by the author.

Cover by Mibilart

Paperback ISBN: 9 7 8 - 1 - 9 5 4 2 5 3 - 4 5 - 2
Hardback ISBN: 9 7 8 - 1 - 9 5 4 2 5 3 - 4 7 - 6
eBook ISBN: 9 7 8 - 1 - 9 5 4 2 5 3 - 4 8 - 3
Audio Book ISBN: 9 7 8 - 1 - 9 5 4 2 5 3 - 4 9 - 0

Library of Congress Control Number Available from Publisher
Printed in the United States of America
FSC-certified paper when possible

Van Velzer Press
Central Vermont
director@vanvelzerpress.com

VanVelzerPress.com

Where I live,
there's a lady who walks everywhere on her hands...
Doesn't trust where her feet want to take her.
- Tanya Donelly, *Judas My Heart*

Despite all this talk about imagination,
we are implacably real.
- Peter Straub, *Ghost Story*

For Jennifer.

The author of my Chapter Two...

Shadows of the Cape

Excerpt from the Cape Cod Times, July 18, 2020

Soaking in the beauty of the Cape while watching the sunset over Old Silver Beach, it is hard to think about this place as anything but a quiet, picturesque summer escape. But nestled among the hydrangeas and cranberry bogs, more than 50 nuclear weapons once sat ready, their operators waiting for the end of the world.

As we mark the 75th year of the nuclear age, it's worth reflecting on Cape Cod's nuclear history in a world still rife with nuclear dangers. As the Cold War was gaining speed in the early 1960s, concerns of nuclear attacks by the Soviet Union grew by the day. Bunkers and fallout shelters popped up around the country, and President John F. Kennedy's frequent visits to the Cape meant one was needed in the area, just in case.

At the time, there were missiles on the Cape designed to ensure a nuclear weapon didn't come close. In late 1957, the Air Force located a Boeing and Michigan Aeronautical Research Center (BOMARC) missile site at Otis Air Force Base, one of eight, designed to fend off a potential Pearl Harbor-type attack on the East Coast. The site had 56 nuclear-capable missiles that could be in the air within 30 seconds of a launch order and strike a Soviet nuclear bomber 400 miles offshore.

It's unclear how many ordinary residents knew that some of the most destructive devices ever created were sitting just a few miles from their favorite beach spots.

This lack of nuclear knowledge is not solely a Cape Cod problem. Nationwide, nuclear education is lacking. Most people do not know the United States government conduced 1,032 nuclear tests that sickened and killed thousands of people around the world. It is not general knowledge that the United States and Russia still possess more than 90% of the world's remaining nuclear weapons — about 6,000 each.

Seventy-five years after the United States dropped atomic bombs on Hiroshima and Nagasaki, it's easy to feel far removed from the nuclear threat. The bombs have gone from our sandy shores and the threat of nuclear war seems distant and antiquated.

72nd Street, Upper West Side Manhattan (present day)

SPLAT!!

Forsythia's vomit erupted across her neighbor's door. "Valerie!" she yelled smearing yellow bile off of her chin. "L-lemmee in... Jus' lemmee..." Fory's arms flailed two right hooks at the steel door while yearning for her neighbor to fix her. She knew she'd crushed two knuckles and wondered if she'd broken her hand. She decided there wasn't enough pain to worry about.

Fory's poison was not in the form of leaning over a mirror or tapping a syringe. Rather, she needed a shot of rum, and needed it fast, lest her next seizure was to be right in the archway of Val's Upper West Side condo.

The door swung open. A very pissed off Val commandeered the archway. Her poodle, Copper, barked uncontrollably as a show of protection at the inconvenient visit.

"Shit! Are you friggin' kidding me, Fory? It's three in the morning," said Val as she ripped fingers through tightly curled black hair. "Go home and dry out! You just turned thirty-five for chrissake, and you're still pulling this high school shit!?"

Forsythia established one knee and stood herself up to where she was six inches from her friend and confidante. Val just rolled her eyes. The ever patient friend was not surprised at this binge.

"Val, I just *need*," Fory paused to spit a maroon stream onto the left side of the door, but quickly returned to meet Val's eyes with a deep breath, "I just need somewhere to sleep. But, a knock first."

Fory looked sheepishly up at her neighbor and best friend in the Big Apple. Val was a successful bond trader by day and served on two Manhattan philanthropic boards in her spare time. She admired Val's accomplishments and tenacity. Moreover, while Val was six years Fory's senior, her soft, ebony skin radiated that of a much younger woman. Fory thought that while it would be great to look twenty- four again, she more wished that one day she could actually *feel* younger again. The addiction was already writing the first chapter of a sad autobiography across her face.

Val shook her head in mild disgust. "Fory, you live next door! Go sleep in your *own* bed. If you stay here, I'll end up waking to your cranky, hung-over bullshit. You're gonna puke all morning. Get in your own bed. Maybe you'll get lucky and pass out for a few hours."

Fory shook her head. "No, Val. I canna be alone. Tonight could be the night. This could be the night."

"Damn you, girl. D' hell you talkin' about?" asked Val.

"I'm just... nervous," whispered Fory.

"Among other things," quipped Val as she reluctantly resigned herself to the fact she was going to have a guest for the few hours left in the night.

While at first glance Fory appeared to be a laid back Manhattan desk jockey, privately she lived in a constant state of anxiety. She chocked it up to genetics, but the daily alcohol or weekly withdrawal side effects didn't help.

Out of fatigue, she shifted her weight to her other leg. "Val, I stole the old man's briefcase," said Fory. "Old man Pratt. My boss."

"Who?! What?! You took his *what?!*" said a jaw-dropped Val while rubbing sleepy eyes. "Girl, have you lost your friggin' mind?! Do they know?"

Forsythia answered with a bile-filled wretch this time to the right side of the doorway. She paused to wipe her mouth of bubbled saliva, then rubbed her forehead and chest to regain composure. She waggled an expensive, maroon leather briefcase in her right hand.

"I don't think they'll suspect me Val, but I can't be sure. As of now, I'm pretty confident my footprints are covered."

Val exhaled loudly. "Why in the hell would you let your bony white ass do something so dumb? I mean, just plain, WHY!?"

Fory rubbed her runny nose on her starboard sleeve. "I dunno, Val...I guess for just a few minutes, I wanted to feel important. Be in control of shit, especially my life. The one in command. Ya know, hold the strings for once."

Val rubbed her temple. "Come in, you dope. I'll snag you a pillow. Take the guest bedroom, but please try to make the bathroom when you're gonna puke."

Fory craved a little sleep before she had to face another one of the city's misleading sunrises. Sleep over puking was her hope.

"Next time you'll feel in command will be at an AA meeting," Val said as she turned to go back into the apartment.

Fory was able to stumble a few feet into Val's foyer, only to fall face-first into a shaggy throw carpet. She popped her head up and wiped her face. "Val, they'll kill me. Eventually, they're gonna find and kill me," said Fory as her withdrawal anxiety set up camp. *I know I gotta dry out, I just don't want to wake up with Val forcing me to do it now.*

"For-syth-ia! You idiot! You stole your boss' briefcase! Better yet, *you're* gonna kill yourself if you keep on drinkin' like this!" Val shook her again. "Well, are you going to at least open it?"

"No, Val. It's got some locking mechanism on the buckling straps. For all I know, if I fiddle with it, the damn thing might blow up half the building. It looks old fashioned but the buckles are locked."

While part of Val wanted to toss Forsythia over the fire escape, she maintained some semblance of pity. "Girl, what in God's name made you steal someone's briefcase? I mean, this is ridiculous. If you're fired you'll get evicted, jobs aren't poppin' right now."

Fory was quiet for a few seconds, then responded, "I wanted to know his world. I wanted to know what it was like to be in charge." Fory paused and dropped her head. "Plus, I know he always has a bottle with him."

Val shook her head as she blew a string of curls out of her eyes.

"Fory, you're a smart girl. *Too* damn smart is the problem. I think you are done there because there is no way you can get that back before everyone shows to work. You better not go back to that office, and you should really get outta Dodge. And fast."

Forsythia sat up and twisted a temporary curl in her thin, light brown hair. "Val, where the hell am I gonna go? I know you're right and I gotta get outta here. Shit, I'll be arrested or friggin worse within hours of them finding out."

Val sat in a high top Heppelwhite chair while she watched her neighbor curl around the floor and contemplate the future. As she crossed her legs, the silk of her pajamas slid with a luxurious sound. "Fory, you got any family? Ya know, someone *not* in Manhattan?"

Forsythia paused to dry heave in a small wasp-hemp waste basket next to an old desk where her friend kept incoming mail. "N-no, Val. You know, my dad committed suicide years ago. I was with him, for crissakes!"

Val stared at her neighbor, seeing further into Fory's pain. "You were a kid?" *Why did she never tell me this? No wonder she drinks like a fish.*

"Mom and Dad are long gone. I'm an only child," continued Fory. "So, I don't have any siblings to turn to. Most of my distant relatives have disowned me or written me off as a high-maintenance drunk after some poor performances at weddings and family events. I gotta few bucks, but not enough to get lost for enough time." Fory used a back hand to wipe her mouth, she was at that point of extreme intoxication where she was speaking perfectly but her mouth was getting drier. "Hey, I *do* have an aunt up on Cape Cod. Dad's older sister. She's old, though. And crazy."

"How old?" asked Val. "And more importantly, what do you mean by crazy*?*"

Fory sat up straighter, legs crossed on the rug. "I dunno. Guess she's gotta be in her eighties. Whatever. But she's nuts. Ya know. A recluse. Eccentric. Yells at everyone, when she even speaks at all."

"Does she share your last name?" asked Val.

"Yeah... a Shea. Irish as soda bread." Fory paused, trying to focus in her alcohol-induced haze, then said, "You know what, though? She's a cuckoo clock, but she's helped me here and there over the years. I think she genuinely loved my dad, and kinda doted on me in her own crusty way. She's got a lot of connections somehow. And like any old Irish clan, there's folklore and bullshit strewn about everyone."

"That's the way in every family, I suppose," replied Val with a smirk. *God if you only knew how my sister lives.* "Well, maybe that's a good thing? I ask because while your name isn't common, they could still find you."

Fory waved her wrist at the air. "No way. They could never find me at her place. My aunt lives like a troll. Nobody around."

"What town?" Val asked through a yawn.

"Chatham," responded Fory. "Nothing there but sharks and New York license plates. Actually the one who got me the job at the sucky firm I work at, well used to until today, was her! Weird, cause she never seemed to have any British friends, and my firm is owned by a bunch of English aristocrat types. My boss is even a Sir! Friggin' knighted I think? Like Paul McCartney."

Feeling more like her normal self, since the nausea had passed for a moment, Fory stood up and continued while making her way slowly toward the guestroom. "Anyway, I guess it wasn't exactly her who got me the job, but rather her financial advisor who works in some sky tower downtown. High roller type. Hessian Kerr is his name. Irish, but beyond anything they used to call *lace curtain Micks* back in the day. Drives his Maserati five hours up to see her once a month."

Val nodded, "She must have a big ass account."

"Family lore is that Aunt Mary was involved with the IRA. Do you know who they are?"

"Only from the news," responded Val. "Seems like they raised a lotta hell over the years, but kinda quiet now. I dunno much."

"I don't either." Fory started to nod, then held her head still as she finished the thought. "Apparently my Aunt Mary, in her younger years, spent a lot of time in Ireland and was knee-deep in the cause during *The Troubles.* I heard when she was over there, she became tight with Dolours Price."

"Who's Dolores Price?" asked Val.

"No, it's pronounced and spelled *Dolours*," replied Fory. "She was a bad-ass IRA rebel with the Provisional IRA, which was a spin off crew from the original IRA. The IRA has more damned chapters than the Bible."

Val nodded in trying to understand her friend's unorthodox family history.

"Anyway," Fory continued, "Dolours's a legend, and was violent. Very violent. But from what I hear, she adored my aunt. Anyway, people think the IRA is like one happy, unified group, but they were far from it."

Val leaned in closer. A word she heard finally crystallizing in her sleepy brain. "Whaddya mean by bad-ass?" she asked.

"Well, when Margaret Thatcher pardoned her from prison after a long hunger strike," explained Fory, "not long after her release, Dolours found out which hotel the Prime Minister was staying at. She set off a bomb and tried to blow the joint up. Thatcher walked away, but people got hurt. That's pieced together from stories growin up."

Val chuckled. "Yeah, I'd call that bad-ass. Helluva way to show gratitude."

"The IRA is actually, or at least *was*, made up of a buncha different factions. Each had their own agendas, philosophies, varying levels of aggressiveness and violence, etcetera." Fory leaned back and rubbed the back of her neck which was starting to throb from the day's various trips and falls. "Anyway, overall it sounded like a friggin' mess. And my poor dad got wrapped up in some of it. At least the leftover from the really bad shit during *The Troubles.*"

Val leaned back with a full body stretch. "Well Fory, for someone who claims to know very little about that whole thing, it sounds like you got an education just growing up as a Shea."

"Yeah, I s'pose," replied Fory. "But the old war stores were mostly about Mary. I'll never be clear on how much my dad was involved." Fory paused as acid was jumping up and down in her esophagus. She sucked in a deep gasp to tame the fire. "Anyway, my aunt is a loon." Fory was starting to feel sick again and was tired of the subject. *Time to wrap this up and hit the sheets.* "But she did at least help me snag a job when I decided I wanted move to this Godforsaken city. Like every other sucker who steps off a train at Grand Central with a suitcase, I was going to star in plays on Broadway as my stepping stone to Hollywood…"

Val remained quiet while Fory was clearly in thought for several seconds until she looked up at her neighbor. Fory's sad voice stabbed Val in the heart when Forsythia said, "Dreaming is slow suicide."

Val breathed deeply three or four times until she finally thought, *Fuck it.* She walked over to her mini bar, grabbed two thick, short glasses and poured two shots of Bacardi Limon. She handed one to Forsythia. "Here. Drink this," coached Val. "You'll feel better. If you wretch up right away, bang another stat and that one will stay down. I know from experience how this works."

The two women returned to the living room and drank, and immediately felt warm. Within two minutes, Forsythia's shakes subsided.

Val looked at her friend, while savoring the initial glow of the rum. "Well, you might want to call the old lady then grab a bus. While I don't like finding you puking on my door at three am, I definitely don't want to find you out back in the dumpster at seven."

Fory sat back and leaned on semi-toned, outstretched arms. "Me neither." She tilted her head to the side in thought. "Me neither... Although, maybe that's where I belong? In a damned trash truck, or they can drag me outta the Hudson. Might be easier that way?"

Val took a second shot of rum, not offering a second to her guest. "Nah, Fory," said Val relishing the second bloom of warmth, "the world is way more interesting with you in it. Plus, who the hell is going to let me drink with them pre-dawn? That's a luxury for me. Usually, any interruption in my sleep is some jerk-off that's looking for morning sex."

Forsythia laughed. "Yeah, they do love it in the morning, don't they?" she asked with a bittersweet memory. "I miss those days."

Winslow & Pratt, Ltd.
Wall Street (earlier that night)

"Oh... man..." Fory whispered a groan as she rolled over after what seemed like an endless slumber. She stretched as if she were crawling out of a crypt.

"Shit!" she hissed to herself sitting up and smacking her forehead on what not only served as her office cubicle, but also her chamber for the night. She cursed herself for passing out while working late, again. Like any seasoned alcoholic, she bargained with herself that because she was putting in overtime, she earned the right to invade her purse to find the liter of Bacardí Limón. Hell, everyone else fled the office at 4:59 in order to get home to their unhappy marriages, Augusta-manicured lawns and petulant kids. Forsythia equated southwest Connecticut to Purgatory.

Fory's hazy thoughts day-dreamed back on the previous evening's supposed romantic dinner date that didn't go as planned...

Forsythia freed that tight, little black dress from the confines of her closet. The garment had hung dormant for too long. She felt love for Sid Victorelli. At least as much love as Forsythia could conjure up. She thought to herself: This is the night to save our love. A night of rekindling. A night when passion tossed its shackles and we dive in the deep end.

"Fory, ready to go?" asked Sid.

"Yes, and I have our little friend."

This was to be a night of naughtiness. A night of spice normally known to lovers their junior.

As they entered the cozy doorway of Andiamo Bistro, Fory turned to Sid. "Sweetie, will you get us a table? I need to go to the little girls' room," said Fory as she pressed the small device into Sid's hand.

The two lovers shared a smile. The remote was only half of the apparatus that Fory thought might re-fire the relationship. The remote vibrating device was for the couple to share moments of bawdy chuckles as they were served dinner.

Menus were presented and drinks were ordered. Fory always made sure drinks were ordered before any other business was conducted.

"This will be fun," said a flirtatious Fory. "We're so bad." With Sid having the control button in his hand and Fory hosting the receiving end of the x-rated apparatus, this was sure to be an unorthodox dinner.

The waitress returned with a bottle of Sam Adams for Sid, while Fory greeted her Mojito with the eagerness of a birthday gift. The lovers toasted. To what, they were not sure.

Buzz...

"Oh!" popped Fory. "I see you're trying it out, sweetie." She was excited. The remote vibrating device proved effective.

"Yeah," said Sid. "This could be fun."

BUZZ!

"OH!" exclaimed Fory with a subdued scream. "WHAT are you doing?" Her pleasure center just traded that sensation for pain.

"Honey, I just turned up the volume on this little baby," said an elated Sid. "Remember Spinal Tap? This one goes to eleven!"

Fory had to admit that, at first, the naughtiness was exciting and she found the vibrations tantalizing. But after the next buzz set at eleven, Fory yelled, startling other patrons. "OW! Sid, for chrissakes! What are you..."

"C'mon, buttercup. You love this. I think it goes even higher on the dial..."

"NO!"

BUZZZ!

Fory remembered waking up in the ER at Bellevue Hospital with the on-call physician saying, "Miss, you're showing symptoms of mild electrocution..."

Shaking her head, Fory crawled out from the confines of her desk and rubbed out the wrinkles in her clothes. She then noticed the red display on her clock: 3:45am. "Damn..." she said to herself performing a reptilian slide into her chair and firing up her computer.

Forsythia's Ride

That's when she suddenly heard the crumble of thick paper. Her neck hairs sought the ceiling.

Fory stood; slowly pushing her chair aside and hid behind the cubicle wall. After several seconds, she lifted her head. Roughly thirty feet away, Sir William Pratt was shuffling papers in his corner office. She found it remarkable that he looked so put together at almost four in the morning. She wondered if it was a late night or an early start for the aging mogul.

The remnants of a haze from the previous night left her with the adrenaline rush of fear. She remained quiet as a spider watching her boss' demeanor change from concentration to frustration.

Pratt slammed the last few papers on his desk and grabbed his suit jacket to wrap around his corpulent frame. He kicked his chair.

As her boss rummaged through his desk and grabbed keys, Fory wondered if he was just going down to his car to get something he forgot. However, the grabbing of his anachronistic hat confirmed he would most likely be gone for a while. This was good news to Fory, who desperately wanted to remain in the weeds: hidden, safe. *The last thing I need is to have a slurred conversation with this stuck up bastard.*

Fory was curious *and* still buzzed from the previous night's alcohol, which for her, was historically a bad combination. Being an observant creature, she noticed Pratt didn't lock his office door after he slammed it shut. As Fory listened for any sounds in the office, she shifted the weight of her toned body. Despite her lifestyle, she was in solid shape. Still, being stuck under a cubicle desk for so long would stiffen even the greatest athlete. She stood up and looked around the room. It was mostly dark except for the glow of computer screen savers. In theory, the floor should remain tranquil for another three hours.

Plenty of time for Fory to slake her thirst for curiosity. For the past few weeks, she'd noticed that old man Pratt, who she considered smug and arrogant, as well as the other senior partners, appeared to be on edge. While the senior partners in the firm were never friendly or calm, recently there was something in the air that Fory felt she could grab and rip open. The fact that Pratt was British and was knighted no less, made her resent the man in the corner office even more. She still carried the weight of the historical Irish chip on her shoulder. She was taught growing up that people like Pratt's ancestors would chase hers through the bogs and peat moss carrying torches while instructing hounds.

Since she was a little girl, Forsythia loved the thrill of temptation and curiosity. It wasn't that the actual things which she uncovered were particularly interesting; it was the electric-charge of the constant danger of getting caught and the thrill of victory when an operation was pulled off, that got her blood flowing.

Fory's mom made sure the family's social calendar was always stocked throughout the summer season. She never worked, so the New Hampshire winters were long and lonely. When the weather turned each spring, Fory's mom would immediately get out the date book and begin planning various events. She especially adored summer parties on the sprawling lawns of Rye Beach. On paper at least, and to the neighbors, Fory's dad was a successful banker who was constantly off on work assignments.

Paul Shea had little interest in their summer garden parties, his wife's summer friends, or even his wife, for that matter. Instead, his thoughts always seemed preoccupied with people and places far away. He tolerated it though; it gave the mother of their only child something to do so that her whining ended after Memorial Day once a few outings had been planned.

Fory loved the parties her mom hosted because the adults were preoccupied outside on the lawn which allowed the young girl full access to parts of the house that were normally off-limits. The forbidden destination in the large home, her parents' vast, walk-in closet, was her favorite target. She liked to sift through the long array of drawers and shelves that sat under rows of dresses, blouses, jackets. Over time those drawers had uncovered certain items of interest like handcuffs, toys and various lotions. She had no idea what all that stuff was or what it was for, only that she knew her mom would not be pleased if Fory found such items.

Forsythia's Ride

The only hidden treasures not yet discovered by the curious child lay in the drawers of her mother's makeup table which was at the very far end of the closet. During one especially raucous soirée, with most of the guests dancing and drinking to excess, Fory tip-toed to their bedroom. Even with the windows closed, Fory could hear the sounds of laughter, music and overall merriment. This was her opportunity to explore uncharted territory! She crept across the carpet and sat on a satin padded antique chair. It had a dark pink color with ornate white carvings that, to Fory, made it look old and something a queen might have in her castle.

She pulled at the handle of the first drawer; it opened without a squeak. In it she found trays and boxes full of earrings, pendants, bracelets and other types of jewelry. The young girl made plans to come back to play princess with all these sparkling jewels. She would be a damsel and there would be a dashing suitor to dance with her. That might be the next summer party, for this day she had to finish her exploration. Each drawer held much of the same. Over the years, her mother became obsessed with accumulating accessories that she felt would accentuate her sense of forever.

One drawer left. Little Fory paused before opening it because she thought she might have heard a creaking sound. She turned around only to see Punches, the family bulldog. Fory's dad thought the real boxer shared a face with the animal, hence the name.

Fory noticed a small box speckled with sapphires, it was stunning. A piece that should belong in a museum. She picked up the trinket and admired the disco-ball-like glitter in the natural light which bounced off the combination of gold and dark blue stones. She picked at the small clasp eager to uncover its contents. Due to always being a nervous child, Fory had no nails because she constantly bit them down thus making it difficult to open the piece.

Finally the clasp popped and something small fell onto the carpet. It was a picture. Fory was surprised to see her father in what looked like some kind of shoddy war uniform. Face blackened with soot, his left eye exuded the a violent color and there was a wound on one shoulder.

Back in her office, Fory snapped out of the daydream of childhood exploration and returned to the matter at hand. It was now almost 4:15am; there was no sign of Pratt or anyone else in the office. Not unlike when she was a child, Fory could not resist the temptation to nose around. She pushed open the door and gazed upon a universe of papers, folders, pictures and awards. *It must be nice to be a knight.*

She crawled around toward the old man's chair in order to get a look at what he was grousing at when he stormed out of the office. It was a hurricane of papers. She didn't know which pile to sniff around first. She looked at the first few papers closest to the front of the desk.

"...and be damned them, do they realize who they're..."

Shit! Fory heard the voice and the whirl of the elevator as its doors closed. Two people had just gotten off and were talking in the hallway.

She had to bolt. Now!

In the slightest second of time, with thoughtless movement, she grabbed a leather burgundy briefcase that was under the old man's desk. She snagged it out of instinct, stood up, and ran to the back stairs located in the far end of the office. That exit was designed as an extrication avenue during a fire. For the moment, what she held in her hand may as well have been doused in gasoline, so it was an appropriate escape route for her.

It wasn't until she was halfway down the stairs that she felt a wave of nausea. She stumbled and almost took a tumble, but grabbed the rail to her right and realized that she not only had to get out of here quick, but needed to bang on Val's door as her only safe haven.

Vomit shot across the hall strong enough to take out an eye during a prize fight. Late round.

Fory felt that she had just danced in the ring with Tyson.

Chatham, Cape Cod
Spring (Present Day)

A bridge of moonlight.

Bassing Harbor traded spit with the Atlantic Ocean every six hours. Silver shimmers masoned the steps. The bright path was accented with a peppering of a few boat moorings and diving ducks.

The stars whispered to five-year-old Vicki McAree. Even with the cloud's drape, a path was lit by moonlight. As she gazed out her bedroom window, she felt the invitation.

Vicki tossed her sheets, barrel-rolled out of bed, and was suddenly confused. She came fully awake with a stir. Her dreams were usually full of princesses and promises of candy. Tonight's were more unsettling. She opened her closet and fumbled the hangers in search of her soft, cloth robe. The night spoke to her in cautious tones.

The bedroom door creaked as she entered the hallway. Just feet away, her parents slept and dreamed of her wedding day. The stairs to the first floor also spoke in protest as the aged-dried wood squeaked in pain. The noise of the back door was not a concern. In her young mind, she reasoned that she had made it past her parents' bedroom, so nothing she did would wake them.

The moon bridge... spit light...

A silver print on the sky. Each sparkle invited a step, and Vicki wanted to cross. Nothing could keep her from the other side.

While the night was warm, the sand felt cool. It was comforting on little feet; reminding Vicki of the times enjoyed with pails and shovels. She loved chasing crabs and tasting salt. So many hours on the beach that the touch of the sand was comforting.

She walked down the long beach that was off limits to strangers. Here was a place of safety. Her place of solitude, where protection was provided.

Matt Fitzpatrick

With the tide at low, there was a small trickle of lazy water Vicki had to cross in order to get to Fox Hill. That was the island behind Vicki's house which, in her little mind, served as the gateway to the magical moon bridge just beyond the island. Beams of light banged off ocean ripples, jewels on the water tips. Vicki didn't want to cross the bridge without her favorite companion. She decided to stop by her fort in order to find this friend to bring along.

Vicki walked fifty yards along the beach to her hideaway that was only known to her and the creatures who found it convenient to call home, especially during bad weather. Some not so friendly, like the coyotes, but for now, all was quiet.

She wrestled with thick bay brush and growth which kept secrets safe for over a hundred years.

She opened the heavy old door only to be blown back with a quick wind of damp stink. She entered and felt comfort among the odd, cold contents inside. The moist air tasted metallic.

Human bones never frightened her. She looked upon them as her friends. Older people who loved her, but who had moved on, and who now were the caretakers of her private oasis. When Vicki lost her grandfather, who she adored, in her head his bones now lay in her fort to protect her as he always promised while alive.

During his life, he never got to visit the private beaches in Chatham. He only got to visit the ones in France in June 1944.

Vicki pressed her palm against the bunker's dark grey walls. They were thick, cold and weaved together with concrete and wood. When it was built during WWI, comfort and aesthetics were not high on the list when drawing up construction plans.

At last, she found what she was looking for. Among a few toys and left behind snacks, Vicki remembered where she'd misplaced her best friend who was crucial to this trip over the bridge. There was no way Vicki was going to try to cross without him.

The worn and matted stuffed animal held an uncanny resemblance to the family's golden retriever, Tak, so she figured that was a good name. She smiled as she hugged him—goofy, friendly and soft.

"C'mon Tak," Vicki whispered out loud, only to have the words stolen by the breeze. "I'm going to take you to somewhere magical."

She gripped/hugged Tak walking down the deserted beach. As she approached the bridge, moonlight encouraged safe passage over the still water. The air was soft; both seagulls and diving ducks had called it a night.

The only sounds were her footfalls on the sand and the scratch of little crunching clam shells under her hardened bare feet.

Vicki tested the water with her right foot. While at first it bit with a slight chill, her skin acclimated quickly, Bassing Harbor boasted mild temperatures during the summer months. It was spring now, the lack of the warming sun kept it cooler than comfortable. Vicki ignored the chill, she focused on the bridge and the fantastic places it would take her.

She walked in up to her knees. The bridge appeared solid and the water extended an invitation. The further she walked, the more the bay opened its arms.

She knew the chill in her feet was unavoidable as she crossed the small tidal creek, but found solace in the warmth of the rocks when she reached the island. They hadn't yet fully cooled from baking in the sun just a few hours earlier.

Ten yards to her right, the surface exploded. A particularly feisty school of bluefish cornered some unlucky herring.

Sand and foam whirled up to her ankles, sucking at her legs, slowing her down. Once the bay found Vicki's waist, she felt the first real chill, but shrugged it off; the bridge held the answer. To Vicki, it radiated silver like a magic alleyway made just for her.

It was only after she realized that the soft sand and silt decided to climb an inch over her belly button that she became concerned. With the enthusiasm that can only be shown by a child, Vicki steadily moved forward.

Although, she could not...

She tried to move her right foot, it felt stuck. Thinking she'd have better luck with her left, she tried to hoist her knee up to the surface. Her knee was unresponsive; her ankle had found a home in the muck.

Matt Fitzpatrick

As the thick silt beckoned for more of her body, she looked at the stars.

She still felt invincible.

The sea would protect her.

She felt something on her leg and figured it was just a pesky crab. Then she realized that her shin had sunken into the gritty silt next to a barnacle encrusted rock.

As the bay invited her to surrender, suddenly she was up to her neck and unable to move. Tak watched with whining concern from the shore.

The tide was ripping in now.

The Cape Cod flow is as steadfast and reliable as a Swiss train.

As the tide began to flood, her last thoughts were not filled with fire-breathing dragons and fear, but of an enchanted princess in a flowing gown, being helped onto her white steed by a dashing prince...

> *"In her sepulcher there by the sea—*
> *In her tomb by the sounding sea."*

Rye Beach, NH seacoast
(20 years ago)

"Honey, can you hand me the line?" said Paul Shea as he slowly rubbed a fillet blade over a swath of steel wool that served as the moment's honing metal. On the North Atlantic, no blade could be too sharp.

"Sure, Dad," said a teen-aged Forsythia. She adored her father, and always loved when they worked on the boat together. She loved his movie-ready captain's voice and his sturdy handling of the vessel.

While Paul Shea was a shitty husband by all normal standards, he adored his daughter. Who Paul Shea didn't love was himself. It was an integrated hatred, like a mole or freckle never to leave unless burned off. His self-hatred stemmed from the regrettable work with his older sister who tended to tow an aggressive line in her business dealings.

It wasn't the aging process or ocean air that etched the lines in Paul's face. It was the violence. The profound waste of it all. Nothing accomplished in the end...

Paul looked around his helm station and thought to himself, *Set the GPS course for Hell. Or, at least a heading toward a long-term tie-up in Purgatory.*

"Honey, can you tighten that line on the port side? It got wet with the rain and she's snakin' out." Paul asked this in a normal voice. As he spoke, he noticed the blade he was working on finally came to life. Paul tilted the knife, it caught a rainbow of reflections off of the sun's rays. Instead of blinding his eyes, it gave him peace. That's when he decided it was time for the first cut.

"Sure, Dad. Will do," responded Forsythia who was so proud to be helping her father. After tightening the line, Fory rubbed her fingers over a bubble of metal. "Dad, thank you for my pretty new locket," she said as her fingers fondled the smooth gold around her neck. "I just think I should take it off while I'm working on the boat. I don't want it falling in the bay."

"Y-yeah, sure, sweetheart. Just put it somewhere safe in your gear bag. It's Italian 18 carat. I don't want you to lose it," said Paul.

"Oh, no, Dad I would never, ever lose it," responded the proud daughter. "I promise to always keep it with me."

"Yeah, I got it from a guy in Palermo who owed from a... Oh, never mind. Dear, when you get a second, toss out that second stern fender."

As she rubbed the locket, she had a thought and yelled toward the helm station, "Hey, Dad! What was that thing you made me sign earlier as your new attorney power thing or something?" Fory asked as she wound up lose line and tried to keep busy and helpful.

"Oh, don't worry about it, it's nothing," responded Paul who suddenly felt a mild panic attack starting. "Just a form. You know, legal stuff you wouldn't understand. You don't wanna... Boring."

Paul examined the tip of the blade. The knife's end again reflected the sun, this time making him wince. Paul took a last look at the tip of the blade. Who would have ever guessed that steel would be the end of his life-long, played out story.

Paul's first cut was to his left wrist...

"Ah!" Paul hissed as quietly as he could. He began to unleash what his body had been storing for far longer than anyone would have anticipated. The blood found gravity; it began to puddle fast...lack of food that day made him light-headed.

"Fory, honey," said Paul while trying not to scream, "my shoes are staring to slog around. I gotta swap 'em out."

"K, Dad," said Fory. Then after a second of further thought said, "Why are you so wet?"

Fory asked lots of questions. Paul was skilled at picking the ones he wanted to answer.

Down below, Paul was out of Fory's line of vision. He yelled up to his daughter on deck, "Oh, it's nothing to worry about honey. I must have bumped up against a fish hook or an old knife. No big deal. The last tetanus shot I got was after an Aerosmith show at the Lynn Manning Bowl." Paul ended that lie with an awkward, nervous laugh due to the pain.

"Very funny," was Fory's quick retort as she returned to tightening the lines.

With his left leg sloshing in his own blood, Paul sliced a 360 degree angle around the circumference of his lower leg—approximately 24 centimeters above his right heel.

He was losing a lot of blood and fast, hemorrhagic shock was setting in. But he was finally, for the first time in his life, ready to lay down his weapons and sleep.

While he accepted death as his whole life bled out before him, he found no solace. There was a fitting cloudy, grey color spreading in his vision as he looked at the stunning blue water.

While most people would think that Paul's choice of suicide within such proximity of his daughter was a cruel, selfish act, the old IRA operative didn't see it that way. In his mind, which had been riddled by chaos for far too long, this was part of Fory's life tuition. The most valuable lesson he could give to her.

Paul inhaled and counted seconds never to be regained.

His blade flicked at the curve in the vein on his neck. The target was covered in thick, sandpaper skin, but when pierced, blood shot out like all hopes finally escaping.

He slammed onto the floor in the cabin, knocking over a fire extinguisher with a loud crash. The calamity brought Fory running.

"Dad!!" she yelled as she awkwardly ran across the slippery deck toward the helm station only to half fall down the cabin stairs.

She saw her father laid out flat. His body's crimson river staining the pristine teak and holly floor. In the final moments, Paul accepted his fate without protest, he knew he had less than two minutes to give Fory his last words to guide her.

Paul Shea was tired...he welcomed rest.

Matt Fitzpatrick

As he bled out, the last sounds on Earth that he heard were the sobs of his daughter and the cries of the seagulls. He thought that wouldn't be the worst sound to be his last.

What Fory's eyes saw brought shock on fast; she started to shake. Speechless, she sat on the steps to the salon. She stared at her father in silence while the shock rendered her unable to emit a sound and set her thoughts into a fog-like slow motion.

Paul's final thoughts floated by like a gale's passing clouds. As the sound volume around him was turned down, he began accepting.

Fory, at eight years old, pirouetting though cold sprinkler water with a bursting smile. Every water droplet and beam of sun radiated happiness and life and the world ahead.

"Honey, honey, stop," said Paul with a slight hand up. "Everything will be fine. I just need you to know that you're strong and I'll always be with you whenever you don't feel so strong. Happens all the time as adults," half-cackled Paul as he fell in and out of consciousness.

Fory was frantic, yet unable to speak or move. She stared while her life and world pooled and joined her father's bloody puddle. Crimson memories and future dreams ran down the vessel's scuppers as both painted the floor.

At the same time the fear was racing through her, she felt slight solace. It was the first time that her dad looked at peace in his whole life.

Time stood still; all of his pain and regret was jettisoned into the mist.

In dreamy slow motion, Fory looked for her cell phone on the main deck. Instead, she found an envelope on top of her dad's pile of nautical charts.

She was still for several seconds, then tore the seam.

It's with love that I write this note. I know that it won't make sense now, but it will over time. I've sinned. You may be asked to wash my sins for me.

Don't.

Forsythia's Ride

Will forever adore and cherish you. In every world you or I ever enter.

I know you can't understand right now, and that is my final regret on a long, still running list.

Love you, Dad

In Irish, the surname Shea means "God is gracious." On his last day, Paul not only rejected any notion of God, but he also had little interest in anyone's grace. Deity or otherwise.

Instead, he forged ahead with his last ultimate dance with narcissism. His final victory with a finger in the air.

Maybe it was a last show of regret or maybe selfishness. But for Paul, it was never about succumbing to one's enemy. For him, it was all about surrendering (or not) to all of the horrors that his too many trips around the sun had unleashed.

The tattered remnants of what had once been Paul Shea stopped moving.

Paul started that day knowing his role in the world had ended once he realized that his past regrets had finally outnumbered his future dreams.

A ratio that few can reverse.

Nor'east Bluffs, Chatham
(6 months ago)

Crack! Ding! Bang!

Lestor D. Hines was sailing into early retirement. After breezing through Stanford and Wharton, he teamed up with one of the sculls from his former West Coast rowing team and started a sector fund which only focused on social media companies, their providers and outsourcers. But, where his real money was now stemming from was his ownership interest in cobalt mines in the Congo. That was a lucrative, smooth sailing, cash cow, except for some pesky labor problems the prior summer when the annoying indentured servants started demanding more of a wage than rice and quinine.

He made a fortune and cashed out with a swelled bank account and a belly to match. At the moment Lester was infuriated as to why the construction next door started prior to eight in the morning. There was a town ordinance, after all. In Chatham, there's a commission that governs breathing.

"Dammit..." he muttered over to his wife of ten years who was used to hearing her husband begin most days by whining. She'd learned how to fake a serene, sleeping pose.

"Those pricks aren't supposed to be going at it this early, unless they're working for me! Then, it's 4am!" Lestor barking was met with silence as he got up and grabbed his robe off the closet door. "Do you know yesterday I had to chase away some little hussy neighbor on our beach! She had the audacity to let her friggin' three year old swim on our property! I know that little brat peed in our water! I'll set 'em straight. I'll be at town hall this morning," he said to his wife now feigning a coma. "But first, I'm going over there and heads will roll!"

"I'll alert the media," mumbled his wife during a fake snore.

Forsythia's Ride

The young retiree stomped down the stairs and without bothering with shoes, or even slippers, threw open the front door and speed-walked over to the neighbor's construction site.

The previous home that stood there for several decades was sold by the original owners and was immediately demolished, which fit in with part of the neighborhood's new zoning code. On this morning, a new structure was in the process of being built to a tune of almost ten figures in design and construction costs, as well as illustrating a life-time's pursuit of excess.

"Hey you!" barked Hines at one of the crew busy cutting boards across two saw horses. "There's an ordinance around here! No construction before eight. I plan on being at town hall in an hour to file a formal complaint. This is ridiculous!"

The worker flipped the off button on his table saw and, with a frustrated exhale, ripped off his plastic safety goggles. "Sir, feel free to go to town hall. Call the cops. Matter of fact, why don't you dig up Jimmy Hoffa?" he said with a contemptuous laugh. "Hell, this ain't union work, so he might take up your cause. Better yet, find a cat and swing it wide by its tail. You just might hit someone who gives a shit."

Lestor heard muted morning cannabis-cackles from the crew as the foreman continued, "We ain't stoppin' work, and it's clear you don't know who's movin' next door to you. She ain't gonna appreciate the interruption."

Lestor stared and shook his head. *She?*

Saw-Man continued, "I'd suggest you go back inside and Amazon some fancy headphones."

Chatam, Cape Cod
(5 months ago)

Roke Mangini never envisioned himself becoming a porch pirate, but during Christmas time in towns like Chatham where yuletide shopping budgets were as high as the real estate assessments, the Fed Ex and UPS boxes piled up on front stoops were begging to be snatched. Many of the parcels sported the familiar logo of Amazon, but others were nondescript, yet still held their curb appeal.

Roke loved Cape Cod. He loved the mini-golf, striper fishing at dawn and the vision of a scoop of vanilla being served by a cute, Ivy Leaguer in volleyball shorts.

Roke butterflied away the images in his head and got back to the business at hand. What he loved the most was to steal. He usually pilfered from the snow birds who were off in Florida each winter hitting the links in plaid shorts and knee-high socks. Christmas time always presented new opportunities as many came back for the holiday and New Year's revelry.

Why pay more? was an advertising tag from a local grocery chain.

Roke's mantra was, *why pay?*

Roke approached the old lady's mailbox. Rust and spider webs had commandeered much of the ornate post, but he had his eyes on the box below. He knew from watching that the old lady would only check her mail in the afternoon after the normal mail guy finished his round on this back road.

He pulled his car over to the side of the two-lane road where old trees that needed trimming would provide some visual cover. With the engine cut, he could still run the radio. He selected *Tom Sawyer*. That song always got him pumped up for a grab, much like Kerry Von Erich before a wrestling match.

Forsythia's Ride

After Neil's drum fills, Roke was satisfied. He quietly shut the car door and approached the driveway. Sleight of hand and a snatch of parcel.

Roke fired up the car and ripped a three-point turn with an elegant swish of his driving arm. He headed back to his trailer in the next town. Such anticipation. *This is going to be a nice little shovelful of pay dirt.*

Once home, he sat on his bed and flipped a few curious roaches away. Although they never really went *away*, he never seemed to give a damn. They were like pets that didn't require shots or grooming.

He grabbed a dull knife that was still half-buttered, and started to slice.

Slice and peel.

Pull away the plastic.

"Damn," he said, which was followed by a resounding, "Holy shit!"

In the midst of the packing papers and stuffing was the most beautiful, brand new BR 18 automatic assault rifle. Made in Singapore, this baby somehow ended up in an old lady's Cape Cod mailbox.

As Roke performed a perusal of the box, he realized that it was not really from Amazon. It was a spurious container that came from who knew where. He wondered why an old Cape crow would be ordering a weapon that delivers 650 rounds per minute.

"Candy from a baby," Mangini chuckled to himself while picturing her stumbling backward if she tried to shoot this thing.

"Madonna with meatballs, this job is getting easier."

O'Leary's Stale Ale Pub
Woods Hole, Cape Cod

"Hey Tommy," said the crusty lobsterman at the end of the bar, "you goin' to Lenny O'Donnell's wake tonight?"

"Nah, man," replied Tommy Reyes, the daytime barkeep. "I hate friggin' wakes. The only guy I'll wanna drink with is always laid out in mahogany," he said as the wiped down the afternoon's spilled bar mess. "Or in the case of my crew, the box is usually made of pine."

Reyes snickered with a couple of other afternoon-wet patrons as he worked the rag. Tommy was half Irish which helped his standing with the guys at the pub, but his paternal genes hailed from Tampico, Mexico. Growing up in the heart of the Gulf Cartel country, he had learned several practical skills. With Tommy's rough Boston looks, he could easily be mistaken for a knuckle-dragging enforcer. But, in Reyes's line of work, his biggest flaw was that he had half a brain. He used it to his advantage, yet never let anyone over him know he was more than a ham & egger.

The bar's old rotary phone burst into life.

"Shut up, ya tossers, I need this call!" yelled Reyes with a wide hand-wave across the bar. He not only tended bar, but more importantly was an associate of Monarch's import/export operation. While Monarch was a mystery, he always paid well on jobs. No call could be missed on the off-chance it was an order from Monarch.

Tommy gripped the 70's phone and leaned into the receiver so none of the usual patrons could hear the conversation.

"Listen, Steamer, I'll do my best," said Reyes. "But, don't go bustin' balls or I'll break ya beak over the phone!"

"Yeah, yeah... Alright," replied Steamer while trying to quell an excitable Reyes. ""What's the latest?"

"Listen - our window is tight," said Tommy. "I gotta pick up the cash in New Bedford in the morning. Probably be back on the Cape and at the marina in West Dennis by... oh, I dunno, around two or two thirty tomorrow afternoon."

"Yeah, yeah, I know the drill," said Steamer.

"You better." He exhaled, winked at the cutest waitress to calm down. He got a quick smile back from the chick who could pass for Lucy Liu and returned to the receiver with a grin. "Now, let's talk business, Steam."

"Tommy, relax. You're wound up tight. I miss the Captain Reyes who was only interested in tapping kegs and bikini bottoms."

"Yeah, yeah... Things are heavier these days," responded Tommy. His inherent attention to detail, coupled with his nerves, sometimes got in the way of reason. It was a flaw that always incited an internal scrum. Lately it was getting worse. He forced himself to stay silent for two deep breaths.

Steamer then asked, "So, Tommy, are we meeting at the dock at two or two *thirty?*"

Reyes yearned to reach through the phone to strangle his partner's neck like a rubber chicken, but maintained composure. "Steam, I said around two or two thirty because of, well ya know, shit happens. I'm driving from n'Bedfid to Dennis. I can get delayed. Traffic. Construction. Earthquake. Maybe friggin' Godzilla... Get it?"

Reyes considered shooting his partner on sight the next day. Just setting the time was getting his nerves tight enough for a heart attack. "How about this?" he asked as he needed the exchange back on track. "For the record, let's officially say two-thirty. Ok? Feel better? So, if I so happen to arrive at oh, say, two twenty-four? I promise to drive around the friggin' block just enough times until I am able to pull into the goddamned parking lot at exactly two thirty! Work for you?"

Steamer knew he'd pushed too hard, even though he enjoyed pressing his partner's buttons. "Okay, Tommy. I'll be there for two and will be looking for the van. Let's just both chill out. I know the stakes are high on this one, and if we blow it, the Monarch will hang us both from the Sagamore Bridge by our intestines. Old school pirate style."

"Whatever..." replied Reyes with a calmed down snicker. "Let's just keep our heads about us and get this done. Once the van is empty and the boat has thrown its lines and heads east, the first round is on me."

Steamer caught himself in mid-thought. "Hey, Tom. Don't you think it's a little crazy we're goin' to be transferring a haul right in the middle of the afternoon at a public dock? I mean, shit, they'll be kids tossin' french fries to seagulls! I don't like it; we're gonna stick out."

"Steam, that's the genius of Monarch. He knows how to pull off this shit! We're gonna blend right in with the activity and look like any other local fish luggers. Hell, we'll do it right under their eyes. We're bringing the van in to meet the boat then really replenish their bait, gear and food. That way, they don't waste time on shore doing it. Nobody will be the wiser. If anything, some tourist from Ohio might ask you to take a selfie!"

Steamer made some muffled positive sound through the receiver.

Reyes continued to make sure his friend was locked in. "Again, that's the genius of Monarch. Most hand-offs are done at three-am, forty miles off the coast. Both boats stick out like wounded whales. This way, we blend right in with the Cape Cod stuff always going on. Anyway, it looks like Monarch is bringin' in the usual load that he's been moving the past few months. Nothing major. Kinda vanilla."

"What's he movin' this time?" Steamer asked.

"Dunno... Kind of a mish-mash," answered Reyes as he took mental inventory. "Cases of burner phones. Coupla big crates of surveillance drones. Some techie electronic shit I wouldn't know how to work."

"Guns, at least?" asked Steamer.

Reyes shrugged at the phone. "He's sendin' *some* iron, but they're just pieces you'd see at a friggin' gun show. Few cases of ammo. No heavy metal. I dunno Steam, the guy's becoming more and more of a mystery."

"Weird..." responded Steamer who confused easily. "What's he supplying? A Belfast boy scout troop?"

"Dunno," quipped Tom. "Strange to be sure. There's also a crate of paintings Monarch stole from some wealthy Cape widow in Oster-ville. He somehow got wind that she died and subsequently relieved that house of, from what I understand, some pretty pricy shit. That was pulled off before the kids could start hiring lawyers to fight over the estate. Brats are gonna find some empty walls," chuckled Reyes.

Steamer interjected with a rare deep thought. "Hey, didn't Whitey Bulger steal a bunch of fancy paintings from that museum up in Bos-ton? Legend is he pulled it off and sent the stuff to Ireland so people like the Monarch could sell the merch and buy guns."

"We'll never know. Boston is full of myths and mist," replied Reyes. "All I know is tha contents of this shipment ain't gonna buy too many AK 47s. I mean, it's a strange order. I'm disappointed as anyone Monarch suddenly decided to start buying books from the children's section, but we can all still grab a score."

Steamer spit a pre-cancerous cough away from phone, and then said, "Sounds like a plan."

Reyes realized something. "And no drinking or speeding on the way down. Monarch's got the local cops on duty all paid off, so they know not to go near the marina, but you're on your own if you see Staties flashing the blues."

Steamer's mind stalled, but finally he grunted a yes, then his brain found another question. "Tommy, when do we get to meet this big boss? I mean, the friggin' dude's in the weeds. Shit... Might be easier to grab an audience with Don Corleone. Heard through the grape-vine the Monarch is on the back nine, but that's all I know."

"Steam," replied Reyes in as patient a tone as he could, "don't be shortsighted. Be grateful for the work. Ours is a business that isn't exactly teeming with opportunity these days. Unless you think we oughta start a Google site or some smart phone app shit?" Tommy was trying to bring his mission partner down from unreality

"Alright... alright," said Steamer. "But we know nothing about the old bastard. We don't get to talk to him. We don't even get a proper sit down like the ol' days? Been going on for years, and we just take it in the can?"

Tommy rubbed his forehead. "Guys like Monarch don't meet in person with guys like us. That's how it works. Would you rather be holding a cold knife, in a colder hand, skinning frozen fish up in Guild Harbor? Since when you gone posh?"

"Fine, fine. Whatever," Steamer retorted. "I just think it's strange that we've been doing jobs for someone we've never seen. Never even been introduced!? We don't even know anyone that has actually *met* the Monarch. He's just a friggin' phantom type."

"Agreed," replied Reyes with a tone that diffused the moment. "But, he's a ghost with a checkbook." Reyes let that sink in then continued, "Monarch is a phantom to everyone. No meet and greets. Just do your damned job and shut up. He's the checkbook. You want to stop gettin' the bags of cash?"

Steamer was quiet for a few seconds in reflection. "Nah, I need the work," he finally said, "but it'd be nice to meet the guy and know who I'm working for."

Reyes cleared his throat. This was getting beyond tedious and he was ready to blow up. "Obviously, Monarch doesn't want you to know who's holding the strings. That way, you can't rat him out. Who cares who we're working for? He's obviously some kinda mystery man. Who gives a shit?"

"Hmm," muttered Steamer. "Ever notice whenever you hear from him, he's got that annoying voice changer thing going. You can barely make out what the hell he's saying. All I can do is get the facts down and maybe notice the Mick accent."

"Steam, maybe that's how he's stayed quiet *and* on top for all of these years? Let's just do our jobs and get our dough. That's the way the world spins. Monarch keeps a low profile and uses intermediaries for a reason. Screw it! Does his cash work for you at the pub or your whore's den?"

Steamer kicked a pebble as if in contemplation. "Yeah, yeah, Tommy," he capitulated. "Fine. Whatever... I'm onboard. But while you're at it, will you please go fuck yourself?"

"Sure. Hell, I might enjoy it. Cost effective!" said Reyes as he hunched over in rare, unbridled laughter.

Both hoods slammed the phone at the same time and went about the rest of their day. The job was to be completed in the afternoon when only locals and a few tourists would be at a nondescript waterfront like Dennis, especially in early spring. Fortunately for everyone involved, the weather was scheduled to be unseasonably mild. Sixty-five degrees, clear and with a five-knot wind out of the southwest. It was going to resemble more of an early June day, a welcomed forecast for everyone involved.

Simple project.

Overall, the biggest expense was on Monarch to grease the local constabulary who were always ready to serve and protect the highest bidder.

Val's Apartment
NYC

Forsythia managed to grab three hours of sleep between four episodes of vomiting which, all in all, was not an unusual night. Val headed off to work. Fory looked down at the old briefcase and rubbed the burgundy leather like a lover's chest. *Wish I could open you and peek inside.*

She knew she had to get out of Manhattan, fast and undetected. All she could do was toss a few things in a duffle. The airport was out of the question, so it had to be via car or train.

She thought about what she told Val about her eccentric aunt who lived on Cape Cod. Fory had never been close to Aunt Mary, but nobody in the family could ever boast that distinction. Fory felt desperation while she reached for her phone.

"Shit!" Fory dropped the cell and ran to the bathroom for yet one more wretch. She relieved her empty stomach of a cup of yellow bile, and then felt a temporary sense of relief.

She returned to the bed and dropped her head onto the pillow like a cinder block. She reached for her phone again. She was surprised Aunt Mary's number was still in her contacts list. Fory vaguely recognized the number. The prefix 945 was old-school Chatham. If your home number began with a 945, it didn't guarantee that your ancestors arrived on the *Mayflower,* but it was a sign for local vendors about who to give discounts to and who got the customary summer resident premium fee.

She took a sip of water, hoping that it would stay down, and then pressed the number.

The phone rang.

And rang...

Forsythia's Ride

On what seemed like the fortieth ring, a voice finally answered. "Y-yes?"

"Aunt Mary!" said Fory trying to sound bushy-tailed even though at the moment, she felt like Satan's discard. "How are you, Auntie? It's been a long time."

Mary sighed with a pregnant pause. "I must apologize..." said a frail sounding Mary, "W-Who is this?"

"Aunt Mary, it's your niece. Forsythia." Silence. She prompted with an overly-hopeful voice, "Fory. Down in New York City."

Several more seconds sucked up air space.

"Fory... Fory? Yes, yes. I suppose it is," Mary responded curtly.

Fory scrambled to establish a dialogue. "Aunt Mary. I've been living in Manhattan. It's been interesting and fun, but I was seeing if you wanted some company this spring?" asked Fory. "I'd love to get out of the city, was wondering if I could come up and visit?"

Quiet at first, Mary responded, "I suppose it's kind of you to reach out to an old lady. However, it's early spring, and it's quiet in this little town. Even the sharks haven't returned. Perhaps you should call me as the summer progresses, the beaches will be best then. I hope that you have a good..."

Out of sudden desperation, Fory cut her off. "Oh, I know, Aunt Mary! I know," popped a desperate Fory. "I actually would love the peace and quiet of the off-season Cape. Work's been stressful and I have some vacation time that I need to use up. Would it be okay if I came to visit?"

Fory could hear the woman take a long drag from a cigarette and blow it out directly into the phone. Fory guessed Benson & Hedges.

"Well, I s'pose I don't see much family these days," said Mary. "Actually, I don't see much family ever. Or anyone else, for that matter." Mary coughed a smoker's hack and then returned to the receiver. "Well, I guess if you'd like to venture to Cape Cod, I have plenty of room for a guest for a few days." Clearing her throat a terse tone came out as Mary said, " A *few* days."

Fory exhaled. "That'd be great, Aunt Mary. I promise it'll be a short stay. It'd be great to catch up and see how you're doing. I can take a bus to Hyannis and then Uber it over to Chatham."

"Fory, I'm old," said Mary. "Quite old, actually. However, I am not just off the turnip truck, either. You sound like you're under some sort of stress. Trust that I don't want any drama interrupting my simple life and household. Please keep your jealous boyfriends on the other side of the Sagamore Bridge."

"No, no, Aunt Mary... Nothing like that," responded Fory. "I just thought I'd visit and regroup. Our family isn't getting any bigger."

"Indeed, we're not," replied Mary who hung up promptly with no added niceties.

* * *

Mary fingered the phone with her thumb as anxiety several decades in the making reared its head. She understood the lid just popped off of an old can of family history. That thought made her cringe, even though she had put this set of events in motion. She loved her brother, and missed him every day, but he went rogue and ended up trying to write checks that could never be cashed.

In Mary's mind, the tragedy was that his daughter was going to be liable for the outstanding debt. She reached for her cigarette. It had burnt out while she was rattling the cages of her thoughts about what she was going to pull off. *One last assignment. Unfortunately, my dead brother's daughter is being put in play.* Mary smirked at what an experiment this might be, the challenge was more important to her than the small amount of affection she had for a blood relative.

Her thoughts allowed her one last chance to call the whole thing off. What little softness was left in her heart reminded her that maybe the plan was too dangerous for an aging operative to try to coordinate using an untrained woman and a sociopathic murderer as the hander.

Forsythia's Ride

Then her racing mind ruled against such foolish notions. She was more powerful than any of those media hogging cartels and this was what she decided would be her last mission for her cause.

"Alyce, where's my Pall Malls, dammit?!"

McCarthy Dental Office
Harwichport, Cape Cod

"Okay. Let's see... We should be ready in five minutes," said the receptionist in between snaps of a stick of Juicy Fruit. "You'll be in the first room on the right. Follow me." The stale gum smell was mercy for her patients versus her normal Marlboro bouquet.

After the patient was settled in, the receptionist paged Lamer (pronounced with the French *la-mer*, as in 'the sea') to let her know her next cleaning appointment was ready. Of course the waiting room didn't lose humor on the fact that the hygienist's name spoken with a local slant sounds like "*Llama.*"

Lamer had embraced her new life as a hygienist. Dealing with tooth polish was much less complicated than planting explosives.

It was typical day at the practice. A cleaning here, an x-ray there, along with the occasional plumping of an insurance billing. All in a day's routine. Lamer enjoyed focusing on her job. Over the years, she'd been periodically contacted by players from her former life looking for favors. However, she had managed to keep a low profile so far.

She donned her light blue smock. Next up was a welcomed mid-day appointment. Lamer liked to stay busy. Most of the other staff looked forward to smoking butts during breaks rather than pecking at maroon-leaking gums. She walked toward the room and scrubbed with the stale taste of Jamison still renting her tongue.

"Be there in the one minute," she called into the treatment room. Lamer checked the patient's chart for any abnormalities and was happy to find a clean slate. Nothing documented, so hopefully an easy scrape. She sat down and scooted the rolling chair to the patient.

"Hi Miss. My name is Lamer. I hope to help ya out today."

Forsythia's Ride

Her salutation was met with an odd silence from the patient. She hoped for an easy, quick cleaning. From her past experiences, Lamer realized that over time the ol' *patience for patients* would eroded.

"Hi," said Lamer to the patient she guessed was around eighteen. "What's your name?"

The young woman in the chair kept silent, which was beginning to unnerve Lamer. She decided to just begin the procedure.

Twenty minutes later, after a fluoride polish, the girl spat out the remnants of the cold-water cleansing. Then, she leaned back and staccato-blinked her eyes.

"Sasa..." said the young patient, "we see that you've taken up a new trade."

Lamer's sinew froze. *How could anyone know my real name?* Genuine shock ran up her spine.

"Sasa," repeated the young girl stronger this time to snap the woman out of her trance. "My name is Michonne. You know my father. I don't have to say who he is. You have an assignment from Monarch."

Lamar/Sasa's neck hairs stood up.

"It's nice of you to clean my teeth. Now we need to call you back into another type of service," said Michonne. Then her voice registered dropped down. "And we're not asking."

Sasa's right hand rubbed her left shoulder in a calming, self-soothing mechanism.

"Once you hear me out, I'll be on my way," said Michonne. "If you say no, then I'll politely leave, and you will soon receive *other* new patients. I suggest you warn your colleagues and staff."

Sasa couldn't believe she was being muscled by a girl who should be in a sorority keg line.

"Remember, Sasa. This is not coming from us Yanks. Your assignment stems from someone a little more connected. You know the mantra, *once in, never out.*"

Sasa kept a concrete gaze on her patient. Her mind slot-machined options in her head of what to do next. She couldn't believe her past was coming back to haunt her. So fast. So acute. She always knew her old world might return with a claim check, but she never anticipated it so soon. She was just getting on her feet, had kept a low profile; should have been unfindable.

Michonne had a cold smirk on her face, knowing pretty much what was going through Sasa's mind. *She's thinking about bolting now that the shock is wearing off, time to knock this bitch to her knees.* "We also still have questions about your brother. He's so handsome. So dashing. At my age, finally, I'm beginning to notice such things."

Sasa felt a whole new type of concern.

"Strange, Sasa," continued the patient, "bet you'd never guess a girl sitting in your chair would know so much about your past."

Sasa suddenly felt the need to turn toward the sink, snap off her rubber gloves, and scrub her hands.

"See, my dad had the pleasure of sharing a few jobs with your brother." Michonne's face was now in a sneer. "Your blood thought that he could commit atrocities with impunity and then walk away with a Swiss bank account."

Sasa's eyes bulged.

"Yeah, well. He's arrogant and naive," said Michonne. "Much like yourself. If you think he's gonna remain hidden... Come on, you're not naive enough to think we're not going to use you to lure him out of his swamp."

Sasa began biting at the inside of her left cheek.

"Oh, by the way, while you're finishing my cleaning today, can you give me the Spearmint fluoride sealer instead of the Peppermint?" asked Michonne. "Pepp tastes like a coward's ass. A coward who thinks she can walk away from a life that provided everything she has."

Sasa's mind raced between running away or grabbing the drill and finding her patient's eyes.

"I have something for you. It's in lieu of my inability to pay with insurance. As you know, in our line of work, the pay is excellent, but the benefit packages are lean. I need to take that up with HR."

Sasa stared.

Michonne pulled out a small box and held it out. "Open it."

Sasa couldn't move.

"You obviously know why I'm here gracing your chair," said Michonne. "You see, in order for us, and you know who *us* is, to convince you to assist on this operation we needed some incentive. Just a teaser."

"You little bitch!" hissed Sasa.

"I'm a patient!" retorted Michonne. "The good doctor would not be happy with an assistant speaking to me like that." Michonne actually felt a genuine laugh starting to bubble up at that, and forced it down with a deep breath. "What you are Sasa, is your brother's only hope for survival. We might let him live, but that's contingent upon your performance in this operation. You understand his extracurricular dabbling in running smack was not good for our group's marketing. I wouldn't buy him any green bananas."

Sasa closed her eyes and slightly shook her head as in disbelief.

"Not a big deal," said Michonne. "He's an oaf and you know it, which is why you're really pissed at the core. Obviously, the smart move for you is to work with us. He's a marked man. As we all are at some point in this game, I guess." Michonne's observation fell flat on a near panicked Sasa. "However, you can save him. If you share with us your talents one last time."

Sasa stared at the wall, an alabaster tone cooling her face.

"And, Sasa," teased Michonne, "while you're at it, someone said that one of my incisors is a witch's tooth. Can you fix that?"

Michonne leaned back in her long treatment chair and opened her mouth for the last steps in her cleaning.

NYC Port Authority

As the lumbering Peter Pan bus pulled away from the New York City Port Authority station bound for Providence/Boston, Fory settled in and stretched tight limbs. She was grateful to have an empty seat next to her where she could plop her stuff and, more important, not worry about idle banter and inevitable unwanted attention.

She already felt some sense of relief and safety as the big diesel engine hummed. With every turn of the wheels, she was one step further away from The Big Apple. Only Val knew her plans and where she was going, and it was Val who suggested that Fory not share the exact address even with her. That way she could pass a police polygraph test with flying colors. Fory promised to check in with Val when she got to her aunt's house in Chatham.

It was going to be a long travel day. If the bus stayed on schedule, she would have a ninety minute layover at Boston's South Station before boarding another coach to Hyannis, Cape Cod. Because it was a Sunday, Fory was getting out of Manhattan before her office came back alive on Monday morning.

She had grabbed just enough clothes that would fit into one piece of luggage which was stowed in the bowels of the bus. Of course, her cross-body satchel contained the burgundy briefcase that Fory had no idea what to do with, but couldn't exactly return to its rightful owner. Next to her was her backpack holding her laptop, iPad, a John D. MacDonald novel (she wanted to finish *The Empty Copper Sea*), two bottles of water and a few one milligram pops of Ativan "borrowed" from Val's medicine cabinet.

Of course, there was also the mandatory bottle of Bacardí Limón stashed away, but she wanted to try to hold off on that until the bus passed through Rhode Island.

She powered up the iPad to take advantage of the free wi-fi pro-

Forsythia's Ride

vided by Mr. Peter Pan.

While she grew up in New Hampshire and still considered herself a New Englander, she followed the Boston and NYC papers online. As an avid Celtics and Patriots fan, not so much Red Sox or Bruins, she enjoyed surreptitiously following her teams while watching her colleagues wear Yankee pinstripe tops on casual day and bleeding Giant's blue when their team lost.

She also loved to keep up with Boston current events and politics. Sure, Manhattan was never short on scenery or stories, yet Fory felt it lacked the historical flavor of Boston.

As she scrolled through one of the websites, she chuckled at the typical Boston headlines involving politicians on the take, battles over urban redevelopment and Howie Carr's latest *gotcha* piece.

She then a headline caught her eye:

HYANNIS —

A Mashpee man was found dead in a dumpster behind the converted Main Street motel that served as his rent-controlled apartment. It was a gruesome scene. Police identified the man as Crucifixio "Roke" Mangini. His address is unknown, and foul play is suspected. Mr. Mangini had a lengthy criminal record mostly stemming from theft and burglary. He was under investigation for suspected thefts in several Cape Cod towns, the most recent incidents all involved larceny of packages from the porches of local residents.

When asked for comment, Barnstable Police Captain Mark O'Meara told reporters, "The waste management professionals found Mr. Mangini in the trash receptacle during a routine stop on their route. Unfortunately, due to the increasing level of drug activity in the area, this is not the first time that a body has been found in a large receptacle. The individuals in the vast majority of cases are the victims of heroin overdoses or narcotics transactions gone awry.

"However, the initial toxicology report on Mr. Mangini showed no signs of drugs or alcohol in his system. What law enforcement considers most disturbing is that the victim was found with both his hands severed and removed from the premises. Their current whereabouts are unknown."

"Damn..." Fory whispered to herself. "Someone pissed off the wrong someone at the wrong time."

Nor'east Bluff Beach
Chatham

Seagulls cried, the wind stung. The Simmons family was intent on taking in some of the beauty of Pleasant Bay while the abnormally warm weather draped down from the northern sky. On any given day, Mother Nature could unleash a merciless nor'easter, but at the moment she was content with shuffling the clouds like a deck of cards giving a taste of a beautiful summer to come.

The ocean still gave a taste of the grey winter just past; far too cold for swimming yet.

Tom Simmons had promised his family a day away from Boston and more importantly, a day away from his cell phone.

Ziva, a spry five-year old Golden Retriever, was a loved part of the Simmons Family. The dog was a glue that bound the disconnected vacationers.

Marcy Simmons carried a basket containing a simple lunch.

The boys were already digging in the sand, when suddenly, Ziva ran back down the beach.

"Whatcha got?" Tom coached the pooch.

Ziva, in doggie fervor, almost darted past the family, so proud of today's catch.

Tom knew Goldens loved to hunt and bring back treasures, and in this case, it appeared to be some kind of toy. Most likely left over from a local teen beach party.

"Dad!" yelled the older Simmons boy. "Look what Ziva has! It's a rubber chicken!"

Tom was curious. It *kinda* looked like a chicken. Definitely a party favor, but a little more elaborate. "Ziva! Drop it!" Tom gently commanded the overexcited dog.

The zealous golden dropped the party favor in front of the picnic blanket, only to be met by Marcy's screams.

"EEEK! T-T-TOM!!"

Tom Simmons looked down at a crusted-over left hand. Or was it a right? Either way, it was dropped and positioned as if pointing to the sky.

"G-Good girl, Ziva..." is all Tom could mutter.

What solidified the horror was that last time he checked, most rubber chickens didn't wear a pinkie ring.

Winslow & Pratt, Ltd.
NYC

Old man Pratt made a bee-line to his personal restroom off the side of his corner office. Old bladders just didn't like the town car ride into the city each morning. He pulled and rolled down his pants over a tremendous gut. A five hundred dollar belt struggled to hold everything in. He barely made it in time.

After settling into the large leather chair he punched the speakerphone button, which was one of the few controls that he knew how to negotiate. "Mrs. Wiggins. Where is my briefcase? The one that I left here in my *locked* office. The one that *you* are ultimately responsible for."

After two seconds of silence he heard, "Sir William. I-I-don't know what you're referring to... sir."

A shade of crimson flushed over his chest, with acid then firehosing his stomach. The fiery red raced through his neck and found a home on his forehead. "WHAT! Mrs. Wiggins! I gave you ONE thing to do. WATCH that briefcase!"

Pratt took three deep breaths. "Where is it!?" the knight barked.

Betty Wiggins, on the verge of tears, quickly rushed to the door and looked around his office...there was no sign of it. "Sir William, I don't see any briefcase. Are you sure you..."

"Dammit! Find it, now!" he bellowed. "Or else you'll be in the breadline!" He waved her away and picked up his phone.

Betty's heart rate was redlining. She'd seen Pratt irate on several occasions, but never like this. Josephine, in a cubicle across the walkway, overheard the exchange. She ran into the employee kitchen and wet a rag with cold water. She coaxed Betty to sit back in her chair and placed the small towel across Betty's forehead.

"Betty, you'll find whatever the old bastard is looking for. You're not paid enough to have heart palpitations over this. Just relax. I'm gonna grab you a water and go look for whatever the hell it is that's so crucial. Just describe for me what he's looking for."

Betty gave Josephine a look of gratitude. "Briefcase. Leather. Maroon color. I swear he had it in his office the last time that I went in there to take some dictation on Friday afternoon. He never put it in my hands to look after. But you heard him. I'm responsible."

Betty Wiggins yearned for a drink, sighed and then smiled. "Hey, Jo, is your brother still looking for waitresses at the diner?" Betty gave a rueful chuckle. "I'm gonna need the money, and as much as it would kill my feet and body, my heart and mind can't handle this much longer."

Josephine wiped Betty's cheeks. "Just relax. Lemme look 'round the office. In the meantime, the old son of a bitch might blow a gasket of his own. Better he end up in the ER than you. Sit tight."

Route 6 East
Cape Cod

The bus swooped in at her next and last stop; off Exit 6 in Barnstable, locally known as *da Burgah King.*

After a long day of traveling, Forsythia was exhausted. Eagerness to establish a safe destination, combined with a curiosity to catch up with her aunt had kept her going so far.

Fory saw her awaiting chariot. As the Uber driver headed east on Route 6, Fory sunk deeper into the backseat as she tried to recap the past few days. She'd left a message at HR that she had a family emergency and would be out for a while. She was nervous about what might await her upon her return to Manhattan, yet in a strange way she was excited about the trip ahead. The thrill of the unknown over-shadowed any discomfort leaving her routine and possibly, by her unscheduled absence, she was in a newly unemployed status. Curiosity always energized Fory.

At first, the houses appeared modest and working class as they passed the usual landmarks that one would see in any eastern Mass-achusetts town. There was a Stop & Shop, an Agway, a pizza joint, churches, two liquor stores and the required deluxe Dunkin Do-nuts/gas station combo which, to Fory, was the quintessential symbol of modern New England convenience.

Forsythia watched the house sizes and grandeur increase as she stared out the window of the late-model Honda Accord. She laughed to herself about how the term "summer cottage" was so relative.

Over the course of a few miles, old Chevy and Silverado pickups with lobster buoys hanging off the back gave way to newly monied Porsche Cayennes and old money Packard restorations. The tension of the Chatham culture clash was visible to anyone who opened their eyes, and it was a recurring topic at Cape Cod Planning Board and Conservation meetings. New money wanted knock-downs to be replaced with trophy "cottages," while old money wouldn't dare step on a clam shell or replace rough greying sideboards. Old money ate at a stodgy tavern just outside of downtown. And they ate early. New money ate anywhere where their New Yorker guests would be impressed. The later reservations carried the most prestige. In their minds, only the unwashed dined before eight o'clock.

The two sociological opposite ideologies both had the currency needed to drive the Cape Cod economy. Their culture war could keep the area enduring for centuries. The old timers complained the town had lost its character and sensibility, but they never minded marching down to bank with six and seven figure checks after a sale. No problem selling off land to California types. That is until the locals realized that they had sold off too much of their town's soul, and in a frenzy, jumped onto local municipal boards using their 945 phone number to try to control the rapid growth and culture shift.

However, their visceral frustration stemmed from the realization they did it to themselves. It always stings the most upon that realization.

They grew livid when new money suddenly decided how things were going to look and whose new, fancy rings would be kissed. The longtime Chatham folks just looked south toward Nantucket and Long Island and saw harbingers of things to come. The joke was on them; it had already happened under their noses. The only local four and five-star resorts that were owned by old families and showcased the town were both sold off to corporate conglomerates before the whole picture had come into focus.

Case closed on the town's former history book...

Hot-shot mutual fund managers would level a classic 1950s home to make way for a palace that belonged in Bridgehampton, then sport a pretentious name over the garage. Moniker's like *Spoiled Rotten, Poverty Sucks* and *Heaven Picked Me!* hung on custom designed signs over garages. Some were made to look like they were whittled by the Pilgrims themselves in an ultimate offense to those forbearers who had frozen to death during their first winter on the Cape. Chil-

Forsythia's Ride

dren included.

It wasn't just high-end towns like Chatham that experienced a massive inflow of the gourmet prepared-meal crowd. Postal workers were confused as to why the sudden surge of Boston Magazine subscriptions were being sent over their side of the bridges. If only Wellesley and Weston had enough annoying old homes to raze and proper beaches, their residents wouldn't have to use "summer" as a verb.

Further away from the highway, the area assumed a different characteristic. The Uber ride was smooth (no potholes here), the houses were larger, and there were gates in front of every parcel. Even the shrubs were taller, trimmed tighter and looked like they could speak.

Brittle clam shells covered the driveways to give a satisfying crunch as owners rolled toward their garages. Elaborate lighting fixtures adorned the entrances to most of the homes. In just a month hydrangeas along the lawn perimeters would be radiating blue and pink, now they were that bright green color only seen in spring. Memories of the colors taunted Fory; they reminded her of tie-dye, hippie rock band t-shirts and early mornings waking up in unrecognizable apartments.

Fory looked out the car's right side like a kid on a field trip. She was mesmerized by the concentration of wealth that, at first glance, seemed in the middle of a forested nowhere.

The driver, hoping for a date and a chance to try out a Mickey he'd scored in Hyannis, decided to play tour guide as they took a left onto the only street that accessed the peninsula. His words snapped Fory out of a daze.

"Now we're gonna drive right through a golf course. Look to the left. It's beautiful all year long and your destination is at the very end."

Fory gazed out the window and noticed a group of seagulls staring at a golfer conquering an especially pesky sand trap. The seagulls squawked as if betting.

"Hey, I gotta ask," said the driver. "I don't get out here much. You visiting some kind of movie star? Not that I'm taking any pictures or whatever, although there's great money in that. But, just wanna say that it's just pretty out here."

Fory was silent, she didn't feel like engaging with someone who she would never trust to drink with. She sensed they were close to Aunt Mary's. As she looked out to her left at the driver's urging, she saw a sapphire bay and unspoiled green. Far off tans of some islands floated on the blue. It was breathtaking for someone who had been cooped up in a concrete jungle for years. Fory had almost forgotten the world did look different once you escaped the grey confines of Manhattan's grids.

Fory then asked, "What's your name?"

In the sudden quiet as he realized the hottie in the back finally spoke to him, the rubber of the Uber's wheels rubbed awkwardly along the salt-beaten, wind-ripped road. "Reed. But my friends call me Yellow."

Fory tilted her head in consideration.

Reed kept going to keep her attention. "Now, you might think that someone called Yellow who isn't blonde might be some type of cowardly guy. Not at all. I'm called Yellow by a select few for safe driving like the yellow caution light. My friends call me that cause I rise up every day beaming like the sun." Yellow glanced into his rearview mirror to see if his sharing was winning her heart.

Freak, Fory thought to herself, She flipped her hair. "Hmm. Interesting angle. Maybe you'll be famous someday?"

"Sure. I'm with you!" Yellow again beamed into the mirror so he could see his pretty passenger.

The streets began to twist and turn the further they traveled out onto the peninsula. Fory turned to her right to marvel at a sea of pink tulips next to an antique fountain which served as a yard focus piece for one of Mary's neighbors. At the next house she noticed several stuffed animals and flowers on the deep front porch. What at first looked like an ornate floral display then reminded Fory of post-crash

Forsythia's Ride

highway sites.

"What's that, Yellow?" asked Fory pointing to cluttered porch.

"Ah, my friend," responded Yellow, "I'm not exactly sure of all the details, but it was in the paper that a little girl from right in this neighborhood wandered off into the ocean in the middle of the night and drowned. Terrible. That must be their house."

"What happened?" asked Fory genuinely disturbed.

"Not sure. My guess is your host will know more. I think the girl was only five or so. Some kinda tragedy."

"Awful..." muttered Fory as the doorway fell out of sight.

A few houses ahead, Yellow crunched Aunt Mary's clam shells and made sure not to pull up too close to the long nose of the Rolls-Royce resting in the middle of the driveway which hunkered like a sleeping, white dragon.

"Hey! Whose Rolls!?" asked an excited Yellow.

"My aunt's, I guess." Fory huffed, "She always had nice cars."

"I see... Lemme grab your bag," offered Yellow.

"No, no," politely responded Fory. "I'll be fine."

As Yellow pulled away, Fory was blinded for a few seconds by the brilliant white shining up from the driveway shells.

Fory stepped back and looked at the house. It was very modest compared to the neighbors, many of whom were *nouveau riche* and forever tried to one-up each other by tearing down and rebuilding with ostentation.

The Hamptons had officially invaded the elbow of Cape Cod.

Nor'east Bluff, Chatham
Cape Cod

Aunt Mary's house was relatively nondescript for the neighborhood, still, she lived at the end of a peninsula that held rich history and folklore. It was very private, very exclusive. Any house in this neighborhood was a proud illustration of wealth in one form or another. Decades before, this area was a U.S. Navy dirigible base. It was engaged in both world wars. The military installation spread throughout the neighborhood. Evidence dating back to the earlier part of the last century could be found if one knew what they were looking at.

Steel eyelets which once held giant war blimps were still dotting the beach and backyards. They'd proudly sponsored trip & falls over the years at backyard parties after too many Grey Goose Cape Codders. The average beach scavenger wielding a metal detector would find nirvana while sifting through the local sands, however the level of privacy here was matched only by Tibetan monk retreats. Depending on whose property an explorer might encroach on, the punishment ranged between a tongue-lashing all the way to a hundred dollar fine accompanied by a vagrant's arrest. It depended on the neighbor in question. The more ostentatious the house, the bigger the walking phallus who owned it.

Fory walked up a long stone path and raised a hand to knock, but the old matron startled her by opening the door prior to Fory's knuckle hitting the wood.

Mary stared.

Fory was suddenly flustered. "I-I'm sorry, Aunt Mary. I was just about to knock and didn't mean to..."

"No matter," responded Aunt Mary. "We saw you coming on the cameras."

Fory kept hold of her bags in anticipation of walking in, but had not yet been invited. "So," she was grasping for words of introduction,

Forsythia's Ride

"that's great that you have a security system. Do you worry about burglars?"

"No," said Mary without hesitation, or elaboration. She then reacted to Fory's befuddled look. "The surveillance is a bit of an embarrassment, and yet an indulgence," said Mary. "You see, I have a consummate need to be informed of everything and everyone around me. At my age, I don't care for surprises. Whether it be the town manager or a neighbor with an apple pie." Mary's tone dropped an octave. "Neither is welcomed."

Fory nodded with a fake look of understanding. "Well, Aunt Mary, you're kind to let me visit. I needed a break from New York. Really fun place to visit and all, but not sure that you'd want to live there," Fory said as she floundered for conversation.

"Won't you come in?" Aunt Mary finally offered with a bent index finger. "Perhaps my security resources are excessive. I am fortunate that certain people care to look after an aging Cape Cod lady. Friends suggested that I install this security system with cameras and what have you, but in truth, I don't know how to work them very well. Except when I have a gut feeling that I should review some footage."

"You should learn, Aunt Mary," said Fory begging herself to find the right words to fill the verbal void and hoping she was coming off as helpful. She walked through the door and let her bags lean against the wall under a hall table.

Mary stared into Fory's violet eyes. They resembled that of her dead brother's. The hue was striking, born of a rare bluish, purple. *If he had just done what he was told...*

"Anyway," said Mary with a deep cough, "a neighbor thought recently that she saw someone take something from my driveway. All I've been told is that I don't have to worry about the scoundrel absconding with my parcels again. Anyhoo..." *Watch it Mary, you have to keep it light, you almost gloated about that robber being trussed up like a tuna.*

The old foyer's floor was worn and pocked, like a picture in *Yankee Magazine.* Fory thought it exuded old world charm with sepia-colored wood feeling warm and inviting. Every step unleashed a cracking squeal that spoke of not only the house's history, but also that of its owner.

"Thanks, Aunt Mary. Where should I put my..."

Mary interjected, "Leave your things right where you set them down. Alyce will take care of them and everything will be placed in the east guest room upstairs. My chamber is on the main floor, as you would imagine a woman of my age prefers. You'll enjoy a pleasant view, although at night you must draw the thicker curtains as to block out the early east light or be woke at an ungodly early hour."

While most people greeted the sunrise with hope and a smile, Mary snubbed it as a punctual morning irritant.

"Okay, Auntie, no problem," said an awkward Fory. "Thanks for the heads up."

"It's the beginning of May," continued Mary, "the northeast wind will be chilly, so feel free to shut the windows. While I don't have the most palatial home in this neighborhood, I know how to maximize space. Years of practice earlier in my life, I suppose."

Fory nodded without comment. She was struggling with getting a grasp on why she was even there. At least the conversation was flowing better now.

"In the meantime, come with me into my sitting room," encouraged Mary with a slight wave. "It's my favorite room in the house. I enjoy entertaining select guests and sharing good conversation. And I get to do it while having the Atlantic Ocean, specifically Pleasant Bay, as a backdrop. Indeed, I am spoiled enjoying this view that some consider as luxury."

"Not sure that it borders on anything except amazing," said Fory as she reflected on the sights from the ride into the neighborhood.

Mary smiled as Alyce entered the foyer. The housekeeper gathered up the bags and headed upstairs. She did everything so fast that Fory was left hanging while trying to properly introduce herself.

"Hi Alice, my name is..."

"Dear," interrupted Mary, "her name is pronounced *Aleece*, not

Forsythia's Ride

Alice. She is quite diligent and pleasant, but unable to speak. She can hear you and I'm sure appreciates your attempt at salutations. However, she cannot respond. She's been invaluable to me. I found, I mean I *met* her in Belfast years ago. The reasons for her lack of speech, I do not understand. Follow me."

Her aunt was an enigma wrapped in a puzzle. Brusk, to the point, yet she seemed happy enough to have a visitor. Fory followed her down the hall until it opened into a large den. While not opulent in decor or size, the view of the ocean was one usually reserved for travel brochures.

"Wow, Auntie. This is amazing," said Fory. "You're so lucky to be able to see this every day."

"Fortunate, indeed," Mary responded with a horizontal mouth. "This is where we take tea." She motioned for Fory to sit on an antique sofa across from her which resembled a throne more than a chair.

A full tea set with cookies and fruit was already prepared for them on the small antique table between Mary's chair and the sofa.

Aunt Mary motioned to Fory to pour for herself. "You'll learn while you stay here, just because I have a domestic in my employ does not mean that I expect her to pour my tea for me. Or for you..."

Fory nodded and reached for the ornate server. She realized that with the intricate design on the body of the decanter, plus the shining silver of the moving parts, this pot was an heirloom. What she didn't realize until it was painfully obvious was how bad her hands were shaking from alcohol withdrawal as she tried to perform the most mundane task of pouring afternoon tea.

"Auntie, this is a gorgeous tea set," remarked Fory trying to hide the clatter of the porcelain. "Where did ya get it?"

Aunt Mary brushed both sides of her mouth with fine linen. "Yes it's a stunning piece. It's an original Paul Revere."

Fory's eyes lit up. While she was no art connoisseur, she knew it was a serious antique. Then she realized Mary was taking mental notes of her every move. She was desperately trying to make conversation so Mary wouldn't suspect the withdrawal symptoms. Sure, Mary was not fresh off the turnip truck, but Fory doubted (hoped desperately) that Mary would catch on to the DT signs.

As Fory angled the pot to pour into her cup, Aunt Mary spoke up. Cutting all illusions to the core. "Forsythia, why must you fall into the drinking habit that has become the bane of our heritage? It is a most cliché sign to hang around your neck. Worse, it has become the butt of various stereotypes and late night show satire. Don't throw another log onto that fire."

Fory filled her cup to three quarters and she sat back. "Aunt Mary, I don't know what you—"

"Please," said Mary in a slightly caring tone that belied the words. "You have been partaking of the drink and now your body is wondering where the next one is coming from. I may be old, but I'm not a wide-eyed Mick off the boat. That was only once... At the beginning of time, it would seem. Your father was at least fortunate enough to be born stateside."

Fory was beyond embarrassed. She rubbed her legs together and pulled her shoulders toward her chest. She was trying to jettison the shakes and random sweat as her body squirted out the poison via several avenues. Willpower alone wouldn't win this battle.

"In the interim," continued Aunt Mary, "should you exhibit withdrawal symptoms at a higher level, I will have my private doctor come out and administer Zofran and Lorazepam until you once again resemble a human being ready for an assignment."

An embarrassed Fory gazed in disbelief, so astonished at how the old lady picked up on every nuance of her behavior that she missed the final point of Mary's words. She sensed that this was only the beginning of her cryptic aunt's accepting a desperate imposition.

"Yes, Auntie," said Fory whose embarrassment forced her desire to stay formal. "I get it. I'll be upfront with everything that's going on with me." Fory then rubbed her forehead to steel up the courage to say it out loud. "I'm a little under the weather, but will come out of it."

"Yes, you will because of your youth," said Aunt Mary. "Just kill the footprints of the drink before you expect that I'll take anything that you say seriously." Mary shifted in her chair and addressed her niece in a warmer tone. "Fory, I'm happy to serve as host, but I am a serious woman."

"I know, Aunt Mary, I know when—"

"Mind that you do, m'dear," said Mary with a polite interruption. "It's critical if you're to end up staying for what I deem a prolonged length of time."

Oh thank god she's going to let me stay a while.

Both were silent until Mary pulled out a large clam shell from a side table and a fresh pack of Pall Malls. It appeared strange to Fory that her aunt, despite her valuable furnishings, chose a mollusk for an ashtray, undoubtedly found on the beach fifty yards away.

Fory sipped tea while Aunt Mary smoked.

After several quiet seconds, Mary offered, "Would you like some music?"

Fory was finally settling down. "No, Auntie. Thanks for the offer, but I like the quiet of this room. Your wall and painting colors with the natural light are perfect. They go with the view."

Aunt Mary rose and perused the room. Cushions in the right place, a recently tuned baby grand. Huge window toward the harbor which had been washed and was crystal clear. Mary was a person who liked her things in their place; it gave a false sense of stability.

As Fory rubbed her eyes and finished the tea, Mary saw an opportunity to broach a vital subject. "Your father was my brother. We are blood. We have a certain history. But, as you might know, family lore can be a problem, if publicized."

Fory's mind started to burn kindling but couldn't zero in on what that odd statement might mean. "Aunt Mary. Your life story...I'm sure it's full of some crazy shit," said Fory,

Mary shot her a laser glance.

"No, no, Aunt Mary. I mean it as a compliment. You may be older, but you are anything but stale." Fory shared her first real grin of the day. It seemed to work, because Mary eased back down into her chair and took a sip of tea.

"Case in point," Fory continued, "your kitchen table. I noticed the carpenter or designer missed a spot. There are three parts to the four sides of the table that are smooth, but the fourth side isn't shaved down. If you sit at that fourth side, it could end up scraping your belly on that rough bark. Is that why you bought it? I know flaws in design can fetch big money at auction. What I'm getting at is that based on family lore, you and my dad had some rough times that I'm sure many in the family viewed as flaws. I don't. I look at it as interesting."

Aunt Mary sucked in a dragon pull on her Pall Mall and tapped the result into the clam shell. "Interesting? Nice way to look at it. That table was from a home up in Ipswich on the North Shore. Owned by a pirate before the Crown knew what the hell pirates were..." *Cough!*

"Both the home and said table were built just as the Salem Witch Trials were about to commence. It was an ... *interesting,* as you say ... time in New England. In the fantasy of time travel, I wish I could have witnessed it. Those days! Immigrants roamed the countryside trying to find fertile land to farm, and thus, towns were established and New England was born."

Mary's tone lost all harshness as she relished the topic. "If one was fortunate enough to have an established homestead at the time, you were expected to open your home to weary travelers seeking warmth and a bowl of stew. Mostly, they sought refuge from the harsh elements and the indigenous people who didn't exactly share the vision of a *city on every hill.*"

Mary pointed to the kitchen. "That table is an original and practical. You see, the fourth side was left rough with jagged bark on purpose."

Fory tilted her head and greeted Mary's comments with wide open eyes to encourage her aunt to continue, showing her interest and very glad things were going smoothly now.

"You see, Fory," continued Mary, "during those infancy times of our country, if you were among the tired travelers who ended up on a

Forsythia's Ride

soft bed in my home, I would have invited you downstairs to breakfast each morning as would have been the proper Christian accommodation. I would set up your plate at a chair that faced one of the smooth sides of the table."

Fory nodded with an outward insipid reaction to the history lesson, but her mind was getting the hint.

"However, after a few days, if I grew tired of you or if I felt taken advantage of, I might change my mind and jettison my role as host. On the morning that I'd had enough, I would set the breakfast plate at the same spot. However, I would adjust the table so that the bark would scrape your belly while you leaned forward to eat."

Fory was getting the idea.

"If, on that morning, one found themself at the rough end of my table, anyone of average intelligence would take it as a sign to move along. Immediately. Have you ever heard the term *turn the tables*?" asked Mary.

"Sure," said Fory finally warming to subject.

"Well, now you know its origin. It's a little history lesson that perhaps you should commit to memory. As of now, your breakfasts shall be served with a smooth end facing your way," said Mary with a pursed smile. "Of course, everyone worries about being so bleedin' politically correct. You can't turn on the damn TV without someone whining about being offended. Ridiculous. Years ago, we were candid and efficient. And we all used our God-given pronouns," Mary hissed through a Pall Mall billow.

She thinks like the dinosaur she is, but she's warming up to me. Opening up a little. Fory felt a sudden urge to hug her aunt, but refrained. Mary's aged-sunken eyes were hard to read through the smoky haze, so Fory thought it better to come clean about the huge matter at hand which was her boss' purloined briefcase. "Aunt Mary, this is gonna sound crazy."

Mary's side mouth smirk silently responded. "I doubt it..." *Cough!*

Despite Mary's obvious respiratory ailments, Fory noticed that she always sat perfectly erect with a chin always at least at horizon level.

Matt Fitzpatrick

Well, let's see if her ancient wisdom can find a way out the situation I got myself into. Here goes... "I brought with me something I found in New York," said Fory. "I'd be grateful if you could take a look at it? At your convenience, of course. I'll tell you the whole story tomorrow, but for now, I don't know if the lock is booby-trapped or something. Maybe you can tell so we can get it open."

"I can't figure out if it's your awkward demeanor, or this odd request, but are you're asking if I'll take a look at what you brought?" Mary asked the next question with a stern delivery. "Are you in some kind of trouble, Forsythia?"

Forsythia looked at her aunt, feeling mentally captured in a corner.

"Obviously, this is an odd visit and I was given no advance notice." Mary knew damn well what it was and was struggling to keep a neutral expression on her face. "It's that old briefcase right? I understand that you're curious," said Aunt Mary.

"Well, yes, Aunt Mary," replied Fory. "Have you ever seen lock buckles like that before? I wonder what is in there."

Aunt Mary took a deep breath. "Fory, it's a heavier cargo than you probably imagined. It's almost time to go to bed." Aunt Mary didn't want to give a monologue into a wind gust. Counterproductive, at best.

Looking at Fory's confused expression, the old lady just couldn't help herself. "Dear, we often tell ourselves that we want to entertain with earnest our most comforting and invigorating dreams," said Mary. "Yet, in reality, our minds yearn to explore our most acute nightmares."

"W-what do ya mean, Auntie?" asked Fory.

Mary paused so she could conjure up the proper response. "If one blames the circumstances around her on outside forces, she will be lost. Fory, if you don't find your calling and purpose in life, you'll be a fallen leaf in early November. Wet, detached, forgotten."

A grinning Mary offered, "More tea?"

Merritt Parkway
Connecticut

Pratt barked at the young driver's seven minute tardiness then instructed the hung-over Columbia Law student to disobey all speed limits. "Liam, just get me there," snapped the knight. "And soon!"

"Of course, Sir William," said the driver while a dribble of orange bile oozed out the starboard side of his mouth. He sneaked a sleeve wipe. "I estimate our arrival in just under three hours." He faked that he was straightening his tie and got the end of it over his chin, absorbing more gunk and hoping the darker pattern on the tie would keep any stain from being visible.

Pratt's thick fingers attacked his cell, hitting number one on speed dial.

The line popped live.

"I'm heading your way." Pratt's sudden adrenaline ebbed as he asked, "Is the fly caught in your web or drowned in a bowl of soup?"

"Resting comfortably," responded the callee.

The line went dead..

Pratt was quiet for a full ten seconds; for him an eternity.

"Liam!" yelled Pratt. "We enjoy some sort of diplomatic immunity. Speed this damn bolt-bucket up. And stop calling me *sir,* dammit! That's a tosser's name. The time for posh has passed."

The driver settled deep in his seat while the car headed northeast. His mind was wondering about the numbers for the mid-day lottery draw. More important, if after dropping off his temporary King Charles, would he still have time to catch last call at the Foxy Lady on the way back to the Big Apple.

Nor'east Bluff
Chatham

As Fory woke, she savored the cloud-like feeling of the mattress. To top that off, the comforter felt like the perfect blend of cotton and feathers that could rival a Four Seasons suite.

Fory curled like a serpent within high thread-count sheets. She half-dozed until the door fanned open without a knock.

"Ten o'clock is an unacceptable waking time in my household," scolded Aunt Mary. "I was generous with the clock and have been sensitive to not only your time, but also to the circumstances of your arrival. Now, it's time to get up. You need breakfast and I need you to further explain your sudden desire to flee that hellhole city."

Fory tried her best to sit up at a ninety degree angle. "I'll be right down, Auntie. My apologies for sleeping so late."

"Indeed..." replied Mary who left the room with heavy feet.

The guest bathroom was nicer than anything Forsythia had ever seen in Manhattan. The pampered feeling soothed her. This was not just like a hotel, it was *better!* She washed her face and brushed two-day neglected teeth. For her hair, she figured a quick rinse in the sink, followed by a finger brush-though would suffice.

She smiled at the shining brilliance of the sink area. Back in New York, her own hadn't been cleaned for weeks and her mirror sported apathetic toothpaste flecks.

With a quick tidy, Fory zipped up simple jeans over a sweatshirt and then walked downstairs. With her brain in check for the moment, she finally felt hunger. *A full day sober. Time for food.*

As she walked down pine-creaking stairs, her nose was blasted with Columbian aromas. Aunt Mary only served the strongest coffee. Fory knew her unpredictable addict's stomach would have to build the mug heavy with milk and sugar.

Fory selected a seat at the far side of the table. She spooned chilled peach yogurt onto a plate of fresh fruit. She tried hard to relax, but that was a foreign emotion.

Aunt Mary and Alyce stepped in from the kitchen. Alyce holding a sizzling pan, but not for long. She poured the contents over one of the old oaken table's middle dishes. With a fork, Alyce lured the bacon toward the top of the skillet while she opened the sluice for the grease to escape. All that was left were crispy strips.

"Enjoy! Fresh country bacon," said Mary with a smile. "I hear you young, Manhattan vegan types just eat nuts and twigs, but please try. It's served Irish style. A little flavor might help your stomach." Mary smirked.

Fory slid her chair forward, beginning the construction of a bacon croissant breakfast sandwich.

"I trust you slept well and are rested?" asked Mary.

"Yes, Auntie. I was very comfortable," replied Fory as she broke off a piece of croissant. "Thank you for letting me stay for a bit. The guest room is beautiful."

"My pleasure," responded Mary. They both suddenly noticed the sound of someone approaching the dining room door. "Fory, you won't mind if I entertain another breakfast guest?" Mary asked her niece.

"No, no. Of course not, Auntie," Fory assured her. "I'd be happy to meet your guest." Fory feigned enthusiasm but didn't care either way, she was just concentrating on keeping her stomach under control.

"Have you ever heard of *Earl Grey*?" Mary asked.

Fory was confused and responded, "I have, but I don't drink much tea these days."

"No, dear," laughed the aging aunt. "I'm referring to a different kind of Earl Grey. The original."

And with that, from the kitchen, emerged an impeccably dressed, cleaned and shaven, Sir William Pratt.

Fory dropped her bread and coffee splashed over the rim of her cup. Her first instinct was to jet to the nearest exit. She slid her chair a leg's length away across the floor making a ear jarring noise.

Aunt Mary raised her hand in the air. "Relax, and sit your bony arse back in the chair."

Out of shock and wonder, Fory complied with her aunt's instructions, never breaking eye contact with her boss.

Nobody spoke until Pratt poured himself a cup of tea and took an unusually long amount of time to select a muffin from the tray. He measured a dash of cream and two lumps of sugar for his cup. He followed an inhale with a sip, wiped his mouth with a fine linen napkin, and found a seat.

The creaks from Pratt's chair made Fory cringe.

"Auntie... What the hell... what the..." stuttered Fory without ever taking her eyes off Pratt.

With the exception of Fory, nobody in the room was exuding any stress.

Mary took a chair halfway between Pratt and her niece. "Fory." Mary was using a flat monotone. "I suppose you'd like an explanation?"

Fory gazed around the room. There was no one else to speak to in order to establish clarification. Fory suddenly felt she was deep into something ... something far over her head.

The three at the table remained silent until Aunt Mary, playing host, felt compelled to break the ice. "I understand you may find Bill's presence unnerving and unexpected."

"Bill?" Fory muttered.

Pratt remained quiet; it was already agreed that Mary would set the stage for their plans.

Fory wiped her mouth with a small napkin. "Yes, Auntie. A little bit... What the fuck is going on?"

"Language!" Mary tried for a harsh tone but fell short. Pretending to be a normal old lady was no longer needed and she had been in the trenches with hardest of the IRA assassins. Language of all types had hit her ears and even escaped her lips.

Fory's eyes darted across to the other end of the table.

Forsythia's Ride

"Sir William, am I being fired?" asked a semi-crazed Fory. "I know I'm not a model employee, but I'll be fine with just a little rest and time out of the office. How did you get here? I mean... I mean... Never even mind that... *What* are you doing *here?"*

Pratt elongated an exhale while breaking his silence, irritated at having to explain himself before Mary got to the core of the reason they were all together right now. "I arrived during the night while you slept. No. You're not being fired. You see, I've had a long and prolific relationship with your aunt over the years, and I don't mean that we share feather and oak."

From across the table, Aunt Mary even in old age, snickered at Pratt's bawdy comment.

"Forsythia," continued Pratt, "I belong to an ... *organization*, let's call it for lack of a more appropriate term. A group that runs rather independent of the mainstream. Just a gathering of good people with a common cause."

Fory stopped him with a raise hand and shot a glance at her Aunt Mary. "Shit, Aunt Mary! The rumors are true?! The whole family knew you were IRA all along! Holing up here on Cape Cod? Pretending to be knitting! I should have believed all the crap I heard over the years. And now? I'm sitting here with my friggin' boss?! What the fuck is going on?"

"Language, dear," snickered Mary lighting up and taking a Pall Mall haul. A deadly serious look then settled on Mary's face. "Your father, need I remind you, died by his own hand." Mary flicked ashes in a very small shell Fory hadn't noticed before. "The whole family knows he committed the act in your presence. That was so unkind, so unfortunate for you and this is why we tolerated your drinking and have tried to steer you beyond that trauma."

Fory burst out of her chair and Nolan Ryan'd an antique teacup into the wall just to the right of a hundred thousand dollar Anne Packard oil seascape. Mary's narrowed eyes sucked any remaining calm out of the room.

"Who the hell are you?!" screamed Fory. "What am I doing here?!

Matt Fitzpatrick

My father is dead and I know it had something to do with you."

Years and miles had taught Mary how to remain calm in any situation. Those lessons were hard, but learned well. This little outburst was nothing at all. "I can see where your initial instincts would point you in that direction, however it's a little more complicated than what is printed in your history books and what you've overheard at family wakes and weddings," explained Mary. "Unfortunately, it seems more at wakes lately."

Pratt rubbed his chin while witnessing the exchange. A nod from him was a sign of his contemplation and mild agreement.

After seeing Pratt give the okay, Mary continued. "The Irish tend to speak their truest feelings when among the dead. It's funny that it's where we feel most comfortable. Could it be we like being around those who won't pose annoying questions?"

Mary Shea's Cottage
Chatham

Pratt tapped his pipe signifying it was time to end the banter and get to the point. "Fory, you got a job at my firm for a reason. Yes, of course, you were qualified, barely, but when you were referred in, it was really to establish a platform where I could observe you. Observe who you are. Monitor; looking for the traits that made your aunt a legend."

Forsythia stared. Pratt's eyes were expressionless in response. "Fory, I belong to a group known as *Earl Grey.* We are technically not part of the British government, we are completely clandestine, independent, and old. Quite old..."

Pratt wiped his chin, moved his napkin aside and cleared his throat. He knew he owed his employee a little background, yet he hated to waste time. "You see, Fory, for years, we have traded blows and worked opposite sides on many unsavory incidents with the group with whom your aunt is affiliated. But, in the end, neither side has really gotten anywhere. It's been more of a tennis match that's played with hand grenades instead of balls. A textbook war of attrition, sad to admit. The overall concept of *victory* fizzles overtime with every body bag." Pratt paused as if in half-prayer. His face as thoughtful as Fory had ever seen it. "Anyway, can you understand this, Fory? Two groups of decent people fighting for their beliefs, only to be laughed at by their true enemies who are watching them destroy each other from afar?"

Pratt ripped apart his muffin. "Mary, please take it from here. Tell the girl the truth. I want to eat."

Aunt Mary responded with a condoning hand gesture and, "Bill, I think it's important that she hears everything from you."

"Very well," said Pratt with a napkin drop. "Fory, we all know your aunt has been involved as a freedom fighter for what is known to the world as the *Irish Republican Army*. However, it's not that simple, Mary, please stop me if I start rendering an inaccurate description."

Mary nodded.

"The IRA, like most paramilitary groups, are not exactly run and operated with the utmost discipline nor even a shared vision. Most of the violence has occurred between splinter groups who can't come together on how things should be planned and executed, mostly squabbles regarding the level of violence that's implemented.

"Like many groups engaged in counter-culture activities, different factions peel off in search of their own initiatives. Some members seek an extended peace, while others never want the war to end. Those are the extremists who think peace would take away their very existence, livelihood and identity. The IRA has splinters which are sharp and jagged."

Fory remained silent and stoic for several seconds. "Appreciate the history lesson. Interesting, and I mean that sincerely," she said as she looked over at Mary. "So, what the hell does this all have to do with me?"

Pratt cocked his head and looked over at Mary who felt compelled to explain this part of the story.

"Earl Grey reached out. They extended a partnership offer the likes of which history has never seen. Our groups were already in a détente, hence your job in the city. Bill, tell her more. You're more on the front lines these days."

"In recent years, the endless hostilities between your aunt's organization and Earl Grey have subsided," Pratt explained. "It could be due to the fact that the world is changing, maybe that globalization and new policies need to be embraced. It also could be as simple as that we seasoned operatives are getting, well, just that, *seasoned*...Many members of the old guard are not only getting old, but also are long dead. The funerals are slowing, with no new people to take their place. We want to see things differently moving forward for generations like yours. The fighting needs to stop, and with our combined resources, we need to focus our attention on common enemies.

Those that threaten both our ways of life."

Fory's thoughts were racing, yet she remained quiet. She was overwhelmed, but inherently and instinctively loved the thought of the challenge. Her mind juggled thoughts of how maybe chaos was her home.

Mary nodded at the thoughtful expression on Fory's face. "While you seem to be starting to get the idea, I need to bring you up to speed on a recent event. This might shed more light. And makes the timing of your theft nearly perfect. We are going to need to do something within weeks anyway."

Oh fuck, I forgot about the briefcase I stole from this guy. This spy!

"I'm sure the fancy New York papers wouldn't carry the story, but we had an incident here on Cape Cod recently. Said incident actually occurred only a couple of streets away."

Fory's nod asked for more detail, glad they weren't focusing about what she stole.

"A young girl," continued Mary, "early grade school age. Ended up drowning in the bay around the corner."

Fory's eyes widened. "Auntie, I'm sorry to hear that. What happened? Was it someone you knew?"

"Sort of," said Mary. "She was a neighbor's daughter and was quite lovely. I didn't know them well because I'm not usually interested in 'life beyond the hedges' around here. But what *physically* happened to her is evident, and it gets complicated."

"W-what does that have to do with me?"

"Well, for now the details have been kept out of the press, but it's only a matter of time before someone leaks some details."

With a puzzled look, Fory asked, "Again, what does that have to do with me? Or you guys?"

"Even though many of the findings of the little girl's drowning are still sealed, with our contacts, we managed to get a coroner's report," Mary responded. "She ingested a powerful synthetic opiate that can only be legally acquired via a doctor's prescription. As you might know, these days certain off the path docs hand out painkiller scripts like they're tic-tacs. This particular drug is a rare narcotic known to potentially cause sleepwalking, hallucination, erratic behavior."

Fory tried to slightly lighten the mood. "Sounds like not a great sleep remedy." Her feeble attempt at humor was ignored.

"The most disturbing part of the autopsy report is that the drug appears to have been administered via the child's eyes."

A befuddled Fory asked, "Her eyes?! That's crazy. Did someone poison her on purpose?"

"Hard to say," said Mary, "but the important piece is that when the detectives searched the home, they found in the mother's medicine cabinet a small eye drop container that held a synthetic opiate known as Tsoulio, which is illegal to possess unless under strict medical oversight. Apparently, nobody in the household is under such care. So far foul play on the part of the parents is not suspected. Initial speculation is that the little girl watched her troubled mom take the eye drops, and then imitated her later on. Apparently, the mom was a closet addict; crafty about hiding her addiction from everyone except her daughter. It's happened before. Only with syringes."

Fory slowly shook her head.

Pratt chimed in, "We realize how unrelated to you and us this seems. It also was to us at first glance. It didn't seem so outlandish once we initiated our investigation and learned what drug was involved."

"Okay, okay... This is all interesting. What I'm still asking is, what's this got to do with me? And what's your final plan? And frankly, why the hell do you care about an addict mom and where she get's her drug of choice?"

Pratt's corpulent body creaked as he sat up straight then surreptitiously stretched his legs under the table. He began preparing a much longed for after-breakfast pipe. "Fory, we have a task for you. But, I need to be frank." Pratt was using his famous sternness and it got her attention as it did to everyone.

"Should you decide," Pratt said as he fumbled in his pocket for some Captain Black pipe tobacco, "not to accept participating in this project, then I will be forced to engage the New York City police, as well as the Manhattan FBI field office, to report the theft of my briefcase. Trust that I have several loyal contacts within both organizations. Entrenched contacts. Very old contacts dating back to a couple of grandfathers."

Fory stared.

"And these guys," grinned Pratt, "would love one last payday!" Fory's face reddened as Pratt explained. "That brings us back to the briefcase. It was a gift given to me by Prince Philip, the Duke of Edinburgh," pontificated Pratt. "It's value, I'm told, is priceless. The last time I checked, in New York, your offense would qualify for a charge of grand larceny in the first degree."

Pratt lit up the Captain Black. "Such an infraction carries a jail sentence of up to twenty-five years."

Fory's jaw dropped. "What the Fu... You bastard!" said Fory. "You're blackmailing me! You set me up with that briefcase! You know I'm fucked up!" Fory was breathing heavily, the sudden panic caused withdrawal symptoms to flare up. They ebbed and flowed with the tide, right now they were rushing in like a tidal wave. "What do you want me to do?!"

"Everyone, calm down," said Mary with a stone face devoid of emotion. "Relax, let's regroup."

Pratt sighed. "It's unfortunate that sometimes we need to resort to certain enticements in order to motivate our operatives. Focus on the positive. You will complete this mission with success, and you will be rewarded handsomely for your efforts."

"Dammit, old man!" Fory shot a look at Pratt while demanding answers. "What do you want me to do?"

"You weren't brought here for your charm," snapped Pratt. "You're asking for an explanation as to where you stand on the chessboard? Well, here it is ... valuable, yet ultimately, expendable. So stop the drama, wait for instructions. Do exactly what you are told and you know very well we will only share with you the information you need to know in order to complete this mission."

Matt Fitzpatrick

Fory stared out the massive bay window overlooking Pleasant Bay. While her gaze was primarily fixated on the deep blue of the channel, which she knew held Great Whites stalking seals, the open ocean still inspired a promise of freedom. She turned her attention to Mary's garden and caught a glimpse of a blue and white butterfly laying siege to a daffodil, and suddenly felt a rare tinge of guilt about tossing a fit instead of leaning in and asking questions and being a bit more cooperative.

In the silence as the young woman assessed her situation, Mary felt a tinge of guilt at setting her niece up. If it hadn't been the briefcase, it would have been an embossed wooden box or a bracelet in a Tiffany box. They had placed a half a dozen little larceny traps around Pratt's office. Like any vulnerable emotion for Mary, it quickly dissipated watching her last Pall Mall exhale of the morning. A flat stare was her only expression as the old woman finished her breakfast.

* * *

Forsythia was already spent, mentally exhausted even though her assignment hadn't even been outlined yet, let alone accepted and started.

"Alright, Aunt Mary," said Fory. "Enough is enough. What do you and Pratt want me to do exactly? I don't care if the paint peels off, or if this joint falls into the ocean. I just want away from you idiots and back to my life. What do you spies, or whoever the hell you are, want me to do?"

Mary paused to fire up a Pall Mall while maintaining an outer appearance of patience and decorum. Only she knew she was breaking her rule of one cigarette each morning, one after lunch and two for the rest of the evening. She exhaled her sustenance, and then touched soft linen to her lips waiting for Pratt to get to details now that the young woman realized she was cornered. At least Fory was thinking about survival; hearing them out before deciding to try to bolt or work with them.

"Your aunt has a new neighbor named Anna Mobley. Now, you can imagine in a neighborhood like this, outsiders are as welcome as lepers on the beach."

Fory felt it earlier as a passenger, there had been more than a fair share of scowls at the car and right in her face as they drove by.

"Apparently, said neighbor is here because she divorced very well," explained Pratt between pipe puffs. "It appears that behavior can evolve into an art over time. Anyway, it has to do with her last marriage to some aging British rock 'n' roll star type."

Mary picked up the thread. "This new resident has caused quite a disruption in the neighborhood due to her ostentatious home design and late night revelry with illegal substances as the party favors. We don't do that here," she said while popping ash into a clam shell.

"What do you mean?" asked Fory. "You think this Mobley lady has something to do with the kid taking drugs?"

"Through our intelligence we've learned that this new neighbor didn't just divorce well. Through some of her former husband's shady entertainment friends, she established contacts that allow her certain trade routes."

"This neighbor," continued Mary a little louder since her niece seemed to be checking out of the important conversation and was looking out the window, "has access to some of the outlets that we used to enjoy years ago. At this point, said routes are open to anyone with the highest bid to book safe passage. Through our info network, we believe that our new community addition is using existing off-the-grid trade routes to bring in narcotics."

With a wary look Fory said, "Okay... I guess I get it. You wanna get rid of a drug dealer. Alright. That's noble and all, but why the hell go through all this drama? Don't you people just eliminate anyone in your way. Just go blow up her house!"

Mary and Pratt exchanged looks. Pratt turned to Fory, the floor making that old house creaking noise. "Nobody is blowing anybody up, much to the contrary of your naive notions about who we are. At any rate, that's not important right now. Bottom line is that there's potentially something much more critical here than drugs. Something that warrants immediate investigation and action."

"More?" asked Fory as she turned to her aunt. "So this isn't about drug smuggling?"

Mary shook her head. "The horrible incident with the little girl was just a big eye opener that drew our attention to the fact that it was time to move faster. A show that this neighbor is a loose cannon doing anything she likes to make show-off money. Pratt's group has been tracking some of Mobley's associates for years. Bill, you tell her."

"Earl Grey monitors unsavory characters all over the world, and have done so since the end of World War II. We strongly suspect that Mobley, via some of her ex-husband's contacts, might be connected to a group called *Le Kraken,* who have been a covert thorn in the side of western intelligence agencies for years. They take great lengths to not attract attention or claim responsibility for any nefarious actions."

Fory was silent for a pregnant few seconds deep in thought, still seething at being blackmailed into something they wouldn't get around to telling her. If they kept dancing around her part in this, she was going to lose her manners again. "Le Kraken? Another one of your gun-toting crew of crazies?"

Mary shifted in her seat.

"Fory..." said Pratt while clearing his throat, "Le Kraken is an entity that has existed since the dawn of the Cold War, right about the same time my Earl Gray organization organized."

"Never heard of them," said Fory. "What's this got to do with me?"

"Allow me to finish," said an annoyed Pratt with a slight raise of his hand. The old spy never had much patience, and he wasn't about to exercise any now.

"Le Kraken was formed by a group of western Europeans in the late 1940s who maintained Communist sympathies and who ended up funneling underground resources to hard-line leftist, militant groups via military actions like you Yanks and those Frogs had in Vietnam. Most historians think of the CPUSA when discussing the Commie movement in America, but that group never made any history altering inroads. More of a vocal pestilence."

Pratt paused to tap and repack his pipe, both within five seconds. "But La Kraken is different," continued Pratt with a puff. "They work quietly and covertly, and that's the way they like it."

"O...*Kay*..." said Fory. "This sounds like a movie. And if they are well-trained you have to be bat-shit stupid to send *me* on any dangerous mission against them."

Pratt ignored her drama again and kept on at his clipped pace unfolding the story how he wanted to tell it. "We received intelligence that Mobley procured property on Cape Cod. It was just routine monitoring that we do for everyone on our watch list. Anyway, upon closer investigation, I realized that she had not only bought property down here, but it was in Chatham of all places. That's when I reached out to your aunt. This was about a year and a half ago, maybe a little more."

"Shit..." said Fory who now saw the first connection. "Just in time for me to be sent to you for a job. Damn... You fuckers set me up!"

"Language, dear," said Mary as she exhaled what could have asphyxiated an elevator full of tourists. "Fory, you were selected for the very fact that you have no experience. You're not a trained operative. That's what we wanted. That's what'll make you effective and keep you safe."

Mary then added the cherry on top. "You'll extricate yourself from any legal issues with Sir William upon a successful conclusion of your work with us."

Fory went cross-eyed. "Aunt Mary! Keep safe? Legal shit? This is goddamned extortion!"

Mary let the air clear before continuing. "No," Mary calmly responded. "It's just your turn to help the cause that has helped your people and *your family* for generations. You owe it to those who came before you. You think if you were still some bony-assed Mick picking potatoes in a field in Ireland, you'd be able to just pack up and land a cushy cubicle job in Manhattan? Had it not been for the struggle and sacrifice of those before you? Shame on you for even questioning." Mary stamped out her cigarette in frustration, feigned and not.

Pratt refused to lose control of an assignment meeting. He barged on before the two could sink into a family squabble. "Mary's neighbor has an opening that she won't advertise in the local paper or website job chats. She only wants a certain class of candidate to apply, and your aunt is providing that *indirect* reference. It's perfect for you. *Client Entertainment Correspondent* is the job title. She's basically looking for someone local to assist her with tending to her guests when she has parties. Apparently, she is preparing for an event as we speak. With all her construction going on, she invited her contracting and design team to come over and take in the progress so far, in hopes of picking up more suggestions and flaunting her excess. All the while needing an assistant and trying to find one without going public with an advert."

Assistant? So just hanging around this woman? I can do that.

"Once you are there, you might even get a peek in her Rolodex." suggested Pratt.

"What's a Rolodex?" Fory posed an age appropriate question, and then brushed it away. "Wait! Wait! Let's go back." Frustration was growing again in Fory. "Okay, this isn't about some local drug dealer. Still, from what I know of your past, this is child's play. Just getting in there and knowing her schedule. So ... What's the real story? And how the hell do you know so much about this lady if she just arrived?"

"Your notions about my past are skewed," Mary replied. "I still maintain an information network that has grown many branches over the decades."

"Indeed," Pratt quipped with a laugh and a cough.

"How I receive information is irrelevant at the moment. Time is short," said Mary. "Here's the story, and you're only going to hear this once, so please listen."

Forsythia's Ride

Fory's silence reflected her aunt's solemn tone. The serious threat of jail time if she refused hung heavy on her head. She was embarrassed to admit to herself that most of the fear was connected to not being able to reach for a drink if she was behind bars.

Mary began. "This area of town has so much military history, you can imagine how much folklore abounds as it does in every old New England town. Well a *new* legend has it that somewhere under these dunes is buried a cache of stolen U.S. military weapons that very well may include nuclear arms."

"Holy shit..." whispered Fory.

"Indeed," said Mary. Pratt was happy to let his colleague have the conch as she continued. "A stash of weapons was stolen many years ago from a base roughly thirty miles west of here. It's been well documented and remnants of the story periodically still show up in the local papers. They were never found, and rumor has always been that it was an inside job by some U.S. military mid-level brass who went rogue. Someone who was not high enough in the ranks to get noticed, but they had enough clout to be able to maneuver what was required to execute the theft."

"Wait a minute..." said Fory suddenly understanding, "you two think that those stolen weapons have something to do with why this lady is digging all over her property? You think her construction project is bullshit. She's really looking for friggin' missiles and bombs and shit! How come the crooked generals or whoever didn't sell 'em?"

"First of all, we have to be clear," Pratt intervened. "We don't know exactly what we're looking for, but we have some pretty decent clues. The reason that the scoundrel military officers couldn't sell the weapons is that the government, out of nowhere, shut this area down and began the decommissioning process. Bottom line, the land got sold off to private speculators, and *voilà*, instant coastal community. So whoever stole the weapons most likely stashed them somewhere near the closed base planning to move them when the heat was off; then with the base closure it was impossible to use military vehicles to get the goods out of the area. The thief must have died in some way or another, because none of the weapons have ever resurfaced. That the area now happens to be mostly a wealthy one compounds the issue tenfold."

Pratt sat back and hauled on his pipe.

"Okay, okay," Fory shot back. "So, you're just going to steal this stuff and go use it for your own bombings and shit?"

"Fory," said Mary in a calming tone, "I can assure you that our respective organizations on both sides of the pond agree that the weapons, if recovered, will be immediately turned over to the U.S. government, as they're rightfully theirs."

Pratt nodded in agreement while Fory sat back relieved but not completely trusting them. Then her imagination ran at full speed. "Oh. That's different. That's... That's great! Damn! I'll be a hero! Get a reality show! I'm in!"

Pratt interrupted Fory's elation. "Unfortunately, whether your participation in this project results in either success or failure, you'll remain under strict anonymity for the rest of your days."

"W-what?" asked a confused Fory. "I don't understand. If I—"

Mary interrupted. "Fory, you need to know, while we absolutely do intend to turn the weapons over to the Feds, the government is going to be presented with a bill for our service that's commensurate with the value of the delivery. Once those funds are securely wired as per our instructions, the missing weapons will be returned."

The three sat quietly during a pregnant pause as Fory stared at the others. "Holy shit..." she said. "You're just stealing what's already been stolen, and then extorting our own country to fatten your own pockets!"

"Now, Fory," Mary waved a calming gesture towards her niece. "You understand what you're doing is patriotic, for sure. It's just that Bill and I serve higher causes that we need to consider. Unfortunately, like anything, the resources required to achieve our goals cost money. In the end, this is a win/win for us and the U.S. government."

"I don't believe this." Fory shook her head.

Forsythia's Ride

"Well," said Pratt to further Mary's explanation of the situation's reality, "would you rather we recover the weapons and sell them on the black market? Trust that between your aunt's and my contacts, there are several channels that we could explore who would be more than eager to take our call and own such a unique opportunity."

"Alright, alright." Fory was getting tired and needed a drink. "How the hell do you know there even are any weapons? And if you find them, do you know how to move nukes? And better yet, why the hell do you know they're down the street!"

"We don't," said Mary with a sigh, "but your father did."

Fory's eyes lit up. "What?"

Mary Shea's
Nor'East Bluff, Chatham

"M-my, father?" Fory muttered the question in a hazy mix of bitter-sweet emotions.

Mary paused for a few seconds in thought, then nodded toward Pratt and said, "The world where Bill and I operate is infested with rumor and conjecture. It was always said that when your dad got into his cups, he was known to boast about a secret location that would be the key to his retirement. He would boast about how he was going to extort the U.S. government and how that would be his meal ticket and allow him to stop having to run operations. He yearned for a more peaceful life. Not just for him. Every dream he had at that time was always for you. I guess he envisioned getting a bigger boat and heading south. We'll never know, will we? Unless, of course, you might have some information that could be helpful?"

Red exploded in Fory's eyes. "Are you two crazy? I'm shlepping away in a four by four foot cubicle for Prince Charles over here, can barely pay my rent, and yet I'm sitting on a secret that could be worth like, a gazillion bucks? Ah, not so much, *Auntie.*"

Pratt wanted to diffuse the situation. "It's okay... We're confident that if you can think of something useful, you'll be more than happy to share."

"Yeah, well, I don't know anything. My dad always treated me like a princess and never exposed me to whatever you all were up to," said Fory calmer since she was falling for Pratt's gambit. "But, if I did know something, what's in it for me?"

Mary smiled. It was only a matter of time before Fory's real colors emerged, and here they were. "First of all, if you cooperate with us, you'll avoid jail time. That's for starters."

Fory scowled at her aunt.

"Second," continued Mary, "if you succeed in this mission, *and* most important, take the secret to your grave, bottom line is that you'll receive a handsome fee. You might not live like your generation's heroes, those Kardashians, but you'll certainly be better off than should you continue to work for Sir William or find another plebian cubicle job." Mary turned toward Pratt with a snicker, "Bill, no offense to your firm."

"None taken," chuckled Pratt. "It's the truth. Fory, you'll be able, for the most part, to do what you want in sufficient comfort moving forward if you succeed in helping us."

A sudden massive wave of withdrawal nausea swept over Fory. She turned grey and covered her mouth, inaudibly mumbled, and ran into the bathroom beyond the kitchen. She slammed the door, only to have it pop back open.

"AHHHHHHH!" she gagged into the toilet.

As the two overheard the violent bile-induced retching, Mary turned to Pratt. "So, you're still okay with her as our girl?" asked Mary with dry heaving in the background, followed by a cry of painful frustration.

"She's perfect," he said as he gazed out the window toward the ocean. "I couldn't have built her better myself."

* * *

After several minutes, a red-faced Fory returned. "Sorry about that. Musta been something I ate," said Fory like any proper addict as she wiped a napkin across her face. "So, okay. Let's say we do this. Alright, so I'm gonna get paid if we find these bombs? What if we don't? What if I do everything right and still strike out?"

"If for some reason, our intelligence and instincts are wrong, which does happen, albeit seldom, in that case you'll be granted a handsome wage increase at my firm. More money, fewer hours and your own office. That's the worst case scenario," Pratt answered.

Fory smiled at first. "Okay, sounds fair. But you're wrong!" She then snapped at Pratt, "That's great and all, but it's in no way the worst that could happen. Worst case scenario? I go over snooping around and that crazy lady feeds me to these damn sharks I keep hearing about."

Neither Pratt or Mary responded.

Ah, guilty silence from the spooks. They know I'm right. "Plus," said Fory running out of steam because nausea was creeping back in, "how do you know she's even gonna give me the job?"

"Don't worry about that." Mary waved her hand. "I've already taken the liberty of dropping a few hints on your behalf. You have an interview already scheduled for late this afternoon."

Fory swiveled her head between both of them. "Today! I can't believe you're doing this to me. Aunt Mary, how could you?! What if she gets onto me? What if..."

"Relax, dear. Before your interview, more precisely before any of this commences, there's someone I need you to meet at the Chatham Fish Pier this afternoon. She's going to take point in backing you up on this assignment." Mary used her most assuring tone of voice.

"Who?" responded Fory in confusion. "I thought you were sending me on a solo gig? This is getting crazier by the minute." Although perplexed, Fory wasn't fighting this meeting very hard, just some protest for show. She knew that going out meant being able to duck in somewhere for rum. "You're at least setting me up with someone dashing with biceps? Why not? At this point I wouldn't mind a stiff shot of Bacardí and a stiff..." Fory meant to say that to herself, but delivered it out loud.

"Fory," said Mary with a calming inhale, "we didn't recruit your contact based on this month's cover of GQ, and if you were paying attention, like you need to be every second you are here on the Cape, you would have noticed I said She not He."

"Aunt Mary, this whole thing is crazy! What the fuck am I getting into?!"

"Language, dear," said Mary as she squeezed more lemon into

her tea. "Anyway, you're to meet in an hour down at the Fish Pier. It's locked in."

Fory's eyes rolled with an unabashed look of *Great.*

"Your phone has been injected with a GPS tracker which allows me to review your travel throughout the day. As in no liquor store or gin joints. Not even an honest game of Keno while nursing a ginger ale."

Fory sat back in her chair and looked at the ceiling as if that was going to magically provide better answers or new options.

She wondered if the ornate, silver butter knives would be able to slit a wrist.

Preferably, her own...

Chatham Fish Pier
Shore Road

With the address given to her by Aunt Mary, Forsythia punched the coordinates into the Fiat's GPS. It was a medium blue with a white stripe up the middle. Making the mini-car look a bit sporty. Despite its anachronistic looks, the vehicle was equipped with the latest in navigational technology to the tune of two independent GPS units and even radar for the Chatham fog. Fory laughed to herself wondering if she could press a button and shoot nails out of the trunk *à la* Agent 007, although that would be hypocritical for an Irish operative.

As Fory drove, she reflected on the past few days. From the calamity at the office, to vomiting at her friend's door, all the way to driving in this glorified go-cart going to a training lesson on how not to get shot in a crazy spy's house.

Due to a light easterly breeze, as Fory approached the town dock she immediately caught a whiff of the day's catch. She slowed the Fiat and molested its gears while she worked the stick shift. She peeled to her right, found a spot, and pulled the emergency brake as a mercy gesture to the transmission.

As Fory got out with subtle joy, she heard the cracks and creaks of her bones that were a reflection of not only stress, but also from passing out under her desk one too many times. The last time under her desk had kept her scrunched for over an hour so as not to be discovered; her muscles were still unknotting from that brilliant move. The withdrawal sparks were not helping the situation.

She tossed her canvas bag over her shoulder and walked down toward the east side of the pier where she was supposed to meet this contact. The sun felt strong and reassuring on her neck. But the withdrawal threw her gait. She felt the nerves and shakiness that come from the body demanding its poison and the mind trying to stay clean.

Forsythia's Ride

Fory hoped that this woman was cool and understanding, and perhaps could be coaxed into a liquid lunch. *Just one to settle the nerves, I won't have more and it will help me step down off the booze. I can have one a day for a week. Then I'll go to one every other day. Keep the pukes away and still keep my head clear.*

The old pier boards croaked and groaned under her feet as she approached the far end of the landing. The further she got out, the sweeter the scent that was carried by the light breeze. After so much time in Manhattan, she could not inhale enough fresh, salty air.

Fory leaned against a faded wooden rail and looked out at a seagull engaging in the ancient task of smashing open a fresh clam by dropping it on the deck of a skiff. Fory was amused by the sheer monotony of the bird using gravity to try and crack the shell, followed by the bang when it hit. Over and over, and yet it was met by the same result. Nothing.

"Idiot. Try cement," Fory muttered not realizing the irony trying to fish a water bottle out of her bag as the shakes were in control of her hands. Her dry, sandpaper tongue needed some lube, but her quivering hands were having a hard time sifting through the dozen other useless items she'd brought along.

"Dammit!" she hissed at herself. Finally, her hand squeezed soft plastic.

Even though she wished that the haul from the water bottle was a belt of Bacardí, Fory was grateful for the slaking of her growing thirst. Feeling a bit more relaxed, she looked out in the channel and saw a large grey seal pop its head out of the water while proudly sporting a schoolie striper in its mouth. White sharks had made this part of Cape Cod their home, with a macabre sense of humor, Fory half hoped for a shark strike.

Suddenly, from her stern a young female voice startled the quiet. "Excuse me... Sorry to bother you, but I'm wondering if you could help me?" asked the young woman, who Fory guessed to be in her early twenties with a possibility of being even a bit younger. Feeling withdrawal symptoms kick in more, she didn't have the patience for some college kid looking for a keg party.

"I'm sure I can't," said a curt Fory. "I'm a fish out of water, myself. Sorry, kid, the homecoming parade isn't around here."

The young woman gazed at Fory like an M.E. over a sliced-up cadaver. "Humm, I think that you *can* be of assistance," said the girl.

"Oh, is that so? Great. An optimist. What do you need?"

"What I *need*," said the girl whose sudden change in tone gave Fory the chills, "is for you to take your attitude down a few pegs. You're so in your day-after fog you have no idea what's happening around you. And worse, you're beginning the first stages of alcohol withdrawal. It's visible. Here, have this."

The girl pulled out a pint of Forsythia's favorite poison and handed it to Fory. It was tantamount to mother's milk.

Fory suspended all discretion and didn't even look around. She couldn't care less who this girl was or why she was there. At that moment, all that existed on the planet was the glass object just passed to her hand. She bottomed up the bottle and hauled hard; a flamingo slamming a mullet down its gullet.

The initial blast to the receptors in her brain kicked in after only ten seconds. An impressive professional.

While Fory basked in the effects of the drink, the young girl was quiet, bordering on creepy.

After several seconds, and once Fory felt fortification with the drink, she took inventory. "Thank you for that. How did you know it would do the trick? And at the risk of being rude, who the hell are you?"

The young woman kicked the pier rails to knock some mud off her shoes. "For someone who was just saved from a potential alcohol withdrawal seizure, I find you not especially grateful."

Fory's fingers found her own hair for a twirl and a pull. "Yeah, fine. Thanks for the haul," shot Fory. "You obviously have experience."

"I do. All kinds," said the girl. "Allow me to introduce myself. I'm Michonne, your contact and handler for this operation. I trust that Mary told you at least the basics?"

Forsythia's Ride

"Wait." Fory looked around to make sure nobody was listening, but in the last second, didn't care. "You?!" exclaimed Fory while her eyes scanned a fast up and down on Michonne. "You're my contact? Shit... Ho-ly shit... You're supposed to be helping me?" Rum-dulled senses removed any filter in Fory. "What do they want? Me to chaperone prom night?"

Michonne let Fory's steam pass for a few seconds. "It may appear so," her eyes grew hard, "but trust that's not the expectation."

"Great." In frustration, Fory ran her palm across the wooden rail and picked up a half-inch splinter. "Ouch! Dammit!"

"You okay?" asked Michonne

Fory shook her hand. "Yeah, yeah. I'll live. This has got to be a joke. Candid Camera or Punk'd type of gags. Right?"

Michonne rubbed her jaw. "My apologies. I don't know what those are."

"Great. Just, great. Where the hell's George Clooney or Harrison Ford?" she asked rhetorically.

"I don't know who they are," said Michonne. "I guess I could Google them if you need personal information? We also have a reliable, secure database for unorthodox requests."

"Lovely," replied an exasperated Fory. "You wanna help? Do you have a particularly sharp butter knife?"

Michonne ignored Fory's feeble sarcasm and bluntly said, "I'm the one who's going to keep you out of jail. And with a smile."

Michonne's blank gaze reminded Forsythia of Wednesday from the *Addams Family*. Fory suddenly looked deflated as her upward exhale made her bangs dance. They were quiet for several seconds again. The only sound was the screaming from a flock of seagulls fighting over scrub bait that was tossed into the harbor.

"Listen," Michonne broke the silence, "I'm sure all this is confusing and unnerving. From what I understand, you've had a few long days. Let me buy you lunch at the Squawking Gull. You'll need at least three ounces of eighty proof to ensure you're able to work properly."

"What am I, some kind of lab experiment?" snarked Fory. "And for the record, I prefer 70 proof rum."

"That's great," said Michonne, "You're cutting back."

Fory stared. "Don't judge me you fucking *Mylie*!" shot Fory, who quickly regained her composure. Insulting a possible bar-tab payor was not a smooth move and she really did want a steady supply to keep her from the shakes.

She exhaled slowly. "My apologies... My language can get a little rough."

"Nah, you're fine," responded Michonne. "A lot of stress, I would imagine."

"Can't even friggin' begin..." Fory wiped an eye. "I know you were sent, but you're a goddamned kid! How'd you get mixed up in this shit? Whatever this *shit* really is?"

Michonne replied without a flinch. "My dad and your aunt go way back to their Boston days, and—"

"Great," interrupted Fory as she fought off the twitches in her hands. "What's he, some kinda James Bond too?" She was anxious because the shakes were coming a little faster even after a noble fix.

Michonne's face went chalky.

Fory didn't pick up on the warning in her handler's facial change. "I take it they met while serving at a Boston soup kitchen, or sharing a rosary at the Novena at *Saint whoever's* in Southie?"

Michonne worked through unwanted thoughts of slicing this fool up, letting the silence hold for a few seconds, and then kicked a scallop shell across the dock and into the harbor. "Not quite," she said tightly. "Fory, don't underestimate how much we might have in common."

Michonne played mannequin while Fory looked out toward the fast-eroding outer barrier beach a half a mile to the east.

Both women were holding back and also begging for the strength to cry.

Pratt & Mary, Nor'east Bluff Beach Chatham

Mary Shea pulled her capris just above her knees to avoid getting soaked by a stray wave or a patch of soft sand. Sir William, under much protest, had removed his shoes and socks with awkwardness. He inadvertently did his best Churchill walk as the unlikely pair strolled southward down the quiet, private beach.

Pratt incoherently groused at the ocean as his walking stick plunged into a dead horseshoe crab washed up on the beach. The business end of what was a cherished gift from Margaret Thatcher had just impaled the crust of a species that had been around since before the T-Rex.

"We must look like an old couple trying to recapture a romantic moment," laughed Mary. "Could make for an old black & white movie, would you agree?" she asked the stodgy old Brit.

"*Old,* indeed," grunted Pratt. "Our colleagues, past and present—mostly past—would certainly disapprove of such an outing, no matter how casual or inconsequential."

Pratt fought the urge to smoke, settling on tapping the bowl on a well-barnacled rock to knock ashes and tough old tobacco strings out of it. "Indeed, the world is changing. If for the better, I'm not yet convinced. However, I'm keeping my focus on the matter at hand. And if that means that while achieving our goal we can enjoy a walk on this lovely beach, so be it!" Overall, he hadn't enjoyed such a peaceful walk, or such pleasant company, in many years. Too many.

Mary smiled and held Pratt's shoulder as they avoided stepping on sharp shells. "Bill, I'm sorry, but I need to switch gears. Are you still confident about using a civilian, who just so happens to be my dead brother's daughter? I mean, Bill, normally either of us would have given this to a seasoned player. Someone whose assets are not just her *ass*?"

Matt Fitzpatrick

Pratt walked to the left of Mary, he ended up with his foot half in the water. The spring Atlantic's cool temps put a rare smile on his face. It reminded him of simpler times walking along the shores of Brighton as a boy back in England. He envied the Mods and their motorbikes. Their girls, their Keith Moon, and their defiant freedom...

Pratt's mind recalibrated. "This is such an unorthodox task. The world is changing, so I guess I must do the same," said Pratt. "Her success or failure will be monitored by both our organizations. Interesting, when you think of it. Her success in this type of field work could be the death knell for you and I. The Forys of the world might just send us old players out to pasture once and for all," said an introspective Pratt as he gave in to himself and committed a wad of Captain Black to his pipe. "Dammit, you know there are many among our colleagues who wouldn't mind seeing both of us vacate our posts. Leaves room for them to move up. It's as natural as brea... (cough) *breathing*," he struggled to say as he blew a fresh billow from the pipe, followed by more hacking.

"I can't speak for you, Mary, but there are plenty around me in the shadows who would not be disappointed to have a big layer on the totem pole suddenly being forced into retirement."

Mary squinted into the sun, the rays bit her eyes. "I'm impressed there's that much demand in the ranks these days. I wish some of the younger players on my end showed as much passion. I bet they're plenty on both sides who wouldn't mind a change."

Mary was interrupted by screaming across the lawn abutting the beach. "HEY! HEY YOU! YOU'RE ON PRIVATE PROPERTY!" a neighbor shouted.

Mary and Pratt both immediately stopped short. There are few people with less tolerance for being accosted in public and drawing attention than two aging spies. Especially true when the angry neighbor in question was so irate at the trespassers that he marched across the lawn in his skivvies.

Mary's neighbor, the often verbose Lestor D. Hines, was barking at them as he ran across the lawn of his ten million dollar, newly constructed mansion that the surrounding residents mockingly dubbed *Chathamworld* due to the exorbitant size, melodramatic design and overall tackiness. Said neighbor didn't resemble the corporate raider he supposedly was, but rather a frantic terrorist in a third-world hellhole screaming, "Death to America!"

Whatever was ruining Lestor's day was about to shatter the peace the unlikely duo had established. Pratt was disappointed; he was enjoying a moment with no pressure and no immediate need for a decision of some sort, but moreover, he responded poorly to threats. As, of course, did Mary, but her responses were usually more diplomatic. At first.

As the consummate male, Pratt always met confrontation with a quick switch to playing offense. Those who shared company with the old Brit knew well that if his walking stick suddenly pointed horizontally in your direction, it may be time to duck.

The irate neighbor stopped short of invading Pratt and Marys' personal space once he realized that the pointy end of the Brit's cane was at his eye level.

"Dear sir," quickly snapped Pratt before his newest nemesis could open his mouth, "we are in the middle of a pleasant spring morning walk. A gentle stroll that would normally include getting soaked and sand ridden, as expected, but not verbally accosted."

Lestor's facial expression abandoned scarlet, and eased down into a pink hue. He suddenly seemed aware his attire was one step below pajamas. Yet like most men of his trade, he had to have the last say. "I own this beach! This is private property and you are trespassing. So, unless you want me to alert the authorities, I would suggest that you both move along."

Lestor was surprised that neither Pratt nor Mary showed the slightest reaction. He was enabled in life; when he raised his voice in the boardroom, bodies shifted in seats and boots quivered! When he raised his voice at home, everyone hustled. These two were just staring calmly at him, waiting for him to finish.

"We do not mean to trespass," said Mary with as much deference

Matt Fitzpatrick

as she could muster. Lestor didn't realize that it was in his best interest to not fire up the old lady's furnace.

"It's actually my understanding," explained Mary, "and not to nit-
pick, but that you actually only own to the high water mark of the
tide. Doesn't the Atlantic Ocean remind you every six hours that you
don't own everything in sight? I've been taught the ocean will take
whatever she wants, when she wants it."

Lestor wrote Mary's words off as geriatric gibberish. "Sorry, lady.
Some law was trying to be passed by that Billy Bulger years ago that
would have made your claim true. As far as Chatham is concerned,
that law doesn't exist. Bulger never quite had the power to swing it. I
own to the *low* water mark. Now, get off my property!"

With that, the *nouveau riche* D. Lestor Hines turned and swatted
at his yipping Havanese who came to see the commotion. The pooch
sported two pink bows and an attitude.

"You tourist types are always coming out here and chipping away
at our navy slab so you can sell them as friggin' war souvenirs on
eBay!" Lestor felt emotional momentum and was totally unable to get
of his own way and read the room, or beachfront. "I know what you're
up to poking around out here."

Pratt politely straightened with distinction and touched Mary's
arm in an innate act of chivalry.

"I don't understand. I live just a few houses away, and I'm never
pestered with intruders," said an icy Mary. "For *long*, anyway..."

Pratt half-coughed as he tried to suppress a chuckle. Of course,
the sarcastic snip went right over Lestor's head.

"These tourist pricks," continued the neighbor, "keep chipping
away at my seawall, and it can't be replaced!"

Pratt and Mary caught one another's eyes, half in understanding.

"They chip pieces off and then sell them. And, I gotta lawyer down
here. An albino, no less, so he's pissed off to begin with! That freak
won't leave a piece of meat on your bones!" the neighbor's voice faded off as he began to lose steam, almost realizing the ridiculousness
of the exchange. The last feeble strand of humanity in him reminded

that he was screaming at a couple old enough to be his dead parents.

"Well," said Pratt after the easterly breeze settled the air as he doubted the veracity of the neighbor's contention, "you really ought to get this site recognized by the historical commission. Then nobody could come near here, and your land would be priceless."

Money appealed to Lestor. "Maybe you're right," he muttered as he scanned the concrete landing base while his demeanor softened. "I dunno... I'll look into it."

Pratt offered a soft tip of his cap in expectation that the exchange had run its course.

Then Lestor's nature kicked in. "However, in the meantime, I must ask that you move along." He motioned toward the small waves. "And, I must insist that you walk along the low waterline."

After three seconds, and an eye glance exchange between he and Mary, Pratt responded with a forced smile. "We would never consider any other route."

Satisfied, Lestor turned and clomped over sea grass to get back onto his putting-green trimmed lawn. After about ten yards, he looked back toward Pratt and Mary. "I just don't like people messing with my piece of history! I own it, dammit!" Lestor's voice trailed off as he blew out his flip-flop nearly crashing to his knees. He hurried inside to pretend he had some dignity left to preserve.

The air stilled. A half-dozen seagulls cried and crashed into the current searching for a few herring who were playing hooky from their migrating school.

"Yes you do, sir. You own it, indeed," Mary mumbled in Lestor's direction knowing she wouldn't be heard. She and Pratt turned and walked away.

"Mary," Pratt whispered a chuckle into Mary's cheek, "apparently, they tapped the wrong Bulger brother to take care of their tidal law issue..."

Squawking Gull Pub
Main Street, Chatham

Fory and Michonne paired to nudge the age-swelled door and were met with a wooden groan while entering the legendary Cape Cod establishment. Stale, spilled beer stuck to their shoe soles from oak planks creaking in pain. They chuckled at the splash of license plates adorning the walls. Dropped off and mounted by visitors from all over the country with the Lone Star state's contribution, *TEX T&A*, as a fan favorite.

"Classy joint..." Fory whispered to her chaperone who responded with frozen eyes.

"My guess is you've darkened worse doorways."

The battle of wits had begun, and would be an exchange not easily won by Fory who marveled at the girl's demeanor and command of diction, both of which exceeded what was expected for her young age.

Several pairs of eyes tracked them as they sought the last available high top table. Michonne, looking younger than her years, wouldn't be allowed to sit at the bar without ID. It was laughable, the thought of trying to come up with authentic credentials of age or otherwise. She never had a driver's license, social security card or birth certificate. It was as though she never existed. *Even I don't know my exact age. Thank heavens Dad has a great forger working for him. I've got all I need for any age I want to be.*

Fory was a bit grumpy because the high-top table felt like a barrier between her and the next drink. The service was always better at the bar. Before and after.

A waitress approached with fresh napkins and silverware. "Can I get you anything to start?"

"Ginger Ale, please," said Michonne, which was met with a not so subtle frown from the server. The Squawking Gull only made money one way, and it wasn't from selling ginger ale.

The waitress turned toward Forsythia. "And you, ma'am?"

Ma'am? Dammit, thought Forsythia then shook off the perceived slight since she wanted nothing slowing the nectar the waitress would bring.

"Bacardí Limón and Sprite. No ice. Less Sprite," said Fory with the delicate approach of a mugger.

"Lime?" asked the waitress.

"NFP," replied Fory. "And I don't think we'll be having food." *That would be inefficient,* Fory said to herself as a well-trained addict. *Maybe we should order something to eat, I'll decide after the first drink.*

"Roger that," replied the waitress as she scooped up the menus like poker chips. At least she had one live one at the table who was showing signs of a pro.

As the two awkward partners looked around the room, it was Michonne who broke the silence.

"Listen, I'm not here to judge. Actually, I was instructed not to." Her charge's eyes rolled with a *here we go* look. "You seem to enjoy your cups," said Michonne. "Kinda early in the day, isn't it?"

Fory molested her napkin. "Listen," Fory tried to explain, "I have an evil twin sister, and as much as I like to keep her locked away, she doesn't require much coaxing to enjoy a furlough." Fory exhaled. "When possible, I try to leave her at home."

Michonne sat back and laughed. "Funny! I have one of those, as well." Her demeanor chilled a half notch. "Hopefully, you'll never meet her."

The veiled threat was not lost on Fory. She didn't know whether to be intrigued or just overall pissed off at her aunt. Or maybe, herself. Or maybe this girl/woman who was trying to take charge. Hell, somehow her dad was connected to this spy mission and her being blackmailed into some spooky job, so maybe she should be pissed at him too.

Michonne remained quiet studying Fory as a scientist does a fossil.

"What's it like?" she finally asked.

A puzzled Fory stared back at Michonne, who realized that she needed to clarify.

"I mean, to get so taken over by the drink?" Michonne's tone really did show only curiosity. "I've seen it with some of my parents' friends, but I don't get it."

Fory's initial reaction was to puff up her back then snarl out a snarky reply, but she could sense intellect combined with a non-judgmental approach, so she squelched an outburst. She exhaled, putting her hands by her side. "It's kind of like a bear trap attached to a chain. A long chain..." explained Fory.

Michonne's eyes reflected the pulsing from the ceiling fan. Forsythia had her full attention.

"You see," continued Fory, "the trap will snap on your leg. Grab you hard! It hurts, and it bites! All you want to do is escape! Anywhere, but here..."

Fory was trying to explain deep emotions and needs, things that must be foreign to the woman sitting across from her.

"You walk, and you walk, and keep trying to trudge," Fory described with waving arms, "and the further you think you're getting away from the bear trap, you notice the weight of the chain gets heavier and harder to maneuver. It's an open field, so you run toward the horizon. You run into an expanse, which in your mind promises escape. But, the further you run away, the heavier the chain links get! You're trying to run, but you're actually going slower!"

Michonne felt the weight of Fory's description, and respected the honesty.

"It's a long metal tether, so you don't think it will snap your life to a standstill anytime soon. At a certain point, you feel the confidence that you're miles away, and despite the ever increasing weight of the long chain, you'll be alright! I'll be okay! There's nothing wrong with me!" Fory was almost yelling and touched the sweat on her forehead.

Michonne rubbed Fory's elbow, calming her down a small bit. "But, then you're not alright?" she prompted, fascinated at this look inside another person's mind.

With a slight head shake, Fory continued. "No...Then, it tightens around your leg more, and the spikes against your calf penetrate. Then, you bleed. Pain floods in as blood flows out. It wets the pavement faster the more you fight and struggle. Eventually you realize you've surrendered to the bear trap. There is no escape, unless you can find a six-foot hole in a field!"

In exhaustion, Fory wiped her right eyebrow. "Anyway, that's what it's like. And I just got squeezed in the calf, because all I can think of now is why is the waitress so slow bringing our drinks?!"

The waitress had given up early on the girls' lunch order, seeing them intensely talking and she had them pegged for low tippers. They were not her priority. Michonne reached over and stole two menus from the next table. She realized that a little air cleaning might be a good idea. "The waitress is miffed that I didn't order a cocktail," said Michonne, "but maybe take a look at this and get some food?"

"Here you are," said the waitress when she returned with Fory's fortification and a ginger ale for Michonne. "Oh! I see you have new menus? I thought you were just..."

"Actually, we changed our minds," said Michonne in a bogus upbeat tone. "We'll have an order of buffalo wings and some potato skins."

The waitress nodded as she wrote in her pad. "On the wings, ya want hot, honey, barbecue..."

Before the woman could finish the litany of flavors, Fory spoke up, "Honey, please."

The waitress looked over her pad. "Hollah if you want somethin' else."

Fory thanked her, and after the woman turned her back, Fory attacked the cocktail with a baby bird's fervor. "Ahhh..." sighed Fory after draining half the glass. "Sad to say, but it only takes a few seconds to start to feel normal again."

"How are you going to feel in a couple of hours?"

Matt Fitzpatrick

Fory couldn't immediately respond because a group of fishermen at the table behind them erupted into laughter after a particularly off-color joke. Fory hoped they were fisherman due to the blood splattered clothes and a rather odiferous waft. Either that or they were serial killers.

As the jukebox came to life and called for Hendrix to play the wah peddle intro to *Voodoo Chile*, Fory already felt better. All it took was that second haul of rum. "Do you like Jimi Hendrix?" asked Fory while moving to a rum groove.

"Who's Jimi Hendrix?" asked a genuinely confused Michonne.

"Oh, gawd..." Fory muttered to herself. She'd heard enough. "I see. Anyway, I'd like to know more about what the hell we're doing here and who you are and how you know my aunt? Wait," said Fory as she noticed her glass had been reduced to a wet glare at the bottom. "Miss!" She yelled over the crowd's din to call the waitress three times. She finally got the woman's attention and pointed to her glass. The server nodded in understanding, she realized this customer was hitting it hard and early, that meant a sloppy big tip! She hurried to the bar to place the order.

Like most addicts, Fory immediately calmed down once she realized the next drink was on the way. With that anxiety quelled, she asked, "Now, where were we?"

"Okay..." said Michonne very glad to get to business and end the lunch date. "Obviously, you wanna know more about me and why you're in this position?"

"It would help," semi-huffed Fory as she kept one eye in the direction of the waitress and her proximity to the drink ordering station. The jukebox paused and moved onto a Black Crowes track. Fory smiled. *Somebody with solid taste is feeding the machine.*

"Well, Forsythia," said Michonne, "I'm eighteen years old, maybe twenty. I could be a little older. I live with my mom and dad, and I now have a baby brother."

"You *think* you're 18?" asked Fory. "No offense, but you act like someone older, but look kinda younger." Her own words made her chuckle. "Shit... my best friend in Manhattan would love that compliment."

"Thanks, I guess." Michonne had a flash of a thought, *I wish I had a best friend.* Then viciously snuffed that thought out. *I can't be weak. To be weak is to die in this business.* "Like I said, I just have an age range. Anyway, I grew up fast, not in the US, and have spent the last few years surrounded by adults. I guess I just learned differently than most kids."

"I see. That's why you don't know our stars and musicians. Do you...did you go to school?"

Michonne tilted her head. "School's a relative term. My mom taught me certain subjects. It's fine being homeschooled and all. I learned math, science, English, blah, blah. Nothing useful in the real world. That all came later."

The table behind them came up with another one-liner. Volcano laughter erupted again.

Michonne waited until the boisterousness dissipated into typical pub din. "Being orphaned so young, I was lucky to find my adoptive parents. They saved my life and have taught me a ton, especially my dad."

"What did he teach you?" asked Fory who was eyeing the room for the waitress. Her internal clock said the cocktail was about a minute late.

"My dad coached me on many subjects. Some dealing in metals."

"Hmm... a sheet metal guy? Like construction?" asked a naive Forsythia who was too distracted to be focusing on the type of person sitting across from her. Little did Fory suspect, this very distraction allowed both of them to be a bit more honest with other than they had ever bothered to be before.

"No, he deals in other kinds of metals," said Michonne, "and I don't mean collectibles and coins."

Fory was quiet for a couple of seconds while the other table quieted down only because they were filling their gullets with infusions burger and fries.

Matt Fitzpatrick

"Shit... Before that you were in like orphanage and foster care type places?" asked Fory. "Must have been rough?"

"Had its moments," said Michonne with a nod. "I met my folks after an especially difficult time. I don't believe it was fate—no such thing—but it worked out. Anyway, a man hurt me in ways I don't care to discuss, so let's just say my folks saved me and changed my life."

Fory kinda got the idea where this story was going, yet had to ask the question. "What happened to the bastard that hurt you? Did he go to jail?"

"No." Michonne's response was quick between aggressive sips of ginger ale. "He didn't get the opportunity."

Fory had a feeling there was a more accurate version. Perhaps not so pretty. "What did you do?" Fory asked probing and half-acting. While to Fory, the girl seemed like a stiff and boring woman, her instincts told her that Michonne was the real deal on the inside with some grit and fire. Otherwise, she'd never be working for Mary.

"I can't really divulge. Let's just say that the guy might have been happier in prison? Doesn't matter, he'll never know."

"W-Why?" asked Fory tentatively. Despite her chaotic existence, this was not a usual conversation.

"Oh, that's cause he's burning in Hell." Michonne's voice and facial color were a matching grey. "Prob'ly saving me a seat. We owe each other one last swipe."

Mary & Sir William Chatham

Pratt squeezed a lemon wedge into lukewarm tea as he opened the local paper. "I know you're convinced that your new neighbor has something to do with the death of that little girl. You sure about the correlation?" Pratt reached for his pipe then pivoted his hand to pick up a spoon and stir his tea. He didn't want any smoke in the way of what Mary was about to say.

"Yes, Bill, I'm stone cold sure. The whole mess is too much of a co-incidence," responded Mary as she placed her glasses and her phone on the table with one hand while rubbing weary, aging eyes with the other. "I'm not even sure why I'm so adamant about stopping what-ever is going on. As you know, there's a bunch of moving parts, and I'm not sure what takes priority at this point. What I *do* know, is that I don't like living just a few houses away from anyone who had a con-nection to my brother's arms dealing; even if it is once removed from a divorced husband."

"How are you feeling about your niece and her capabilities?" asked Pratt.

Mary folded her hands and leaned back in a porch chair facing the surf. "Michonne has Fory covered. She's in good hands, and we're keeping her just enough out of withdrawal so she's effective."

Pratt twirled the spoon exuding indifference as Mary continued. "I instructed Michonne to take her to a local watering hole so she could have a few and stop shaking before she meets with Mobley."

"What's your neighbor's first name again?"

"Anna. We're still trying to gather intelligence on exactly what her MO is and because she's picking Chatham of all places as a base of operation that seals the deal that somehow she has intel connected to the information my brother took to his grave. She's basically just a professional divorcee with hardcore leftist leanings. New to any business like ours. I know that Fory, if she keeps it together, can gather new intel."

"So, you're confident that a clueless, desk-jockey will be awarded the job, infiltrate Mobley's operation, and not falter in the process?" Pratt laughed and coughed in tandem. "I envy your optimism."

Mary drained her tea in graceful ladylike fashion. "I think her flaws, awkwardness and eccentricity are a perfect cover. From what we hear, Mobley is trying to endear herself to the community, so she's going to want an assistant with local contacts. Michonne will coach her on how to not blow her cover. And being the niece of a neighbor got her the interview. She'll be competent in her duties as long as she avoids too many cups. Her quirkiness will take Mobley off guard. She'll never be suspected for having any other motive than a paycheck."

"Hmm." Pratt said, "Mary, we've known each other for a long time, mostly as competitors. And I've always admired your tenacity and success rate." Pratt shared a one-cheek smile. "Yet, with the mission nearly on Go status, I am having a few doubts. Can this be pulled off by an untrained operative?"

"I know what's involved here. I've been in this game for way too long, and while us getting old has toned us down, I've not lost my gut instincts."

Pratt actually took comfort in Mary's confidence. She was a proven survivor in a world where life insurance was unavailable.

"I've no idea if the old story is true." Mary wanted to convey the story while keeping her guest relaxed and confident. "But I think the pieces are coming together. I think somewhere next to us is a buried stash of World War II armament. Once the war ended, they gutted this town like a bluefish. In the opinion of government officials, anything worth finding has been dug up and most likely has been stolen or sold years ago. I think if the nukes were taken, they have been brought right back to be hidden in a spot the military has checked off their list," said Mary as she caught herself remembering back to more exciting times. "I know there's something big under Mobley's hood. So do you. Selling this drug is just because she is a novice and giving in to quick money."

Pratt nodded. "Well, this is gonna be one helluva reconnaissance mission, Mary."

"Indeed. We're lucky to have Michonne along to assist under the radar. I have to call Justin later to update him on his daughter. McGee is confident she's ready for her own assignment despite her young age."

"His reputation precedes him. Justin's a cunning bastard. We could never quite snuff him out," muttered Pratt.

"He's beyond a pro, Bill. I'm not at liberty to start sharing resume items," chuckled Mary, "but it's vast, and he taught Michonne everything she knows. For better or worse."

"She may be a worthy asset, still, I'd bet her father didn't teach her *everything*. I'm guessing that her most important skills, unfortunately, were learned at a much younger age."

Xanadu
(home of Anna Mobley) Chatham

Dressed in black spandex, and with an attempt at a normal new yard design, Anna Mobley watered her tulips along the driveway in the front. With all of the spring moisture from morning dew, she waited and cranked the hose around 1pm when the eastern sun was high. Anna had been preoccupied lately. While she zoned into her thoughts, she failed to hear her neighbor, old Mrs. Gant, bumble over a small garden fence.

At eighty-seven, Gant's mind had left ten years ago with an outgoing tide, but her sandpaper voice still could shred an ear, "You're ruining this neighborhood!" screamed Gant. "I'm a *swimmer*! As in *one who swims!* This is an outrage. You're churning up all the natural protection from the dunes, in order to what? Build a wine cellar?!"

At this early stage in the exchange, Mobley thought death by kindness might work. "Mrs. Gant, I didn't mean..."

"Shush!" hissed Gant, "we swim here. Your new dock out back is a complete disruption to the coast. It's dangerous. Unsightly. I demand you move that dock closer to the middle of your own property so our family can enjoy the same sand and water that we have here for four generations."

Mrs. Gant paused and gathered her composure, then went on in just a touch calmer tone thinking that Anna's silence meant Gant scored the first round. "Tomorrow I'm going to the conservation commission and having this *raping* of our landscape held up under a cease and desist order from the judge!"

Mobley walked over toward her disruptive neighbor. "Mrs. Gant, my advice to you is to walk back to your property, and at this point in your life, dream of a quiet, happy death."

The neighbor's pupils exploded with adrenaline, she was speechless, never having encountered such a strange response in her life.

Forsythia's Ride

"We never know at what moment it might be smart to just move along, and enjoy the day," said Mobley as she picked up a dead crab that had floated ashore. Anna touched and viewed the creature with care. She then stared at her neighbor, and smashed the decades old crustacean into a rock. After two dozen dried up pieces smashed and were caught by the wind, Mobley nodded and said, "Some old people naively think they're gonna be here forever. If I'm granted even one more day more past eighty, then I'll be a lucky woman. Perhaps you, not so much..."

Squawking Gull Pub

"Sure, one more please," said Fory to the waitress who had come over to pick up the remnants of their lunch.

"Fory," snapped Michonne, "you said that two rounds ago. You do realize you have a job interview in two hours? We need you at your best." That got her only a frown as a response so she pressed on. "Not passing judgment. Just doing my job."

"What, as a babysitter? And you take an alcoholic out for a liquid lunch? Great job Mary Poppins!" shot back Fory. "By the way, I like your pin." She pointed to a small, sterling silver shark fin on Michonne's lapel.

"Oh, thanks. It was a gift from my uncle. Anyway, listen, I'm not here to babysit. I've been briefed on the fastest way to extricate you from alcohol withdrawal symptoms. Right now that is to feed you more of the poison. Only to the point where it will help you function better for a few hours. After that, it's not my problem. You do what you want."

Fory rolled her eyes as she drained the last of her glass. The urge to lick the inside of the glass clean came over her, Forsythia had just enough dignity left to resist. Barely.

"What brings you to Chatham, anyway?" asked Fory trying to not think of another drink. "From what I understand, your dad has kinda had you traveling since day one?"

"We moved around, but I'm lucky in that my parents always kept some semblance of normalcy. Different perhaps, but I'm sure they loved me and gave me a good routine."

Michonne gave quick head shake to shoo out the creatures in her mind. "Alright, enough of this. Let's focus. Let me brief you some more. At least with what I know, which is not everything at this point. We've got to get going soon."

"Fine," said Fory. "You can start by telling me how your dad and my aunt even know one another."

Forsythia's Ride

"It's not a long story. Basically, your aunt is a legend in certain underground circles. I can't say which ones of course, but I think you realize your aunt has a history of being involved in various projects that might not always be considered legal to local authorities and the government."

"Yeah, I know of her past. Family stories and lore shit," responded Fory.

"Alright, so you know at least part," said Michonne. "Well, my dad has been involved in several assignments of his own over the years. Some of those assignments put him in play with helping your aunt. Missions definitely not condoned by the normal powers that be. Kinda like when he tried to assassinate my mom. Shot her in the head."

Fory's eyes widened. "He WHAT!?"

"Shh!! I know, I know. Long story," calmly responded Michonne. "That's not relevant here. Another tale for another day."

"You people are out of your mind! All of you!" snapped Fory who pulled a haul from her ice and wished it was Jamison. "Who *are* you?"

"Oh," responded Michonne, "we run with a tight narrative. Sometimes when I watch old TV shows, I realize we could be viewed as odder than the Addams Family. But, to me, I think we more resemble a modern day *Leave it to Beaver* Cleaver family that happens to take on a murder for hire or an extraction of valuables once in a while. All that means to me is we have to travel a bit more than the average family to scope out the job."

"So," said Fory with a half-laugh, "you're like this junior operative in training? But you're so young. Shouldn't you be worrying about getting a prom dress?"

"Nah," responded Michonne as she drained her second ginger ale and fidgeted in her chair as if signaling Fory it was time to go. "I think the prom would be more worried about me."

Fory was about to take the hint when she noticed the couple that just walked out had left a full and just opened beer bottle on their table. It only took a small twist to the right to be aimed at that table. She started to reach for the sweating beer bottle; poor thing left alone with discarded napkins, that could be considered alcohol abuse. Right before her fingers curled on the cool bottle ... Suddenly they were greeted by an uninvited lunch guest.

"Hey, ladeesh," said one of the fish-gut covered patrons from the next table who had clearly already had a long day with his Coors. "I wanted to come over and properly introduche myself. I'm Sh-haan. I mean, S-shawn."

Their new luncheon friend sat next to Fory, who barely reacted. Her mind was on what their server would be providing. His mind was focused on how the rest of the afternoon would turn out with this chick on his boat.

"I don't recognize you... Cute little thing. You on vacation? Wanna boat tour of the habah?" said Shawn as he placed a hand on Fory's left thigh further up than was in any way proper. Fresh beer, stale marijuana and staler codfish wafted around the beast. There were small specks of brown: dried fish blood splattered from the morning's work.

Fory's eyes widened as she snapped back to her circumstances. "Shawn, I think we're about to leave and I'd ask you to do the same, without us."

Shawn's hands started to gently massage Fory's upper leg, while Michonne looked on with frustration. *Damn! It's way too early for this nonsense. I can't kill this prick in front of a lunch crowd. Maybe break his shin with a foot grab and a missile kick with my boots?*

"C'mon schweetie," he said in the drunken mode of I-am-perfect-everyone-thinks-I'm-hot stage of sloppy and beyond buzzed. "Don't be like that. You're on vacation. Don't you want to experience a little of the local flavah?" Shawn's groping hand was now inches from Fory's panties.

Suddenly, her suitor's demeanor changed drastically, to the point where he picked up a few notches on the sobriety scale. "What the—!" he yelped.

While Shawn was wooing his target, Michonne quietly reached under the table and jabbed fingers into his eager crotch.

Forsythia's Ride

"Oooo..." said Shawn. "Another kitten with claws. I see. Whatchya do for fun when you're not grabbing me a little too hard?"

"I'm good at skewing actuarial tables," said Michonne with such coldness frost should have been misting out of her mouth.

He was quiet; processing took a while in his thick beer haze. He then started to chuckle at what he thought was a young girl. "Whaddyagonnado, Goldilocks? Tag me right here in the middle of the day? In front of a packed joint? Doubt it. Why don't ya just go back and help your troop sell more cookies? I'm busy here with big sister. I'll give you a few bucks to go watch a matinee. Won't take me too long with this hot, pretty thing."

Michonne pulled her hand away, and set it back on her lap. Shawn smiled with satisfaction as Fory stared in shock at what was transpiring in the middle of a restaurant.

"See, that's better," he said. "Now, run along. There's a candy store across the street. Get yourself a lollipop. Good practice!" Shawn roared into laughter, his only regret was that his buddies couldn't hear his one-liners. And see how he snagged this pretty little thing who was going to give in to him soon. He was envisioning the quick cab ride to his place. Then he had a better thought, "Or you can join us and get some on the job training."

Michonne made a point to stare at Shawn's protruding beer gut. "A threesome sounds great. You, Ben and Jerry. Bet we could sell the copyright to all your pals over there."

Fory looked on in semi-shock. She wasn't convinced that their guest would just leave them alone if they walked out, he certainly still had his hand on her thigh.

"No, deary. I got the tab," said Shawn. "Perhaps, you'll get the tip?" He laughed, pulled out a toothpick, and began working it. At first glance, it appeared he had about half a set of teeth left. Crystal Meth had claimed the rest.

Michonne reached in her purse but didn't pull out a wallet. Instead she fumbled around until she found a brand new Integra 15-22 silencer. She pulled out the piece and surreptitiously attached it to her Glock under the table. *So disgusting, if he hadn't taken it to a threesome with someone he thought was underage, I might have just sprained his ankle.* She pulled back the hammer and pressed the weapon to Shawn's pelvic area without emotion or a change in facial expression.

Fory was starting to sweat. She was able to glance to down and had seen what was going on. "Michonne, what are you doing?"

"Nothing really," said Michonne. "Just relax."

Shawn was quickly finding more sobriety as he understood that this wasn't an act or rehearsal. He stared at Michonne, who gazed back with lifeless eyes. *Like a doll's eyes.*

Her stone face gave him the shivers.

"Crazy little broad..." is all Fory and Michonne could hear him say. The young girl responded poorly to insults.

With a move that confused both Fory and their new friend, Michonne slipped the gun in her pocket, walked up to the bar and snagged the spiked holder for all the paid bar tabs. She placed it on the table and said, "Time to settle up, guys..." In a viper motion she grabbed Shawn's right hand and impaled the middle of his calloused palm on the metal spike.

"Ah!! You little bitch!" he yelled but was not heard with all of the bar commotion.

"Come on, let's go!" said Michonne as she grabbed Fory and bee-lined it to the door.

Once outside, they speed-walked toward the car.

"Get in!" snapped Michonne reaching in her other pocket for the keys. While she didn't peel out, she exited the parking lot as fast as she could without drawing too much attention.

Fory was in a semi state of shock and remained quiet until the two were out of downtown and headed north back toward Aunt Mary's neighborhood.

"What... what did you just do?" asked Fory.

"Stuck him with the check," giggled Michonne.

Mary's Guest Room

"You polish up nice! Yeah, you're gonna knock 'em dead," said Michonne. "Got your resume?"

Fory fixed her collar and rubbed her fitted skirt. She hated the stuffy, uncomfortable business attire Mary had picked out for her, but had to admit it was scarily tailored to her exact dimensions.

"All set," said Fory as she tweaked her hair in the mirror. "Mary wanted me all dolled up,"

"*Voodoo* doll, maybe?" Michonne chuckled at her own joke. They went silent immediately. *What's wrong with me? I've laughed a few times with this woman. She may not know how to survive, but I know better, we aren't here to make friends. Got to focus better.*

"Very funny," said Fory with a frumpy glance not noticing the change in her handler. "Makes me look like I'm a personal assistant for Jeff Epstein. But an older version!" sighed Fory in half-feigned frustration. "At least a Voodoo doll might look pretty."

"Ah, c'mon... you look great," assured Michonne. "Our recon tells us Mobley often has very attractive men *and* women coming in and out of her place at sporadic times. She might take a fancy to you."

"Oh, yeah? For what purposes?" Fory asked with a cackle.

Suddenly, the addiction called. "Listen, I need a friend," Fory blurted. "I know we've got time to shoot over to the liquor store to snag a coupla nips for my purse."

"Not a chance," replied Michonne without hesitation. Her eye stare punctuated the response. Uncharacteristically she softened so added, "And I don't want to find out what Mary and Pratt would do if I let their Trojan Horse walk into her interview half in the bag. Not gonna happen."

Fory itched along a sleeve as they walked down the street toward Mobley's driveway. Fory sported the awkward discomfort of an eight year old boy when forced to wear his first coat and tie.

"Looks like auntie dolled you up with the finest the Pilgrim Shop can offer," laughed Michonne. "You look like an ad for the Chamber of Commerce!"

"Funny..." quipped Fory. "I feel like a mannequin."

"Ah, it's all part of the costume," replied Michonne. "You've got to really convince Mobley you're true-blue Chatham. Even though you're half-shanty Mick, you need to exude the air of someone whose ancestors' feet walked the decks of the *Mayflower*."

"Great..." said Fory. "Me, with all my old world charm."

"Remember your back story. You're staying with your aunt down the street and you're looking for interesting and fulfilling work locally because you didn't like the city. You have vast experience working with Manhattan executives," coached Michonne, "which, by the way, isn't a total lie. Sir William is not exactly a two-bit player. In New York and London he's well known and carries a pretty big stick in the best circles on both sides of the pond."

"This is crazy!" said Fory. "With all the power and connections between my aunt and Pratt, you'd think they'd hire some hotshot James Bond type to break in undetected at three in the morning, or some type of shit like that. Steal whatever they want."

"Doesn't work like that—only in the movies.. Listen, you're gonna do great."

Fory felt like she was going to the gallows. She could bumble in so many ways and get caught snooping.

"Anyway, did your aunt or Pratt give you any last minute instructions?"

"Nah," said Fory. "It was weird. I was at the house and showered and whatever, but there was no sign of either one of them."

"Hmm... Most likely a late lunch or a tea at her country club up the street. That's where Mary takes her meetings with people she doesn't a hundred percent trust. In her business, she deals with unsavory characters at times, and doesn't care to have them cross her threshold."

"Don't blame her," said Fory.

"With Pratt in town and so many balls in the air, I'm guessing she's using the time with him to strategize."

"Does she really meet with these spy guys?" asked Fory.

"Yeah, sometimes. Not just guys. The international relations business has become an equal opportunity employer," laughed Michonne. "Plenty of woman on the circuit now, which is good news for us. Before now, Mary was pretty much the only one with top power who cared about female operatives. If I make it past a few more years I just may carve out a little empire of my own."

As they approached the Mobley home, two bright, rust-colored foxes trotted across the street toward the beach. One had an especially wide smile, its mouth was stuffed with a mouse. Dinner in the dunes.

"Those things look wild," said Fory. "Do they bite?"

"Nah, they're skittish as hell," answered Michonne. "Especially those two cause their coats look so healthy. It's the ones that are drab colored and matted you have to avoid. Most likely rabid."

"Great."

"Fox aren't a big deal," said Michonne. "Just stay away from the coyotes. They're a different breed, so to speak. Aggressive, especially if they smell fear. If you walk the beach or one of the trails at night, make sure you bring a flashlight and good stick. Personally, I have an old K2 ski pole I'm partial to. I sharpened the end and removed the plastic guard. So I can penetrate the skin much deeper and actually cut it to the bone."

"I see," said Fory, "an animal lover..."

Michonne chuckled. "Nah, just a survivor."

"I thought this neighborhood was all fancy and posh. Don't they have, like, animal control guys to shoot them or something?"

"At times, but you'll notice the residents of Chatham, especially the lifers, kinda like things the way they are. The coyotes were here before us, so they can hang out until a bulldozer takes out their den to make way for another behemoth like the Mobley house here."

"Hmm..." Fory had a sudden thought. "Didn't native tribes live here at some point? You know, Pilgrims and Indians?"

"Sure," said Michonne, "until we introduced them to whisky and smallpox."

"Lovely," muttered Fory in nervous thought. "Alright, I should go in."

Michonne nodded as the two arrived at massive stone pillars that served as sentries for the Mobley property. In Chatham, they called them cottages, but that description was a quaintness, an empty nod to community. This was an ocean-side estate. Most of the houses in the neighborhood were large, updated and would fetch well into the seven figures; the Mobley house was in a class of its own.

While most of the other homes illustrated a traditional Cape Cod veneer (with salt-weathered wood shingles for siding behind hydrangea-lined driveways) Mobley had used all of the latest modern building materials. This place looked like it belonged in Malibu versus an old New England coastal town.

The visitors also noticed the intricate fence that surrounded the property which was unique to the area. They were walking toward a large, double wrought-iron gate between impressive pillars. The cold-faced enclosure didn't beckon with a warm invitation. Everyone else's lawn had no such barriers. If they had anything more than shrubs, it was a small and unattached section of a white picket fence to boarder a flower garden.

"Looks like a fortress," noted Fory. "What's she hiding?"

Michonne smirked. "That's what you're here to find out." She grew serious. "Okay, I'm heading to Mary's for a meeting with Sasa. Text me once you're wrapping up with Mobley. You're not to leave the end of this driveway until I return. I'll be at your aunt's and can be here in two minutes."

"Okay," said Fory in a higher than normal octave.

Michonne touched Fory's forearm. *Why do I care about what this fool feels?* "Remember, there's a lot riding on this, but don't be nervous."

"Yeah, right," responded Fory,

"Be yourself, and give it hell!" said Michonne with a wink as she turned to head back to Mary's.

Fory was silent as she rang the buzzer on the towering pillar on the left, where drivers would buzz to get their cars observed and let in. As she waited for a response, her immediate involuntary action was to rub the locket her father had given her as a kid right before his suicide. Despite the circumstances in which the jewelry was given, it always helped her relax, not nearly as much as a shot of Bacardí, but still therapeutic. It was a touchstone back to times of innocence and feelings of safety. She loved the feeling of the gold and the picture inside of them during happier times. She missed him every day, and had never understood what lead to such a tragic ending. Next to the picture in the locket, were engraved what Paul Shea told his daughter were her lucky numbers: 95941714 95366996. The numbers seemed gibberish, but her dad was never frivolous. Those numbers often haunted her dreams.

She noticed small letters engraved above the numbers and to the side, which resembled where an engraver might stamp a serial number of some kind.

Weird... she thought to herself. *I guess I never looked at this in bright light like this freak has shinning down like sun in front her gate.* The letters were GNOLTAL, all in caps. Fory's mind pronounced it with a silent G ... no-tal. She had no idea what it meant.

Because the sequence was so long, but Paul told his daughter that the numbers showed up in a fortune cookie at dinner at Harry Mook's, something had always not added up. He assured her that someday it would prove to be a number that would bring her luck and fortune. She craved both now more than ever.

Xanadu

As Fory waited for a response from the keypad speaker, she watched Michonne walking back up the street. The young girl not only acted older than her years, but her gait listed slighted to the right. They were the steps of someone who had worn out a lot of shoes.

She reminded Fory of someone who the world had laid a burden on, someone with a set of shoulders too young to bear such weight. She wondered what this spy had seen in her short eighteen years, and doubted much of it had been pretty. She bet that Michonne's past held a deficit of Barbie dolls and party dresses.

"Good afternoon," the speaker finally crackled into life. "I trust that you are Forsythia?"

"Y-yes, sir. I'm here to—"

"One moment, please," interrupted the speaker. There were only a few seconds of silence. "Yes, Ms. Mobley is expecting you. Once you're buzzed in, please proceed to the southwest entrance. Please remove your shoes immediately after you enter the door."

"Southwest..." Fory muttered to herself, "great. They didn't give me a friggin' compass."

She was nervous and pissed. Mad at her aunt and Pratt for roping her into this, and mad at herself for falling into their trap. Most of all, she was furious at the fact that she needed a belt of rum and needed one fast, lest the withdrawal beast raise its ugly head again, and always at the worst time.

She approached what was her best guess at the correct door, and was pleasantly surprised that her booze-deprived instincts were still intact. She heard the click of a latch. As the door opened, it revealed a man in his late twenties in a tight, Euro-styled, big-collar button down. Fory liked the eye candy. She guessed he was some kind of body guard or security.

"Please come in," said the man curtly. "Don't forget the sh—"

"Yeah, yeah," said Fory. "I know. You don't like shoes." She gladly

Forsythia's Ride

removed the new Eileen Fisher slip-ons. She'd already started two blisters just on the walk over. Fory placed them into an antique hand-woven basket.

"This way," said her grumpy greeter who introduced himself as Dane. "Please watch your step. We have renovations underway, as you can see."

He gave a slight bow and then led Fory down a long hallway which spilled into a vast living room. The entire rear side of the house was a wall of tinted glass. Fory felt like she could smash through and dive right into the bay. To the left side was the kitchen whose new steel appliances were blinding with the sunlight's reflection.

Fory laughed to herself. *I'm not in Manhattan anymore Toto. Or Kansas.*

"Welcome, I'm Anna Mobley," said a striking raven-haired woman standing two steps down in the sunken living room. Mobley's olive skin tone radiated in this décor that must have been chosen for just such a purpose.

"As you gaze around with a look of awe, I feel complimented. Do you like my decorating?" said the would-be employer. Appearing to be around forty years old, both Mobley's dress and demeanor boasted confidence and sexuality. A suitor could be easily lied to if she said thirty-five.

"Y-yeah. I mean, yes. Beautiful," said Fory secretly referring to not just the house.

The living room wall was a bold splash of purples with burnt orange tinges as accent marks. A quick survey of the room uncovered several works of modern art which Fory figured cost a fortune. One painting appeared to portray a naked nymph erotically caressing a horse. Another looked like a plate of old Spaghettios.

"I see you notice the pieces I'm testing on the walls. I'm not sure they'll stay, so I'd appreciate your feedback," said Anna. "What do you think?"

"Ah, ah," stuttered Fory, "very beautiful. I-I don't know much about art."

Matt Fitzpatrick

Looks like someone puked on your purple wall, was what Fory wanted to say out loud, but kept to herself.

She then noticed a swimming pool off to the side of the living room. In it was another perfect male specimen swimming laps, but he wasn't moving forward. She'd never seen a lap pool inside someone's house. Through the rippled water, she also noticed the Adonis-like creature was fully nude.

"As you can see," said Anna, "I provide my security with all the tools they need to keep their bodies in the shape to perform their duties. Or rather, my demands." she said with a fake hand-guided motion toward the swimmer and a light, meaningless laugh.

Fory was at a loss for a response, finally coming up with, "Y-yeah, yeah. I'm sure you want the best protection."

"Among their required tasks," said Anna as she took a sip of what appeared to be red wine and then interrupted herself, "Oh! Would you care for a cordial?"

Fory's eyes lit up a little too fast and a little too wide. Right away, she caught herself and knew she had to play it cool. If she sipped a glass of wine, it would be devoured in seconds, there was no doubt she would not have enough self-control to sip it to the end. "Um, no. No thanks, Ms. Mobley." The demon in her brain was irritated, but had no fear. Fory would return.

"Pity. Life is short," said Anna. "However, I'm sure your diligence is one of the reasons you're here. Standards of not drinking on the job are appreciated. Please, come in and sit down," said the host as she patted an aging, obese poodle in her hands.

"This is Bubble," said Anna who had followed Fory's gaze. "While not a puppy anymore, you can see that she still has a fondness for treats."

Fory felt beamed into a *Twilight Zone* episode. She found this lady odd, yet the surroundings were strangely comforting. They had an old European feel. Maybe Greek.

"Ya know," said Fory, "maybe I will take you up on that drink."

"Excellent," said Mobley, who immediately finger-snapped.

Forsythia's Ride

Dane approached. "What would you care for, Miss?"

"Oh... Would you happen to have rum and cola?"

"Of course. Excellent," he said as he walked away toward the bar. Fory's mouth nearly watered at the clanking of ice cubes.

Mobley waited and caressed Bubble. While the dog may have gotten fat, Anna Mobley was anything but. As she slithered onto the Montauk sofa, Fory noticed toned muscles that tested the tight the constraints of sepia colored yoga pants. Her sculpted breasts strained a tight black shirt, and when Anna turned away to place Bubble on the oriental rug, Fory felt a natural warmth below her waist as Anna's chiseled ass was shown to perfection. Fory wondered if this was a job interview or a seduction.

Before Fory could offer Anna the resume paper, Dane took the papers from her hands just as the indoor swimmer emitted a loud grunt as he changed strokes and kept on swimming.

"Here you are. Enjoy," Dane said exchanging the cocktail for the papers.

Anna looked at her guest and simply demanded she come over and sit close. The two woman were now four feet apart, three feet below the surface of the rest of the house. Fory thought the living room felt more like a web than a visiting area.

Mobley drained the last of her glass and tapped a finger against the crystal. Upon hearing the *Ding!* a new minion approached to tend to the refill. "So, Forsythia..." she began.

"I-I'm sorry. Please feel free to call me Fory. It's easier."

"Very well. Brevity is a virtue I admire," agreed Anna. "In certain instances, anyway. Now, I understand you already have a general idea of what I'm looking for?"

Fory nodded. "Yes, my aunt briefed me on the position. Although she wasn't big on detail, I kinda got the gist."

"The *gist?*" Anna said with a slight chuckle. "Yes, perhaps you will in time. Fory, I like to entertain. Better yet, I *need* to entertain for my business. I need a reliable right hand-woman to assist with making my guests comfortable. As you can see, I have a penchant for hiring very capable men. My definition of capable is their ability to meet my wishes and expectations while also looking very attractive. Do you understand what I mean?"

"I-I guess. Sure," said Fory needing to change the subject because she really wasn't sure if this woman was making sexual innuendos about her male staff or just about their quiet efficiency. "You mentioned your business. What is it? Must be interesting?"

"In time," Anna responded with a slight hand wave and without a smile this time. "What I need is someone smart who can multi-task. Basically, somebody who will tend to my guests' wishes while treating them as if they are visiting a palace. You'll not only tend to their needs, but also learn how to anticipate them. Someone who is painfully loyal. Could that be you, Fory?"

Fory knew exactly why she was there, no time to search her soul for an honest answer. "Sure, sure, I can do that. Might take a little time to get to the anticipation part, but I'm willing to give it a shot." Fory paused, faking that she was thinking something over. "Um... I imagine you entertain a pretty high level clientele and, ah, you know..."

Mobley blank stared at her prospective new employee. Honestly clueless. "To what are you referring?"

Fory felt the heat of Anna's eyes. She forced down her nerves. "Oh, no. No, nothing. It's just that I'm very much a G-rated girl. I-I just don't know what some of the guests might be looking for?"

Mobley belly laughed. "You're too much! You think I brought you here so I can take my precious time to interview a prostitute?!" Mobley laughed in a good natured way. Dane joined in the chuckle as he delivered Mobley's refreshed drink.

"You're funny. No, Fory, No." Mobley wiped her mouth. "If I hire that type of escort for a guest, I don't waste my time interviewing them, I go directly to their manager and order what I want. You see, I need a woman's intuition. A woman's attention to detail. A woman's eye for beauty, and also her sixth sense to know when a situation is deteriorating and how to fix it. Men don't possess those skills. However, they do have other utilizations. This particular position would not require such from you, I assure you."

"Okay, cool. Thanks for clarifying," said a relieved Fory who wasn't faking it.

Through the corner of her eye, she noticed the swimmer climb out of the indoor lap pool. His nude body shamelessly walked (while soaking the floor) until he found a puffy, orange towel and started to dry himself without the slightest show of shame.

Anna noticed Fory's innate interest. "I see you admire Julian's natural form. What's not to? You see, men since time began have kept women around as window dressing. *Les objets d'art,* for their viewing and carnal pleasure. I'm merely returning the favor. If you stick around me long enough, I'm happy to allow you to borrow one of them for an afternoon."

Fory was silent.

Anna sensed her new employee's discomfort and got back to business. "I want someone local," explained Anna. "Someone with ties to the community. I understand that you're not a true Cape Codder—nor am I—however, while I don't know Mary personally, I certainly know *of* her. And she is Cape Codder to the core. Being directly connected to her will suffice for what I am looking for if you can do the actual work."

Fory's instincts told her to keep quiet while Mobley was discussing her aunt so she just nodded.

"Let me be frank, I'm eager to get to know Mary better," said Anna sipping lightly from her refreshed glass of wine. "Your connection to her is an interesting twist to your candidacy."

"But not the only reason I hope?" Fory asked in a manner that was forward, but Mobley didn't seem to mind.

"If you're unable to fulfill your duties, then I wouldn't care if you were Mary's Siamese twin, you'll be terminated."

Forsythia thought it might just be in her head, but she didn't like the dark inflection Anna put on that last phrase.

"Fory," Anna asked back to a business tone, "what did you think? I did a nationwide search and your skill sets and experience blew me away over everyone else? I know you have New England roots, and so you know nepotism is how this part of the world was built. From the king's land grants, to cushy Boston financial gigs, it's all in who you know. If that's insulting to you, then maybe this isn't the right—"

"No, no," interrupted Fory with a gentle hand wave. "No, I get it. Just trying to fully understand what you need and want."

"Fine," said Anna. "You will understand much more as we work together. Anyway, I'm sure you want to discuss compensation."

"Sure, please," Fory responded awkwardly. *Damn, this could be good, I'll get paid from Auntie* **and** *this rich snot and end this job with enough to do whatever I want. Okay, I think I better concentrate and really convince this woman I'm the one for her.*

"I'll start you at sixty dollars an hour," said Anna standing to walk toward a side room where she had a small work station. Not her full office which was located above and in a more private area, but she did need some basic business work done with the occasional visitor.

Fory's eyes sparkled. "That's very generous for a starting salary." Fory couldn't believe this pay was going to be almost double what she made at Pratt's firm.

Anna smiled. "I can tell by your reaction that you're satisfied with the wage. You should be, as it's way above scale for this type of work on Cape Cod. However, your hours will vary depending upon when I hold events, especially because I understand you'll be staying up the street with your aunt. I'm anticipating you being available at flexible hours to do various duties. You will be earning that amount by being available to me on short notice and working during party hours. Is this acceptable?"

"I can stay at Aunt Mary's for a while. Shouldn't be a problem," said Fory. "If my hours will vary, does that mean I can't go shopping or to the beach?"

"It's important that you'll be close by. Certainly you can shop or sun yourself on the beach. If I call, you will have time to wrap up whatever you're doing. Just please stay within a fifteen-minute drive of my home unless you have cleared a longer outing with me. I hope to not have to do it often, but I may feel compelled to call on you if a situation arises where I require your assistance. It could be on Christmas Eve at 3am, and I'll expect you to respond. That's what I require of my people," said Anna with a firm glare. "What I demand."

Fory adjusted her necklace in a brief moment of thought. "Yeah... Yeah, that's fine," she responded. "I have no kids, so a holiday crunch won't be a problem."

"Excellent," Anna said as she motioned to a minion to freshen up Fory's drink which happened to be already drained.

"Sure," said Fory. "Honestly, these days, things like Christmas are just another calendar flip."

"As I figured," replied Anna. "Then, if all is agreed, you'll start right away. We usually start our days around ten unless a specific party is planned; then you don't have to show up until noon because the day will be a longer one."

Fory's eyes lit up as Anna further explained. "You see, we tend to not be early risers, I prefer to work well into the evening, which you'll be expected to do."

"I see. And, I understand," responded Fory with canned words. Her brain was still trying to process the situation, feeling it was a match made in heaven. *This is going to be cake.* All thoughts of the danger involved disappeared with the thought of working parties late into the night.

"I have an event in a few days where I'll be entertaining some big potential clients, and I also have some of my design people coming by. Going to be an eclectic group, for sure, but should be fun and requires my best."

"Okay, I'm happy to help," said Fory. "Ms. Mobley, I mean Anna, it would help me out if I knew exactly what you do. I don't have a full grip on what your business is. These people might have questions. Don't you think I might need a little more information to do what you're asking? I don't mean to pry or offend you."

"A woman in my position is rarely shocked or offended. All you need to know is I'm in the import/export business. Most important," quipped Anna, "I divorce well, which has always afforded me both the capital and the contacts to continue my work now that my short-sighted, dimwit husband has been jettisoned. Poor man."

Mobley's face soured. "The world, it seems, was a little too rough for his constitution. While the world lauded his work, behind the scenes he was a defeated child. A pathetic little, puke! His coddled upbringing didn't prepare him for the horrors of how the real world works. He was weak and ran off to play pop star or some silliness. I broke the news to him while he was at Wembley waiting to go on with his band in front of seventy-five thousand screaming fans." Mobley slugged from her glass. The anger belied the flippant way she had joked about divorcing as a means of making money.

I've got to change her mood fast. "What do you buy and sell?"

"Whatever people perceive as valuable. Items that I and others find desirable," was the vague response. "You'd be surprised what people are willing to pay for. To sacrifice for."

"Well, I'd love to embrace the opportunity."

"That's it for today then. Start time is ten tomorrow. Make sure you tell your aunt to come by and visit," said Mobley standing up.

"Indeed, I will," responded Fory realizing she had been quickly dismissed.

Anna nodded at Dane to show Fory to the door.

Fory nodded and turned to head out.

"Oh, wait. Fory!" Mobley called from the couch. "Maybe you can start right now by running a small errand for me?"

"Yeah. Sure," responded Fory, "it's just that I'm not very mobile right now, I'm kinda borrowing my aunt's car when I need it."

"Oh, no, no," Anna responded. "It's just a small package I need you to bring to a neighbor."

"No problem then," said Fory. She welcomed the assignment as a sign she was in Mobley's good graces.

Mobley got up, went into the kitchen and retrieved a small leather case. "Here. Please take this small item over to Mrs. McAree just a few houses away."

Fory's thoughts blazed as her mind raced. She knew she needed to stay calm as stone. "Okay. Do I need to tell her anything?"

"Oh, no," responded a casual Anna. "She's expecting it. Thanks! See you tomorrow."

Mobley headed toward the back of the great room to inspect the condition of the new lap pool after Julian's intense swim.

Dane smirked as he let Fory out into the late afternoon spring sunshine. He knew their new associate had just blood oathed into a world that only had an invisible entrance sign over the front door. A door that was only an entrance, no exit from this lion's den. And the fool didn't have any idea of what she just signed up for.

She walked down the street toward the address stamped on the package. *This can't be...* Fory thought to herself.

Once out of direct sight of Mobley's cottage/mansion Fory untied the rawhide strings around the case and looked inside.

The peek inside only confirmed her suspicions.

The case contained a half-dozen vials of what appeared to be eye drops that one could pick up at CVS.

Mary's Cottage
Chatham

Sir William sat at the antique dining room table. He opened that morning's Boston Herald. He enjoyed the editorials and was a long-time Peter Lucas fan. The habit was so ingrained that he instinctively scanned any available American newspapers for editorial content, especially in places like Boston and New York for the reasons of who settled there during the decades that shouldered 1900. Those families were still shadow powerhouses that moved the world.

He scanned a few articles, then yelled into the kitchen, "And you Yanks whine about our Daily Mail!" The old knight flipped the paper and settled down once he realized he was being served. "Thank you, dear," said Pratt as Alyce set a plate of warm croissants in front of the plate of fresh fruit.

Mary joined him at the table with tea and toast. He beat her to the dialogue.

"I do enjoy your local political news—your papers are amusing. From the Boston Massacre to the Molasses Flood, you Yanks forever provide interesting fodder," chuckled Pratt. "Even those poor Rosenbergs..."

Thirty years earlier, Mary would have reached for a hidden knife as a reply to that. Today she was just calmly solid about her political goals and nearly so about her past. "Yes, Bill," she said while wiping some stray jelly from the side of her plate. "We have plenty of odd history here, as we do on both sides of the proverbial Atlantic Pond, and also the Irish Sea. Your political media observations are duly noted."

Pratt sipped coffee followed by a grunt as he kept reading.

"Let me ask you," Mary leaned toward the knight with more energy than normal, "how's it that your average British tax payer is burdened each year to fund that *ridiculous* farce of a Royal Family?

Forsythia's Ride

Bunch of spoiled ribbon-cutters."

Pratt raised his hand. "You have a point. Let's not bicker. We're on the same side of the table on this one. Rare, but for once our goals are in sync. Speaking of which, have you heard from your assassin friend in Ireland?" Pratt's tone held a touch of contempt.

"I expect a called in update around noon, our time," answered Mary. "I know Justin McGee wasn't your favorite candidate to consult on this operation, but he's a proven and trustworthy quantity. It's his daughter's first true ownership of a job. As you know, these days intelligent and talented players are not easy to find. People don't give a damn about any actual causes outside of their own selfish, obsessions while checking their X feeds. It's not like the 70s when people had real passion about the world and their futures."

Pratt was silent, stuck in thought. She gave him a few seconds before she finally asked, "How are your London boys feeling about all of this?"

"As ornery as ever," replied Pratt focusing on her again from wherever his mind had been. "But they're smart enough to know we're the ones on the front lines. The point of the matter is that I believe everyone on either side of the *Irish* Sea will be relieved when this task is finally executed and put to rest."

Pratt's thoughts switched lanes. He wanted to better understand the progress so far. "Does Fory know enough about her assignment up the street?"

"Michonne will keep an eye on her," responded Mary. "This is a lot on Fory. It's a huge first jump into the deep end of the pool. Not sure it's a great idea to place her in an open bar setting. If she blows up this piece of the job tonight, it's on you."

Pratt placed his coffee mug on the table and rubbed his napkin to his lips. "I suppose that it would be," said Pratt with minimal sign of concern. "But we need her *au natural* to keep Mobley off our scent. And moreover, effective. If that means she self-medicates, so be it."

Mary began to respond, but Pratt interjected with a bit of heat, "Regarding your question about tonight, may I remind you that it was your idea to get your old soldier, O'Heara, involved. What makes you think he's got information he's withholding from you?"

Mary let a brief pause hang in the air while searching for a proper answer. "Again, Bill, it's my gut. Why he's suddenly on Cape Cod after being on the lam for so long, I really don't know. What I do know is his cancer is terminal. His liver finally called the fight in the eleventh round. But, he seems hell-bent on enjoying the last months of his life. I wouldn't put it past him to have a few vendettas hanging out there as well."

"This is an unfortunate wildcard," said Pratt through a puff of smoke.

"I know you think because he's a part of my so-called *side*, that he'd give everything up without coaxing. As you know, Bill, our world doesn't work that way anymore. O'Heara is gonna play out whatever card he's holding, but not until his very last hand. And he's only going to play it for his own benefit. Grander causes are out of style now."

Mary pursed lips pulled on her cigarette. She watched the smoke dance into the fading puff sent up by Pratt. The smoke and this mission; it reminded her of a million years ago when her father taught her how to waltz.

"Bill, if he's withholding information, he's going to give it up for the sake and safety of his family," said Mary. "No matter what the man's sins were to the world, he still adores his daughters. His days are numbered so he making his last, best play. O'Heara just needs a little piece of ass to drink it out of him. Nobody's more qualified for such an assignment than my lushy niece."

"Where's the big party?" asked Pratt as he tapped his spent pipe into a blackened quahog shell.

"Chatham Dunes Hotel," replied Mary. "I booked Fory a suite and ordered her a Stella McCartney designer dress. I called in an old favor. Figured you'd be proud," Mary said with a wink.

"How the hell'd you pull that off?" said Pratt as he was cleaning his pipe bowl while coughing and longing for another full bowl yet knowing he had to hold off for at least an hour. It suddenly struck him how much of a similar addition he was fighting while sending Fory back into her alcohol infused playground.

"O'Heara would have to be blind or dim to not notice her. It works out well cause he's only in town for a couple of days, and Fory is starting at Mobley's tomorrow to get know that woman's routine."

"Hmm... Chatham Dunes Hotel in a new custom gown, you say? Quite fancy," scoffed Pratt. "Great. Two drunks with our credit cards. I trust that this unforeseen expenditure comes out of your half of the budget?"

"Oh, please, old man," laughed Mary. "If you were twenty-five years younger, *you'd* be begging me to let you tag along as an unsupervised chaperone."

"Indeed I would," chuckled Pratt. "I understand not many men can ignore a pretty young woman in a McCartney gown, but how do you know O'Heara is gonna seek her out?"

"Oh, you men are so predictable. So *manageable*. I told O'Heara I sent my niece to show him around and keep him company."

"Excellent," Pratt managed to say while savoring the smell of Captain Black as he folded the pouch. "We're running a damned escort service," he grimaced. "Churchill would not have approved."

Chatham Dunes Hotel

Forsythia stretched her neck to release herself from that state of half consciousness which can hang on after a cat nap. Of course, within a few seconds her body began looking for the next drink, but at least the withdrawal symptoms were staved off for the moment as bones cracked and muscles stretched. That afternoon, Michonne had handed her a hotel key, instructions for a job and a false name that would be recognized at the desk. She assured Fory the bar would welcome an endless tab.

Fory intended to take to heart the freedom, already imagining the renowned resort's forty dollar martinis.

Those two old spies were going to have one hell of a bill at the end of the night.

She got out of bed and opened the curtains. She grabbed a bottle of spring water. What normally would be a refreshing drink made Fory's stomach spin.

She ran to the bathroom and wretched yellow bile that had been pooling while she slept. She spooled the roll of toilet paper, noting the fancy triangle fold at the end, and then proceed to dry heave for a cruel three-minute eternity.

She leaned back and inhaled tears and snot that had rolled down her face. She was concerned what the other guests might be hearing. Star-headed and dizzy, Fory got up and went to the door and peered through the eye-hole into the hallway. She was grateful to see it was empty and quiet.

She slowly opened the door and looked up and down the corridor. At her feet she noticed a large box with a card taped to it. She lifted the box to bring it inside, surprised at how light it was.

After placing it onto the mussed bed, she opened the envelope.

Forsythia's Ride

Forsythia,

If you're reading this, it means the initial stages of our operation are running smoothly. This box contains part of your assignment. I know you have been overwhelmed by all the events that are transpiring over the last few days.

The time for shock and disbelief has passed. We now need you to don the face and attitude of an operative. Financial rewards upon successful execution will surpass anything you could have imagined back in New York. However, like any great reward, there is significant risk involved.

In the box, you will find a dress you are to wear to a charity event downstairs in the ballroom which begins promptly at 7. There will be a gentleman there, Chip O'Heara. He is expecting you. Technically a friendly. O'Heara is an operative, but a questionable one as of late. In recent years, he's pulled contract work from both sides of the Irish Sea. His loyalty is solely to his bank in the Caymans. The fact that out of nowhere Anna Mobley moves here and suddenly there's an international hired gun on the scene is too much of a coincidence. O'Heara comes from a high profile Dublin family who've been generous to our cause. We just need him occupied for a bit. We need him off the grid for a few hours so we can focus on another task. The one thing that can preoccupy O'Heara is a charming young woman.

We need you to extract whatever information

he might have about Anna Mobley and what the hell is she doing in my Chatham. So get him so piss-drunk that he needs to convalesce in his hotel room for a day after confessing all to you. Just keep him out of the way while we process what you share after debriefing.

Try on the dress to make sure it fits. Call the concierge if you need adjustments. You'll look stunning at the event, and your target knows that you'll be looking for him. My guess is he'll find you first, as he knows what color dress you'll be wearing.

If you feel ill or nauseated, which I assume could be the case, please contact the woman at the number on the other side of this card. She'll provide you with Ativan and Zofran for the withdrawal symptoms. However, you have an open tab at the resort if you want to try to stave off your symptoms the old fashioned way. Stay in enough control that you are the one extracting information and are able to pass it on to us.

Good luck, Fory. Michonne is your contact in case of an emergency. You understand that "emergency" is a relative term in our world. Use it carefully.

More instructions will follow. Enjoy the party and the company of Mr. O'Heara.

- Auntie

Fory exhaled and shook her head as she looked down at the box and began to slice the tape with a pocket knife given as a gift on a family camping trip in the White Mountains. She smiled; that was her first trip to Story Land.

"*Auntie*. Yeah right... Great," she whispered to herself. "I'm gonna be the only broke chick at a charity event."

She opened the box and sifted through the mounds of glittered tissue paper. At first glance, the dress seemed rather drab in color for such a posh function. Until she pulled it out, and examined the contents more closely.

She lifted the garment in the air.

It was a striking purple cocktail dress.

Fory tossed the dress onto the bed and ran into the bathroom to throw up again. This time she had to grab the handicap rail because the heaves were so deep and strong. Her retching sounded like an animal dying.

Ballroom
Chatham Dunes Hotel

Fory stood at the entrance of the grand, opulent ballroom. She found it anachronistic in a calming, classy way. The chandeliers shimmered and wood trim glistened; it was like a scene from an old Hollywood drama. She thought the room colors matched perfectly with her dress, but she felt self-conscious due to the amount of skin exposure. She knew that would pass with the first forty-dollar martini and the knowledge it would serve to lure her quarry to her side faster. *Just drinking and talking, this is an easy one.*

She patted her hair and rubbed her sides. Her energy was coming back as her monster whispered her on the path toward a cool cocktail.

As Fory crossed the threshold and walked into the room, she immediately felt that familiar warmth of men's glances. While she was in many ways a hot mess, she was pretty, not a knockout, but nicely put together. She wondered if they would care if they knew she was only skinny because she rarely ate, drank daily, had nightmares at least weekly. Well, looking good tonight was going to get her some of the best mixed drinks of her life. That thought bounced her mood up higher than it had been in weeks.

Her immediate attention was stolen by the bar which was at the far end of the expansive dance floor. Fory figured making it her first stop would kill two birds; crossing the room to score her nectar, she would be noticed by her mark.

"Bacardí Limón and Sprite. No lime, please, and no ice. With a cherry if you don't mind, lest I starve," she said smiling. Being flirtatious to the handsome bartender whose facial angle was fixated on her sculpted form, could only be a good thing. For someone who consumed as much alcohol as she did, and only worked out a couple of times a week, Fory still could pass as a hot number when she tried.

Forsythia's Ride

In the back of her mind, however, she knew Father Time would catch up with her at some point if she didn't tone down her lifestyle. Fortunately for Mary and Pratt, she still could still polish up like a sapphire.

"Here ya go, miss. Enjoy your evening," said the bartender with an elongated stare as he placed the freshly built drink in front of Fory. She downed a third of the glassful relishing its immediate warmth.

On a small stage, four musicians in black played Mozart's *String Quartet #14* as Fory walked away from the bar toward the cheese and cracker table. She was halfway across the room when an eager young waiter approached her.

"Miss, would you care for a shrimp cocktail?"

Fory nodded with a smile, and whispered some words of gratitude. The young waiter began to blush. Fory was concerned that she might be attracting too much of the wrong attention. She considered herself at work and had to strike a balance between getting noticed by her mark and not fawned over by every male in the room. *I guess I did clean up nice today,* she laughed to herself feeling confident, *it must have a little to do with this expensive dress.*

She bit into the chilled prawn and heard that distinct *snap* that's only felt from the freshest shrimp. She laughed to herself again thinking of the soggy, freezer-burned rubber souls she would order during happy hour at the corner bar in Manhattan.

She folded the tail into a cocktail napkin. A handsome, older man's eyes lock with hers. Instinctively, she knew this was O'Heara. Confident she had established non-verbal communication, she thought it best to stand still and pretend to be enjoying the droning classical music.

As she waited for him to finish his conversation, she noticed another set of eyes taking stock. Although, this was not the usual carnal male assessment of Fory's form. This glare had other intentions, and feeling it made her nervous.

As she looked around, someone invaded her space.

"Good evening, miss. My name is Chip O'Heara. I was told you'd be joining us this evening. What a pleasure," he said as he offered his hand.

Fory politely shook while admiring the James Bond-like distinction of the older gentleman. She couldn't help but think of the crush on Sean Connery she had watching early Bond movies, all the way up to *Red October.*

"Pleasure to meet you. I'm Forsythia."

"Yes, I know. It would be cliché to say that the pleasure is all mine, so I will refrain. However, It'd be my pleasure to freshen up your drink, and we can chat for a bit."

Fory realized she'd drained what was a high octane cocktail without realizing it. She knew that while she welcomed the next boost, she had to be more careful. *I've got all night, I need to go easy now and then I can finish the night once this guy is blitzed out; once I have what I need, I can blitz out myself.*

"Yes, of course, Mr. O'Heara. Lead the way."

"Please, call me Chip," he said with a head tilt. "Another cliché would be for me to say that *Mr. O'Heara* was my father. That, I cannot say with certainty, as I never knew the man."

Is he trying to be funny? Should I laugh? Or is he sharing a real piece of his life? Not knowing how to respond, Fory motioned for Chip to lead the way to where they might be able to speak without arousing suspicion. They found a high top cocktail table.

O'Heara pulled out Fory's chair. "Make yourself comfortable," said Chip with a soft wave of his hand which unveiled a fifty thousand dollar Rolex. "I'll be right back after I order our drinks, I assume you want the same?"

A nod sent him off to the bar, he was quickly back and set the drinks down.

"Mr. O'Heara, I mean Chip. Before we chat, I need you to know that I think there's a guy staring at me, and I don't think it's because of my pretty dress."

O'Heara smirked. "My guess is it's a combination of male curiosity and also his duty."

Forsythia's Ride

Fory was a bit shocked. "What do you mean? How does anyone know I'm here or what I'm supposed to be doing?"

O'Heara sipped his scotch. "Forsythia, they always know we're here. This cat and mouse game has been going on since way before your dad handed out cigars at the hospital. It's just that they're not certain what kind of threat you pose. Don't naively think your movements are clandestine."

Fory warily nodded.

"As long as you play it cool, you'll be fine. Don't panic, and just go about the business of enjoying a pleasant evening. I'm confident that you'll not be disturbed."

Fory was quiet for a moment as she scanned the room to see if the roving eyes still sought her. She didn't notice anyone looking at her. She said to her contact, "Pratt and Mary told me I'm your guide while you are here and that you were to help me with next part of whatever this crazy mission is."

O'Heara was quiet for several seconds. Too many. "I do have vital information. Data that will help with your assignment."

Fory looked to both sides, then at O'Heara. "How the hell did I get myself into this?" Fory asked rhetorically letting a little anxiety show.

O'Heara smiled. "In this business, compromising positions are par for the course. All I can say is that to have garnered the faith of someone like Pratt, you must be a stand-out in his eyes." O'Heara's tone and gaze shifted.

"Did Pratt tell you what the next step is?"

"Well, no," responded Fory. "I thought that was your role?"

"Indeed, it is," said O'Heara. "But, ah... He said nothing? Not even a clue?" His tone changed again, sharper, stonier.

"No, Chip." Fory was suddenly really nervous. "W-what's going on?"

O'Heara's cell phone vibrated. "Forsythia, I have to take this. It's important you remain right here. Please don't leave this spot. I'll be right back." O'Heara placed the phone to his ear as he left the table and headed to the other side of the room.

Fory's instincts screamed it was not wise to be idle. Maybe another trip to the cheese table might be in order, or better yet, the bar was just as close.

She crossed the room feeling some of the same probing eyes. Most were businessmen or politicians enjoying a night out showing off their finery. She was three steps from the bar when someone intentionally blocked her path.

"Oh, excuse me, miss."

It was the man who had been staring at Fory earlier from across the room!

His smile showed concern. "I'm sorry, Fory. I didn't mean to startle you. Please let me introduce myself. I'm Chip O'Heara."

Fory felt ice running in her veins.

"Word in our little world is that your aunt and old man Pratt are not happy about my sudden arrival in town," said O'Heara.

Fory's empty glass slipped through her hands and tumbled onto the parquet floor. "What the hell's going on?" Fory lasered the question toward her second newfound contact. "I thought *that* was O'Heara who I was just talking to? How do I know who the hell you are?"

With a hand lightly placed on her shoulder this Chip O'Heara tried to calm her down. "Simple, Fory. The stakes here in this little Cape Cod hideaway are bigger than even Pratt or Mary know. They probably told you you could work under the radar and sniff out information at your leisure. Those days are over."

Fory's eyes whirled around the room.

"There are too many players circling this town with their eyes on the prize. Your aunt and the old man are used to when they were the biggest players and could command intelligence and control over any situation. That time has passed. There's a lotta cooks in the kitchen, and your aunt's new neighbor holds the spatula."

O'Heara paused and wiped his mouth as his right index finger dried a tear. "And I'm dying, Fory." O'Heara stared with intensity as he spoke. "Time is short and there's still work to be done before *I'm* done. I gotta clean up a few messes before my demise so maybe my daughters can have a better shot. I know that sounds trite, but in the end it tends to be a universal, genuine wish for most guys."

Fory took a deep breath and five second self-assessment. "Okay. Okay, then. Well, who the hell was that guy!?" Fory was trying to hold it together, but a mini panic attack was setting in as she tried to remember how much info she shared and the possibility this guy was the fake. *This is fucked up. I'm in big trouble. This was supposed to be easy with cocktails.*

"You're going to find yourself rather popular over the next few days, especially in light of your new employment."

"What the... How did you know *that?*"

"I can't disclose the identities of everyone who will be seeking your acquaintance, but I can assure you that your new friend won't be the last one trying to play you."

"Where'd he friggin' go all of a sudden?"

"His immediate departure is indicative of a two-bit operative who realized he got made by me," said O'Heara. "Most likely, you'll never see him again. Curious who he's working for, but it doesn't really matter. At this moment, they're most likely three other men in the wings who will approach you in a similar fashion."

"Friggin' great," said Fory. "Now I got that to look forward to..."

"That, and a fresh drink in the fireplace room," assured O'Heara.

With that, the aging spy politely, yet with intention, touched Fory's forearm in a silent request to walk with him.

Fifth Floor
Chatham Dunes Hotel

Fory half-stumbled coming out of the elevator. The rum fortification was rendering expected results. Even after another two Bacardís while talking at the fireplace, she was not overtly inebriated. With the exception of a couple of mis-steps on thick carpeting, Fory's drink tolerance rivaled a southie ironworker, but the adrenaline overload and exhaustion from the past few days was going to set in soon, and she knew this. It created a growing unease, something was going to go wrong soon if she didn't wrap this up and leave. *I'll act just a little more buzzed than I really am, maybe he will finally let some info slip and I can end this night with a cold one in my room.*

O'Heara sensed Fory's unsteadiness. He gently guided her in between intermittent stumbles. She was regaining her wits, but slipped on a corner of rug almost falling into an Out of Order sign hanging on an ice machine at the vending station. "Wanna Coke?"

"Nah, all that sugar is bad for you," said Fory as she straightened up both herself and the middle of her dress. "Unless it's a Sprite with a little somthin' added, I'm not interested." O'Heara didn't respond.

They got to the room and Chip scanned his key. The welcome cool of the A/C and the TV that was left on a 24-hour news station greeted them. A Botox-injected talking head was droning on about a violent uprising in some remote hell hole.

> Joining us tonight is General Malcolm Young from the U.N. Peacekeeping Force to give us the latest. General Young, the world wants to know your thoughts on the recent...

Fory walked across the room and grabbed the remote. She killed the volume and plunged onto the luxurious bed. Her slight neck roll and grin would have made a great commercial for the hotel's next ad campaign.

For a second, the primal part of O'Heara was disappointed in the lack of sexuality in her movements, then his scattered thoughts snapped back into place. The old operative could still feel the blood flow beneath his belt, but knew that if he didn't focus on the matter at hand, the maroon might have to flow in other ways if he wasn't careful.

Fory stared at the ceiling for several seconds and gathered her thoughts only blurt out, "How the hell do I even know you're the right contact?! You're all a bunch of liars, my aunt included."

Chip shrugged with indifference. "Good question. You probably want to see how I was a tattooed on my chest as a terrorist in Belfast?" he asked.

Fory was silent.

"I'd much rather prove it by asking *you* a question," said O'Heara with a challenging tone.

Fory looked into the older man's eyes with her own challenge. "Fire away."

"Alright. This will be quick." O'Heara paced the bed at a respectable distance. "Please tell me. Did the imposter say Pratt and Mary's names first, or did *you* bring them up first?"

Fory had a little trouble processing with a head full of rum. "Shit." was all she could whisper. "Shit!... Dammit."

O'Heara crossed the room into the loo and poured tap water into a glass. Chip cleared his throat after a needed wet slug. "Pratt and Mary are mythical to the players in our business. That's one of the keys to the their longevity in this godforsaken game."

Fory rubbed her temple. "Well, then... Who *was* that guy? Who's he work for?" Fory as she smacked her own forehead. "Better yet, why's he trackin' me down? Da fuck?!"

"He could be working for a number of shops. Most likely a freelancer sent in to gather information. You've already provided him with an important slice by sharing's your boss' identities, which is unfortunate," said O'Heara as he slid into an oversized chair across from the bed. "I'm sure Pratt won't be happy with that piece of intel."

"What could I do?" said Fory as anxiety kicked in. "I'm not exactly trained in this spy shit, and I—"

The old hired gun interrupted with a palm toward Fory. "Listen. I want to cut to the chase. I'm here as an independent contractor on this one. For whatever reason, the old man and your aunt think they're still relevant enough in a younger, changing world to be the only ones really calling the shots. We gotta move now."

Fory's mind began processing all avenues in her head, however they were blocked by cobwebs, withdrawal and anxiety.

"Fory, I'm here to earn a buck. I can't share the particulars, but I'm also here to help you."

"Help me? *Help* me!" hissed Fory. "How the hell are you friggin' gonna help me? All you're doing is testing me with names and bull-shit to see what I know that will help you." Fory's eyes glossed and stared. "Honestly, you damn Paddy, I'd have more respect for you if you just dragged both our asses up here for a good ol' screw!"

O'Heara didn't respond.

Fory calmed and dropped her volume. "You said you wanted to help me. The big question is why?"

O'Heara got up and walked to the mini-bar. "How 'bout a drink first?"

"Thought you'd never offer." Fory scowled, but turned it into a fresh smile. "How about you tell me who *you're* working for?"

"Fine." said O'Heara as he got up and moved over to the couch that was even further away from Fory. She expected him to already have crawled next to her by then. That was how her dates usually worked.

"Bottom line is I'm not working for anybody, probably to your aunt's dismay. I'm here 'cause I have important information on what you're caught up in. It's unfortunate for you that you are stuck in this mess. I want to make some money to set my daughters up for life. Like your dad needed to set you up to be strong when he was gone. Well he did more for you than you can imagine."

Forsythia's Ride

Fory's alcohol dulled-eyes lit up. "My d-dad... You knew my dad!?" Emotionally drained, it was all Forsythia could do not to sob. "How the hell did you...?"

"It was long ago.. We did work overseen by your aunt."

Fory was quiet and gave him eager eyes, encouraging him to share more information.

"You see, via Mary, your dad and I were hired to procure goods, meaning *steal* things, of value. We then had everything sent across the Atlantic to be used to purchase weapons for our cause. Your dad and I did all kinds of work in that world, but we were also in the information business, our world was not always bombs and terror and mischief that the world saw on television."

"Mischief?" coughed Fory, "*That's* what you guys called it? *Mischief?*"

"Yes. We did. Anyway, our handlers charged us with buying and selling items that would benefit the arms re-supply effort back home. We'd obviously move the usual suspects around for resale when we could get enough of it, namely coke and heroin."

Fory was stunned with Chip's candor. "I see." Fory pulled at her own hair in thought. *Drug dealers.* She deflated. Her father, nothing but a drug dealer. "Must have made your people proud?" she asked with bitter sarcasm only an Irish lass could deliver when in her cups.

O'Heara bit his lower lip. "Back then, we *all* did things we're not proud of. In some bizarre, twisted way, it's encouraging to see Pratt and Mary work together on a project for once. Their two teams have traded more than body blows over the years."

"So, what's your deal? Why in the hell would you tell me any of this?" asked Fory who was slowly losing the alcohol buzz and craving another. At Fory's senior level, normal speech and functioning or withdrawal could come fast and with little warning. The monkey needed to be fed on its own timetable.

While coming down ensured a clearer head, it also ushered in a shorter temper. "Cash? In the end, don't all you spooks just money grab once you realize your time is fading?"

Matt Fitzpatrick

O'Heara chuckled. "I see time has already hardened your young heart. In many ways, it will provide you with a proper defense, you can thank your dad for that. In other, less concrete ways, it's a pity and this outlook will eat away at you over time and squander your opportunity. Unfortunately, the aging process comes faster than we think it will," said Chip as he walked over and built Fory a new cocktail banging three ice cubes into the glass. "Here, you're gonna need this. And I need you more alert. Get your buzz back, and you'll have your wits. You'll pass out later which is fine."

Fory laughed as she grabbed the drink like she would a gold bar. "Well, if your pouring, Mr. Bond, I'd be rude to snub." She took a fresh cocktail haul. "So, what are you offering, and what are you looking for?" Fory tossed the drink's ice cube contents on the floor next to the bed in drunken disgust. "Waste of water..."

"Forsythia," began O'Heara in a gentle tone, "years ago, your father and I were put on an assignment that was to be an incredible source of arms revenue for our cause. One of the biggest scores we'd ever made, and your dad was knee-deep in the planning. We were under instructions from people like your aunt to do whatever it took to find what we knew was coming on the market. Back in the day, our organization was constantly scrambling for funding and resources. Regarding that score, well, your old man and I found a source. And your dad led the charge."

"What were you going after?" Fory asked as she climbed up another level of buzz. "Why didn't you just stick to selling drugs on school buses like y'all did with Whitey?"

With a noticeable wince, the Irish operative ignored the insult and said, "Chatham is not exactly a hot bed for international espionage and operations."

"No shit," spit Fory. "Bunch of hydrangea planters. Screw them and that Lily Pulitzer while you're at it."

"I see..." said Chip. "Nonetheless, your father and I stumbled on an opportunity..." He then paused and stared directly at Fory with eyes that iced whatever fire was in her belly at the moment. "Your

Forsythia's Ride

prick of a father got shit-faced and told me where the friggin' clue is! I've stayed loyal to him up to now, but now my own daughters' future hangs on it. Literally. The secret is around your bloody neck, you drunken bitch!"

The grey-haired spook lunged at Fory while she was still lying on the bed. With outstretched arms he screamed, "Give me that locket! I'll kill you and leave ya for the gulls!"

Fory rolled just in time for Chip to crash against the headboard hard enough to be stunned and draw a small amount of blood. It also afforded Fory just enough time to lurch/stumble for the door.

As O'Heara shook off the pain from the smack to his head, he was already getting up and moving toward the door. Fory threw it open and in slamming it behind her, caught O'Heara's hand in the door-frame.

Fory heard two bones snap and low warbling noise as he tried not to scream. Despite the painful strike ripping up his hand, he didn't want to alert the other guests. As he clenched his teeth to quell his seething fury, he jerked the door open. Fory almost turned to stone from his stare.

"That goddamned thing around your neck is MINE!" O'Heara hissed.

Chip's fumbling to get the door all the way open gave Forsythia a window to run down the hall and away from a sudden enemy who was supposed to be a friendly contact. However, the old spy was quicker than anticipated; he rushed into the corridor while his quarry was only halfway down the hall.

With lightning thought Fory raced to barricade herself in the vending room. She hoped to grab a few minutes of safety while the other guests on the floor would hear the commotion and hopefully call the front desk.

She flailed her arms and grabbed the door to the vending room. As she was half way in and swinging it closed almost on top of her own legs, O'Heara caught up and grabbed the back of her hair.

"You bitch!" He was spitting saliva drops in his intense anger.

Matt Fitzpatrick

As Fory's hair was being wrenched by her pursuer, her right hand managed to return the favor. She used the leverage on his head to smash it against the side of the wall.

Chip was beginning to tire, and now was bleeding from two places. While he was still a formidable spy, the illness, normal aging and a few drinks were causing him to lose a physical battle with a much younger opponent. His fury rose.

Fory slammed the door and flicked the twist lock just as O'Heara crashed into the door. Fory hoped security was being called and alarms were ringing. Chatham Dunes Hotel was not used to hosting a spy vs. spy wrestling match.

With O'Heara sitting in the hall nursing his wounds and regaining his breath, Fory knew she had to act fast and flee. She also knew she needed to report back to Mary and Pratt.

During the ruckus, Fory sustained a cut. Despite the calamity she didn't want to walk around with a visible wound, this one was only slowly oozing blood. She opened the ice chest in order to get something cold on her face, only to find herself staring at the spurious Chip O'Heara #1 from downstairs. While good and dead, he reminded Fory of the final scene in *The Shining*, with a frozen Jack Torrence.

She screamed in surprise, but the only one to hear her cries was the killer still sitting in the hallway.

"Screw you! You'll never know the secret!" O'Heara hissed. "It's gonna die with me, then maybe you, someday. Hopefully—" he let out a short screaming bark that shot up blood from his mouth which dribbled down his chin. With much effort, O'Heara pulled out a gun, but never got to aim it at Fory.

As Chip's internal systems began to send him to cardiac arrest, his body exploded all its air, gas and waste. An epic body shut down left him in a pool of different fluids gasping like a fish.

Fory fled down the hallway not stopping to call housekeeping.

After the Ball, Mary's Cottage Chatham

Mary and Pratt made perfect dinner companions, both appreciated the tradition of a quiet meal over which they could discuss the day. Pratt entered the dining room as Alyce was serving the salad.

"I just heard from my plant at the hotel," said an annoyed Pratt, "O'Heara made contact with Fory, but not without incident. It seems she was intercepted by some imposter, dropped our names and then managed to turn the night into mayhem."

Mary looked up as she placed her napkin calmly on her lap as if not surprised. "That is unfortunate. No matter, Bill. We've both been around too long to pretend to enjoy our past anonymity, and we're too far along to harbor such concerns. Care for French or Roquefort?"

"French, of course," replied Pratt as Mary handed him the antique ladle. "I want to be able to adopt your lack of concern. But Mary, can she really handle all this? Things are going to get more complex, and fast."

"She'll be fine, Bill. She's the perfect operative for this one. Naive and clueless. Drunk and promiscuous. The tangle she got in just now is with our competition, Mobley has no idea about what is going on around her, so our main agenda is going forward as planned."

Pratt interrupted with a feeble attempt to lighten his own mood. "I see you'll be sponsoring her for an ambassador's post!"

"If we sent a pro in there, they'd stick out upon arrival." Mary was ignoring Pratt's comment, not knowing if it was jab or flat attempt at humor. "Forsythia will appear dimwitted and it won't be much of a stretch role. Trust my instincts on this, Bill. I've been at this game a while."

Pratt smiled. "Indeed you have, Mary. A living legend."

"Flattery will get you everywhere," smiled Mary as she tapped

Matt Fitzpatrick

Pratt's hand. "Another piece of news is that Michonne convinced our old friend Sasa to come aboard."

Pratt grunted in approval.

"Apparently, she was enjoying her retirement from the 'life' but our girl can be persuasive, as you know... At any rate, Sasa's in."

"What do you have in mind for her to do?"

"Well... It seems last year she took up with a clerk at her local town hall. She tossed in his bed for a few months until she learned he'd been lying to her about being single. Not only is he married, but he's been living with his husband for over ten years in Truro, much to Sasa's chagrin."

Pratt sat back and smirked. "Ah Mary, how times have changed. So, Sasa had an affair with a gay married guy? Interesting twist. That stuff didn't happen back in our day."

"I beg to differ, you old coot," laughed Mary. "Nothing has changed. It's just that back then, one had to be more discreet, lest facing consequences would...

"Anyway," Mary tightened her thoughts, "Sasa initially threatened to rat her lover out to his husband, but decided having it hanging over his head would be more valuable in the long term. She's smart, and right now fortunately, we are the beneficiaries since we control her. She's gonna approach her Romeo and lean on him hard to see what the hell is going on with the building permits at the Mobley place. Could be a nice break in our situation to have blueprints."

"Wow," smiled Pratt. "Wow! Nice little arrow in the quiver."

Pratt took a sip of scotch. "You never cease to amaze me. Imagine, us old crows ... Still so many balls in the air and pieces on the chess-board."

"Yeah," said Mary with pursed lips. "We're not rookies anymore, for sure. But unlike some of our peers, we're not gathering moss or barnacles." *But why not? I'm old, coughing and smoking. What more do I want?* With a feeling of imperious anger she answered herself. *I'm still one of the biggest dogs in the pound dammit. No one's going to undercut me on anything, I AM IRA power. Fuck them all.*

159

Forsythia's Ride

Pratt was quiet for several seconds watching her face tighten and darken. "You're right, Mary. Most of our peers are in the dankest of prisons or long underground."

Mary finally smiled, like a shark.

"Well, at least we have that look to look forward to as part of our retirement package."

Night Moves Under Moonlight
Chatham

Fory gave the hotel valet a dirty wink and a false promise about what would happen if he would drive her the few miles north back to Aunt Mary's. While he was supposed to be at his station the entire night, the opportunity presented was too enticing to pass up. He was very embarrassed when she shoved some bills in his hand and gave him a peck on the cheek, then rushed off. She rewarded his false hopes with a lofty tip, but still, the frustrated livery spun off with a tire chirp as he abandoned hope about getting this pretty woman in purple to bed.

Luckily, Fory found one of the back doors unlocked. She sneaked up the stairwell into her guest room hoping to not cause a stir. As in every step on this adventure, Fory had no idea she not only tripped a silent alarm that went right to Mary's bedroom, she was locking in a very clear digital recording of her wobbling tiptoeing.

Mary huffed, clicked the alarm off and went back to sleep.

Fory exhaled, looked around, and spun into what some addicts call a Shoeshine:

Splash water splash on face. Stand under shower for 30 seconds. Soap and shampoo not required, but permitted if time allows.

With a boxer's left and right hooks, Fory battled the shower head. She delivered one punch to the metal that she immediately realized was futile. Then still with frustration she saturated her hair with calming, warm water until it hung heavy over her face. The more she cleansed and gathered her thoughts, the more the weight on her head and soul increased.

As Fory snapped the spigot shut, she was shaken by a buckling sound from the aging pipe system. It reminded her of her alcoholic stomach.

She wrestled with the harsh reality that there was nobody in her corner who she could trust. After a few seconds, the brief solace from the shower and thick towel wore off.

Not only had she left her so-called contact banged up and bleeding in the hallway of a posh resort, but his competition lay dead on ice cubes in that same posh hotel. *Hell, the mess Chip was oozing out probably means he's dead too.*

"Damn! What the hell am I doing?" she said out loud, but took a deep breath as she tried to regain composure. *Recriminations belong under a granite headstone,* was her quick thought.

"Dammit!" she yelled into the towel lest Mary hear. After years of self-abuse, even a stubborn Fory knew the remnants of bad behavior always emerged at inopportune times. She felt it happening now as her stomach gave a clinch and roll.

Fory's prison called. With the normal withdrawal gods calling in their chits, Forsythia launched face-first into the bathroom and aimed her head over the toilet. Hard. Piping hot, *Exorcist* bile missile-shot from her throat and splashed the porcelain. The visual aftermath reminded her of Hampton Beach spin-art collected as a kid. She gathered it all summer until Labor Day washed everything away.

Fory stepped back while coughing and exhaling. Next would be two minutes of dry heaves and yellow acid spitting onto the sides of the commode.

Maybe, this is the end, she thought as she wiped her mouth again. Fory power-coughed into a fistful of toilet paper and then faced the mirror. Some of her phlegm was still stuck to her fingers as she tossed them through her wet hair.

Stinging acid filled her stomach. It ran down her insides like a serpent.

Fory sulked at the mirror. She knew O'Heara had been adamant about what he knew and what he was willing to die to find.

She peered back into the glass, rubbed her sternum and opened the locket. The small picture of her father still reflected the image of the strong man she once knew.

Fory gave the whole thing a much deeper inspection than she had ever done, now noticing the clasp on the pendant was loose. A memory shot through her mind in a flash, and for a long second, she felt the gentle scratch of her late father's two-day stubble...

* * *

Sudden knocks smacked the door. Fory rolled over. More knocks.

"Shit," said Fory as she wiped her face and ran her hands down her robe. She had fallen asleep in it on top of the covers. Her stomache growled letting her know she probably missed breakfast.

In a strange way, she hoped it was Michonne, who might be the only person she could even try to trust. In her awkwardness and desperation, Fory wanted to find solace with her handler. Socially odd, Fory did sense the girl was legitimate, she hoped it wasn't all an act. Luckily for Fory's anxiety level, it was exactly who she wanted to see. She opened the door and the two exchanged equally awkward smiles.

"Thought I'd check up on ya," said Michonne as she entered sans invitation. She took quick inventory of Fory's appearance and smelled the stubborn stench of stale booze and vomit. "We know you've had a long few days. You okay?"

Fory breathed a couple of quick puffs out of one cheek. "Yeah, I'll live," she said. "I was lucky to get back here, I suppose. Just getting a second wind and tryin' to process all this shit."

"You've been sent to the wolves, but you're doing great."

"Yeah, great," coughed Fory. "I got one guy on ice and another I *wish* was friggin' dead and very well may be. This is insane!" she all but yelled as she paced the room and abandoned her fear of being too loud.

"Fory, we understand you could be feeling duress," said Michonne in a monotone, "but you have us in your corner, and we are all gonna see this through." *Why is it hard to deliver this crap company line?*

Forsythia's Ride

I'm getting soft, wanting a real friend out this.

Fory's adrenaline surged. She had picked up on the flat delivery. "*WE*? Who the hell is *WE*? I got sent on a goddamned suicide mission, and I'm just supposed to play Babe in the Woods?" Fory noticed her temple sweat was beginning to mat the sides of her hair.

"I'm DONE! Fuck this! No more! I'm going back to New York! Get me a friggin' Uber!" Fory began rummaging around the room and tossed clothes, both dirty and clean, into her luggage. "Buncha pricks!" her outburst continued.

Michonne was silent for several seconds while Fory scrummed with her belongings.

"Fory," said the young handler in a steel tone, "you do realize that you're not going anywhere?"

Fory's froze. Not only because she was being threatened, but more so because she knew the people involved and how far they would go.

"There will be no Uber. No bus." Michonne cleared her throat half for emphasis. "And, no Superman or magic carpet for an escape." She punctuated the next statement with laser eyes. "Unless of course, you'd like to hire private livery at your own expense?"

Fory's exhale was half spit.

"Fine! That's all I needed to hear," said Fory. "Yeah, I'm broke, but I'm gettin' outta this scene from Cuckoo's Nest and heading back to the city."

"Speaking of a cuckoo's nest..." Even the usually stoic Michonne took pride in her occasional wit as she motioned toward Fory's wild hair and twisted robe. One of the few movies she saw, her dad telling her it was a classic as well as having some valuable life-lessons.

"You do know who will be there to greet you upon your arrival at your apartment in New York?"

"What are you talking about?" asked Fory as she pulled a worn brush through her hair and wrestled with a scrunchie in preparation for tossing on some clothes and making an exit.

"This assignment has larger ramifications which trump your concerns," said a serious Michonne. "Unfortunately, any deviation from the plan will not go over well. Not well at all, especially for you."

"You're giving me a veiled threat, you little freak of nature!" Fory seethed.

"Not so veiled." The words came from a blank face. Inside Michonne was nearly falling apart, the person she was threatening was the closest thing she had ever had to a normal girl friend. To a normal life. To just sitting around and chatting. The longing to just belong somewhere for who she was, not what job she could pull off.

"Wow!...Wow!" Fory pulled her hair so hard she could taste it. "You know... you're a lunatic! You look like a sorority sister, but you act like a geriatric. Talk like a friggin' normal person, will ya?!"

Michonne ignored the outburst. *I wonder if I can save this? If Fory knows this isn't my fault; I'm only doing my job.* "I'm actually older than Constance Greene..." she finally said with a tight smile. "That's an inside joke..."

Fory threw a firm hand up in exasperation and walked away with purpose, but quickly realized she had nowhere to go. She sat on the bed and rubbed her eyes.

"Listen," said Michonne, "we've got to get you put together and ready for your first day at Mobley's."

A deflated Fory looked up. "This is insane. I can't believe this is happening, and I can't believe that it could be my dead father's fault."

"Nobody's fault," said Michonne. "We just have to get to the bottom of what's going on down the street. The stakes are too high to ignore."

Fory got up and stared out the window. Even the ocean seemed apathetic.

"Hey, your aunt's a warrior. A hero and someone who has tenfold *saved* more lives than destroyed. Fory, it's an old war, and she's an old soldier. This is her last hurrah, so to speak. Just help her this one time and you'll be rewarded. I'm here to help you get through it. Truly I am."

"Rewarded," muttered Fory. "What? In some heaven with harps and shamrocks, and all my dead relatives who I couldn't stand when they were alive?" A crazed laugh burst out of her and then Fory rubbed her face with a sob.

"Fine. Whatever." Fory's emotions suddenly drained from her face, as her gaze stiffened.

"When do I have to go over there? I'm friggin' exhausted," responded Fory as she reached back to rub a tight shoulder.

"We're certain you are," said Michonne with an intentional pause. "That's exactly what we want."

"Course, you do," quietly snapped Fory.

Michonne took advantage of Fory calming down. "We know something is going on at Mobley's. Everything that went down at the hotel last night is all connected to Mobley's construction project. We know that for sure. What you need to find out are the exact details. You're going to go there, and find out if your family's legend is true."

Fory was confused. "Legend? What are you talkin' about?"

Michonne stared at Fory's chest. "We need to see what's around your neck."

O'Leary's Stale Ale Pub
Woods Hole, Cape Cod

"Shut up, ya tossers! I'm deaf as a haddock over here!" A frustrated Tommy Reyes was trying to take his partner's call over the din of the late afternoon crowd. The usual sods were rambunctious since they had just gotten paid.

The roar tamped down to a dull roar. Reyes held one ear shut and said, "Yeah, g'head, Steam."

"What's with this new work all of sudden? We just did a haul for the Monarch," said Steamer.

Gawd he is so easily confused. Lord give me patience. "Don't complain," said Reyes. "Summaht's comin' and we both need the dough, but Monarch was light on detail with this one. He's planning something over in friggin' Chatham of all places. We need to bring a boat over there that's big enough to store whatever he's haulin' this time. But, we can't attract attention."

"Chatham?" laughed Steamer. "Whadda we gonna sneak in a stash of stolen Dom Pérignon and crates of adult diapers?"

"I doubt it, you idiot," said a nervous Reyes. "Let's just friggin' do this, and worry about contents later. Shit, man, we both need the money, and I need a score to get me through to Fourth of July. After that, if history holds, with summer in full blast, we'll get plenty of work running stash over to the fancy mucks on Nantucket. We'll be golden with that, but we're still a coupla months away."

"Okay, I hear ya," said Steamer. "I know a guy with a 38 Rampage over in Falmouth. Nice boat! Fast, plenty of storage. More importantly, he owes me a favor. He banged one of my ex-wives and refuses to pay proper tribute. I consider him in my debt."

Tommy Reyes eye rub moved up to his temple. "Whatever, man..." said Reyes with a laugh. "Glad I don't live on your planet."

"Hey, man. Screw! I'm gettin' us a vessel." Steamer was insulted.

Forsythia's Ride

"Fine, fine. Just get the goddamned boat!" barked Reyes. "And get it over there and tied up in time. Monarch said we should get positioned in Chatham and then wait for instructions. We could be called up in a day or in weeks, so we need to be ready."

"No problem," replied Steamer. "I'll bring her over. Take me a coupla hours. I know another guy I can lean on for a slip for a few days at the Chatham Fish Pier. Meet me there, and then what?"

"Not sure, Steam. Not sure," honestly responded Reyes. "I think we just do it, trust Monarch and do what he says. He's never let us down before. Hey, when I meet up with you, I'll even bring a fresh bottle of Jamison to calm you down and shut you up 'til it's go-time."

"Alright! A little J always helps," replied Steamer as his gears turned. It seemed like a typical gig, but the end instructions were vague.

Reyes realized he could be stuck waiting at a dock for a couple of days while plans got adjusted. The biggest challenge could be keeping Steamer occupied. Could be a dull assignment, for sure. *Maybe dull wouldn't be a bad thing,* he thought as he was interrupted by his partner's request.

"Think ya can bring a coupla broads?"

Mary's Cottage

Michonne followed her assignment into the bathroom. Fory leaned over the sink and fingered the locket gifted from her father. She held the piece to the mirror, and opened the clasp.

"It's lovely," Michonne said leaning toward the shinning gold with genuine curiosity. "Can I see?"

Forsythia opened the locket to reveal tiny pictures of a young Fory and her dad. She tilted her shoulder so her handler could see.

"Pretty," said Michonne. While she was now blessed with two adopted parents who adored and treated her like their own, that tug of the truth about her real past would never leave her. It was always a gale wind in her head. *My parents may love me, but they are still using me; making me into what they want so I can take over their work. I know deep down, they mean the best, but I'm kept so alone, can't really have friends, and always have to keep moving. I wish I had what Fory did with her dad before the tragedy.*

Fory had been twisting the pendant in the light. Now she pointed to the numbers engraved on the other side of the locket while Michonne's brain immediately began processing. She rubbed her lips in thought. It didn't take long for her figure out the answer to those numbers. She was half-expecting it, and luckily for her, it all clicked into place.

"You play the lottery?" Michonne asked with a quick laugh that bordered on sarcasm.

"Nah, I've had enough bad luck." Fory chuckled. "What are you talking about?"

"Here," said Michonne as she handed Fory a mini paper pad and pencil.

"Okay," said Fory in an awkward tone.

"Read the numbers in the mirror," said Michonne. "It inverts them. Just write 'em down as you see them in the mirror."

Fory held the locket up to mirror while balancing the pen, pad and mostly herself. The stretching and wobbling caused some withdrawal symptoms to bubble up. Her eyes tightened as she peered into the glass and began to write:

48711714 3576996

Fory tossed the pen into the sink and stepped back. "Okay, Miss DaVinci Code, what next?"

Michonne normally would have tried to challenge a stranger with a snarky retort, but this was too important, plus she still entertained a subconscious desire to have a friendship with this woman; at least she could be honest about what she did for a living with Forsythia.

"This is it!" Michonne exclaimed with rare, happy hand-waves. "We have it!"

Fory was talking to Michonne through the mirror's reflection. "Cool. Great... But what does it mean?"

Michonne returned to serious mode. "My guess is that your father was involved in communication and decoding for your aunt's organization."

Fory was goggled, mouth and eyes.

"From what Mary's told me, your dad could have deciphered the Rosetta Stone," said Michonne into the confused eyes blinking in the mirror.

"Bottom line, Fory, in addition to the other things he did, he was a coder/decoder for IRA intelligence," said Michonne. "Don't you get it?"

Fory inhaled before speaking, "Alright... but what did he decode here?"

Michonne took a quick breath to calm down. "It means your father was not only a key player, but he had an eye for script. A more than valuable trade in this day and age. Script is a trade word for being able to manipulate messages and information. Your dad was a master by reputation, and this supports that."

"My dad had a reputation?" asked Fory.

"These numbers are simple enough to interpret," said Michonne with a rare grin. "Your father had information he wanted to pass along to you via the engraving on your locket. The digits and message are simple. They're latitude and longitude numbers! Your father taught you how to navigate as a kid on his GPS on the boat, right?"

Fory was quiet for a few seconds. "Yeah, yeah..." she muttered. "Okay, so what's it show, I mean what's there?"

"We just uncovered a secret your dad was keeping to himself. Selfishly."

"*Selfishly?* Screw you!" yelled a suddenly jarred Fory. "He died in front of me and I goddamned well know it's all connected to you, my aunt and all this shit!"

Michonne stared. "I don't know exactly when your dad passed, but my guess is that I was in diapers, or maybe not even born. Anyway, what this *shows*, Fory, is that your dad knew exactly the information he refused to share with his only sister."

"This is crazy. I know nothing about this shit. If he kept something from my crazy aunt, then it was for a damn good reason."

Michonne parted her hands in capitulation to diffuse the moment, but remained quiet as the fumes evaporated around Fory.

"Coordinates?" mused Fory, whose memories immediately turned to the day her father dissected himself in her presence. Dissection was an appropriate term. He must have wanted to be peeled open so his daughter could finally see the true him that day.

Fory shot a hand in the air in a wave of frustration. "You're outta your mind. This has to be some coincidence, the jeweler just marked it like a logo or something to show who made it."

"No, Fory," said Michonne. "Read the numbers in the mirror, like they're supposed to be read. In order, with the digits backwards."

Fory squinted and read the digits off of the locket first, and said, "It means nothing... Bunch of gibberish."

Michonne couldn't believe Fory'd worn the trinket for so long and had no idea it held a secret in the numbers, even if she had no clue about what they meant.

Forsythia's Ride

"Ever hear of lat/longs? Navigational terms? Used when at sea?" asked Michonne.

Fory blew hair out of her eye. "I'm from the fucking middle of fucking Cow Hampshire. Now, Manhattan. Lucky if I could even find the ocean," said a sarcastic Fory who was done with this dancing around crap. "Luckier, if I ever get to see it again, aside from this Cape Cod dream vacation!" She spit out some contrived laughter.

"I see... well what your dad had inscribed into your locket **are** global navigational coordinates pointing here, to Chatham. I'd bet my bottom dollar those numbers correspond with where Mobley lives, probably exactly where she still has construction going on!"

Fory looked beyond puzzled.

"C'mon, read 'em backwards," said a convincing Michonne, "and you'll get it. He was sharing very precise coordinates with you. He's sending you a message from right before he killed himself."

Fory was silent.

"They really read 41.117 784 on latitude," said Michonne in a monotone to try to keep Fory calm and also to keep herself from going too fast right now, "and 69.967 533 on the longitude."

"Okay," said Fory, "and the price of bananas is what?"

Michonne inhaled deep before responding. "The price of bananas is that you uncovered global positioning coordinates that point directly to a spot on Anna Mobley's new property!"

"So you fucking said. What's that *mean?* Could you just be straight out with me for once?" asked Fory.

"It means, your aunt's gonna call a meeting and you're gonna clean up and get to work!"

Nor'east Bluffs
Chatham

They congregated in Mary's great room that overlooked Pleasant Bay. The wind dancing with the eel grass was a typical Cape Cod spring easterly that felt pleasant at first, but then bit the bones as the afternoon progressed. Gulls were growing excited because tourist season was starting; tossed french fries and overflowing trash bins could now be found.

"Thanks to everyone for being here," said Mary. "I know it's been a long couple of days. We're one major step further toward accomplishing our goal thanks to Michonne and Forsythia."

The two received their nods of approval from the others gathered: Sasa and an uncharacteristically quiet Sir William.

This was the first time that the full group had officially met. Since time was short, Mary wanted to be brief so suspend formalities.

"We've all been briefed by Michonne," said Mary. "Bottom line is the old story appears to be true, and it looks like our neighbor is trying to capitalize."

While the others stayed quiet, Fory was pissed. "Legend? I know the locket Dad gave me has a clue." She fingered the piece. "Calling a drug dealer a legend is pathetic. I know Pratt does it. I know for sure the IRA does it. I guess I accept my dad did it. I don't call that legend. It is criminal. I'll help, but then I'm done with you all. I knew this life was what caused my dad to kill himself. I don't know exact why, and now I don't even fucking care about the details. Let's just get this over with. And by the way, who's this?" Fory finished pointing to Sasa.

Mary raised her eyebrows. She then looked toward her former operative and said, "She's with me. She's temporarily coming out of retirement for this quick assignment. Sasa'll assist you with getting this done, Fory."

Sasa's eyes dropped with lips pursed. She would have rather been back at the dental office sitting in the patient chair with no Novocain.

"Sasa has been kind enough to offer her expert services on this mission," said Mary.

Sasa sported a look of mild contempt, but in the end, she knew Mary owned her in exchange for her brother's life and for knowledge of past sins. Sasa learned that the ones who approached her with love and history, always had a pin to pop in her trust balloon.

After remaining quiet for the group's initial comments, Pratt felt the need to take control. He tossed his thoughts out like dice on the craps table. "Our next step is crucial." Pratt tapped his pipe ashes into another one of Mary's quahog ashtrays. "This has to move fast."

"Relax, Bill." Mary was slightly insulted. "You know I have things in the works—"

Fory interrupted, "Okay, if everything we know are in those coordinates, why don't we just get online and pinpoint what you're looking for?"

Michonne said, "We still need a visual Fory. Old GPS coordinates aren't a hundred percent accurate. We still need boots on the ground to get proper intel before we disturb the hornet nest."

"Indeed," said Pratt while he fired up another bowl of Captain Black. "We're here to establish a unified front, a cohesive strategy." He shifted his girth, leaning back into his chair. "Mary, I think it's time you take full lead on this one now. We're in your neighborhood. Earl Grey has provided funding and all our intelligence, now it's your turn, you have always excelled at the dirty parts."

"No mistakes can be made at this point," said Mary ignoring the possible insult. Into the now quiet room Mary laid out the plan.

"We know that the tales of the missing weapons appear to be true. There's no denying it now, and I realize that my late brother knew it as well," said Mary as she looked over at Fory.

"The global positioning coordinates found in the locket point to where Mobley is doing construction, her excuse is creating a new dock just beyond a new huge guest cottage. We need to stop this now before she can mobilize a transfer of the missing weapons. No doubt she's going to throw them out on the black market. We know she has the channels to do this. It's anyone's guess where they'll end up."

Mary gazed around the room. "We move tonight," the aging spy said with pride. "This is to be my swan song, everything in the past will be a footnote to my saving the entire world by getting these nukes under control. First we send in our people at staggered times; goal one is to confirm the weapons really are there, with so much time having past, it is possible another group found them and moved them. The original thieves seem all to be dead at this point. A coincidence the IRA is not involved with. That they are gone is a low probablity because if they were found, they would have been sold by now. There are still so many impulsive authoritarians around the globe. Still, that makes it imperative before I move my transport into place that we confirm. Once we have confirmation, we neutralize the others in the situation and call for transport, they are waiting in a dock very nearby."

"Neutralize?" interrupted Pratt with a sarcastic smile. "Are you suggesting that we call in a bloody black ops team?"

"No, No. Far from it," responded Michonne who was Mary's point person on this mission. "It's going to be way more subtle, and that's where Sasa comes in." She looked over at the miffed hygienist.

"Whatever. I got you the blueprints. Just tell me where you want me to stand lookout and I'll deal with my attitude. Where do we start?"

Michonne began an impromptu plan sketch on a pad held on a tripod. "Fory heads over to help with the gathering Mobley's having tonight. Not gonna be a huge crowd from what we know, but enough moving parts to create sufficient chaos so nobody is paying attention to little things. Fory gets there right on time, maybe even a little early. She meets the staff who'll be working and Fory is to try to avoid getting roped into a menial project that could limit mobility. We don't want her cloistered in the kitchen chopping onions."

"And you're positive, Mary," Pratt interrupted as he turned away from Michonne and toward their host, "that Mobley isn't onto us?"

Forsythia's Ride

Pratt's question was punctuated with a look of subtle warning.

"As of now, there's nothing to lead us to believe that she's aware anyone knows what she's up to. The reality is we can't really know. Fortunately, that scuttle down at the hotel shouldn't make any news until it's leaked out by someone on staff. Chatham Dunes is careful to keep disturbing news quiet, especially as the season gets underway, which is to our advantage."

Pratt nodded but remained silent.

"So, if Fory can finagle a task at the party that will allow her to roam around," continued Michonne, "I'll arrive posing as one of the caterers bringing in a surprise, last minute fancy wine Fory ordered. Sasa will have the TR7 GPS unit. Brand new. Swiss made. It's the most precise on the market outside of the Pentagon's stash. If Fory gets caught with this type of unit, it would scuttle the mission and put her in danger. That's why we need Sasa to bring it over via an approach from the park next to Mobley's beach. We can't have it on Fory's person when she reports to work just in case Mobley's security does a pat-down."

"Great. Figures," said Fory. "By the way, this gizmo you're talking about. Is that like what's in cars? Will I know how to use the damn thing?"

"Not exactly, which is to our advantage," answered Michonne. "This one is calibrated way better than what you buy retail. By design and government mandate, older civilian global positioning units are intentionally off by just enough degrees to still make them accurate, but not pinpoint where one could precisely land a missile. Nowadays, they're better, but yours should be pristine."

Mary interjected, "Sasa, the crucial piece here is that you need to literally *see* where these coordinates suggest, and if they're exactly what we're looking for. Then, you simply hit the MOB button on the positioning unit, usually used if someone falls overboard at sea. Then, the coordinates are marked. There's a forward button on the unit that's programmed to send directly to Michonne's phone. All you have to do is press it and the saved coordinates go right to her like a text."

"Okay, gotta love technology," Fory said with a snicker. "How the hell do I know if I'm looking at friggin' nuclear weapons?!" Fory rubbed her eyes. "This is fucked—"

"Yes it is," Sasa interjected feeling compelled to join in the conversation since they were discussing her role. If she was going to be forced to contribute to this insanity, then she was going to give her experienced opinions.

"Fory, you're gonna know you're staring at actual nukes for the simple reason that a rich lady playing in the black market wouldn't have a need to hide fake missiles in her back yard. Mostly likely she's under the impression no one else knows they're there and she can dig them up and sell them under the radar."

Fory's emotional chaos was physically showing.

"Sorry... I don't wanna stress you." Sasa sat back and frowned.

Mary said, "Sasa's concerns stem from experience. Her anecdotes and advice will be valuable over the next several hours."

Pratt spoke up realizing Fory really never got an exact answer. "If you actually get a visual on armament of any kind, you can bet it's real."

Fory was processing the situation. "Okay... Mark it and text it. Then what?"

Mary nodded toward Sasa.

"That's where I'm gonna take point," said Sasa, who was feeling some of her former life's spy mojo. "Once you get a confirmed visual on the weapons, and I get the coordinates, Mary will contact the transporters. All you have to do is act normal and keep helping with the party, keeping everyone mingling and talking and maybe close to the house and away from the construction area in the back yard."

"Oh, okay," said a snarky Fory. "So, Mobley and her goons will just let us waltz in there and politely relieve them of millions of dollars of friggin' bombs?"

"Certainly not," snapped Mary, "but we can't exactly storm the beach like Normandy. It has to be a fast and a quiet extraction.

Michonne is in charge of overseeing that part of the operation."

"So, my rent-a-kid sister is in charge of distracting armed guards while we steal missiles and shit?" Fory scoffed. "Sure! Why not? Makes perfect sense." She looked toward the ceiling while slightly shaking her head. *This is too straight forward. It never happens like this in the movies; there's always some explosives or hired guns or something. I'm going in with nothing but a dress on and a GPS gadget.*

Pratt said something that made Fory turn cold; it was like he saw into the very heart of her thoughts. "I know it sounds like we're trying to stage a major theft that would require dozens of hands and heavy equipment to move the cache, but we only need one crate."

"Crate?" asked a confused Fory.

"Yes," responded Mary. "It will only take a couple of strong bodies to move a big crate. If our intelligence is correct, there should be several wooden boxes and our transport guys can easily handle one. We put all the parts we want that contain the actual nuclear warhead components into one crate. That's all we want. They can keep a bunch of old iron buried there forever, as far as we're concerned. We just want the *brains* of the weapons."

Mary look around at the rest of the group. "Okay. Regarding the transportation of what we hope to find, that piece of logistics has already been set in place. The guys who are going to implement the plan have a history of successful missions with me. Not heavy lifting operations, but they're adequate B-level players. I picked them specifically for that reason. They are on standby, they will be at Mobley's dock within 5 minutes of my calling them."

"Who'd you get, Mary?" asked Pratt, "Not questioning, but that's one precious load they'll be carrying. Shouldn't we be using the best guys available? Well-seasoned transporters?"

"I understand your concern," responded Mary with the flick of an ash tip into a razor clam shell. "My answer is no. We're lucky to have access to two guys who will fit in with the local fishermen, which is crucial to our success. It would never work with polished professionals. Not on Cape Cod. They'd stick out and be made before the next tide change. We can't afford any local attention or scuttlebutt, especially in Chatham, where the coconut telegraph is more powerful than the electric grid."

Pratt nodded, satisfied everyone understood their personnel component of the operation.

"They'll be fine," said Mary. "They have experience and Irish luck on their side. Not necessarily in that order."

Xanadu

Fory was careful to approach the Mobley house with as little fanfare as possible. The gate was open this time for guests. The construction crew had knocked off for the day. She hoped to cross the driveway undetected.

She glanced toward the ocean, amazed by the scale of the project. Mobley had hired a full-blown construction crew, who at the moment, were probably out drinking their padded wages. Smart Mass crews always added fees to projects in towns like Chatham and Osterville as a drinking fee because these types of owners drove any sane worker to drink at the end of the day. However, they definitely earned their premium on this one. If Mobley had her way, the dock project would make the Big Dig resemble a kid's sand castle.

Fory pushed back her hair as a bead of sweat began to sting her eyes.

She gained composure and walked to the entrance of the house. She had to trust that Mary's people knew their stuff. There was no other attitude to embrace while walking through the doorway.

While she wanted so much to trust Michonne, she wasn't fully confident in the girl's intentions if a situation arose where Fory might have to compromise her aunt's wishes and flee back to Manhattan. The kid had a crazy upbringing.

Fory feared that Michonne's brain could be even more a plate of scrambled eggs than her own.

Fory didn't have to worry about any squeak of a proverbial loose board announcing her trip up the porch steps. Mobley's wide-cut wood planks were set with oversized metal screws so neither would squeak for at least five years.

Before Fory could push the doorbell, the door opened. "Greetings and welcome," said Dane. "Ms. Mobley is expecting you. Matter of fact, we've all been."

"Oh, great... thank you," said an awkward Fory as Mobley's right hand man ushered her in.

What the hell did he mean by that? Was it a smirk on his face? Now he looks so blank. Shit I can't read him at all. Does he know I'm here to snoop?

Fory looked around, immediately impressed by the transformation of the room. Chrome appliances gleamed, standing out like silver against peacock wall colors.

The lap pool water was still. In place of a perfect male specimen swimming, many floating vanilla scented candles bobbed calmly. Fory's thoughts turned to that hot swimmer guy, her libido had been hoping to see him. Her wandering mind was interrupted.

"Forsythia, welcome!" heralded Mobley from across the room as she approached her assistant. "Do you like how the place polished up? Isn't she delicious?"

When she got within three feet of Fory, Mobley tilted her head while examining Fory. "You look lovely. The guests will adore you as much as I do at this moment, I can assure you."

Mobley's Cheshire grin unnerved Fory.

"Y-yes, I hope they do. I'm here to help out with whatever you need."

"Indeed, you are, and this will be a great night," Mobley said while continuing her perusal. With a look of satisfaction, Anna motioned to Fory. "C'mon in. You know Dane. I'll let the rest of the guys introduce themselves. The guests will be arriving shortly, so please make yourself comfortable while I tell the caterers you're here. I take it you'd like a drink?"

"N-no, thank you... I'm on the clock," said Fory with a fake smile.

"Hmm..." muttered Mobley. "Right answer for the HR department, but wrong answer for me and the rest of the real world." Anna paused in thought. "I'll be back in a moment. You know where the bar is. Worst case, ask Dane for a drink. My guess is he'd be happy to accommodate any requests." Anna walked off with trailing laughter, but she stopped short at the sound of the doorbell.

"Oh, I can tell already this will be an explosive evening!" exclaimed an excited Anna. She then pivoted and briskly walked toward the front door.

Fory welcomed the distraction and seized the opportunity to slip into the background. She knew she couldn't pretend to get through the night without a proper buffer between herself and the nectar. Two shots of Bacardí might do it.

"Hey, Dane!" she called across the kitchen, "You buying?"

Mobley's minion walked over with his best James Bond swagger. "Why, I thought you'd never ask," he said as he walked to the bar and began dropping cubes into a hefty cocktail glass.

"Bacardí Limón, please... Neat," Fory said with a flirty smile. The baby bird begged for her worm.

"I know what you like," Dane said with a smile. "Sorry... Cliché joke. My apologies."

"None needed," said Fory who eagerly accepted the freshly built fortification.

Okay, maybe he is just flirting with me and not being weird about suspecting me. He just wants to impress me by remembering my drink.

She quickly relieved the glass of half of its weight, and she felt the blanket of addiction. The soft brown leather of the Italian sofa across the room beckoned...

"Fory! Fory, I want you to meet someone!" Mobley called from across the room. Fory looked for a coaster, but instead set her drink on an already soaked cocktail napkin.

"Yes, of course," she said as she walked across the room.

"Fory, this is Binky Roberts," motioned Anna. "Forsythia, she's my girl who's going to help me make Xanadu live up to its name," said Mobley flushed with excitement.

"Pleasure to meet you, Binky," Fory said with a head bow.

"Likewise," said the neighbor. "Anna, Peter will be over shortly. He had to take a call as we were leaving. He'll be right here in minutes."

"Excellent," said Mobley. "I look forward to showing off the house to him." Anna turned. "Dane, Dane... Please accompany Mrs. Roberts to the bar and do your best." Mobley smiled.

Within a second of being out of Binky's earshot, Mobley whispered into Fory's ear, "Yeah, Binky's husband did have to take a late call. It was to me. He seems to want to see my progress with the master bedroom later tonight."

* * *

Anna Mobley hoisted a champagne flute like she was lighting the Olympic Torch.

"I'm so grateful for all you've done," she said addressing her contractors and guests, "This project could not have been done without you all." She led everyone with a hefty sip and a smattering of claps.

"Tonight, we celebrate all of your work. Your patience. Your art. Your vision."

Fory felt a sudden wave of nausea more due to Anna's speech than withdrawal.

"Tonight, we celebrate everything that you've done." Anna clapped as her guests joined in. "If not for all of your dedication, *Xanadu,* would never have seen the light of day. Now, this room will face the rising sun every morning."

The crowd clapped with fervor as their eagerness grew. Anna relished their embracing her drama. "Dane and his crew will freshen up your drinks." Mobley boasted, "Time to move down to show you my newest addition, the guest house and then the new dock which is still in progress."

Fory's eyes lit up at Anna's last comment.

She needed a bathroom, fast, this was a great opportunity to slip away from the crowd.

The guests smiled and rumbled comments as they regrouped themselves and belongings, then headed down toward the newly sculpted beach.

"Please walk on the planks lest you get sandy," Mobley shouted

Forsythia's Ride

over the wind. "Make yourselves comfortable."

It was a perfect Chatham Spring evening—just a little chilly.

The stars were coming out and promised to turned the sky into a kaleidoscope as soon as darkness took over.

Such radiance could inspire one to walk on water...

Mary's Cottage

Michonne's phone lit up; an incoming from Fory. This is what she had hoped for. "How's it going over there? You managed to get some privacy so soon?" asked Michonne.

"I'm in the bathroom," said Fory with a loud whisper. "Mobley's all making nice/nice and showing off the place. She sent them to look at some new guest house down toward the water. *THAT'S IT!* I know it. I feel it in my bones! Those damn coordinates in my locket will match exactly where that friggin' new cottage is. Well, that or the new dock."

Michonne grinned. Things were slowly coming together. "Great work, Fory. I'll send Sasa over to get a visual. It's almost dark, so she can approach from that park next door."

"Yeah, but," said a nervous Fory, "she's gotta look out for Dane and the goons."

Michonne chuckled. "Don't worry. From what I know from stories, Sasa has handled her share of goons over the years."

"Okay," said Fory not picturing anyone her size winning against the goons. "So, you confirm the coordinates match where the guest house is. Then what? You just show up and start breaking up the floorboards? *Oh, don't mind us... We're just here to steal millions of dollars worth of bombs and shit?* This bitch is crazy! She'll have her minions just start shooting." Fory started to panic. "The only thing going for you is she can't exactly call the cops."

"Leave that to us," said Michonne in a flat tone. "Just go about your night and help Mobley with the guests. You'll most likely be receiving someone unexpected at the door. Just play it cool and be yourself."

Fory was confused, "What? Who? Who's coming to the door?"

"Fory," said Michonne, "you have guests waiting and your absence will be inevitably noticed the longer you're on the phone. I'll find you in a bit. Be safe."

"But, I can't just—" Fory started to respond until she realized that Michonne had already ended the call.

Forsythia's Ride

Michonne yelled down the hall, "Sasa! Ready for a little recon?"

The reluctant operative's boots clomped down the hall. She poked her head around the door. "I thought you'd never ask. I'm growing cobwebs sitting around here. They were about to relegate me to a seat at the Chowder Society's meetings."

Michonne nodded. "Good to hear. It's nice to see you smile after our recruitment meeting."

"Yeah, well. Mary wouldn't have it any other way," said Sasa. "I'll grab my stuff and be out the door in five minutes."

"Be careful," said Michonne. "I know this isn't exactly the sexiest mission, but your piece is crucial. We confirm if the guest house or the dock matches the coordinates. Your visual will tell us which one is our target."

After Michonne set Sasa loose, she called Fory back for a quick discussion.

The phone rang three times. "What!" whispered Fory.

"Don't act surprised when you answer your phone. Everyone over there will be taking calls. Just show that you're working and that whatever you're discussing has to do with the party," said Michonne. "Just relax and we'll take care of the rest. Keep us informed of any other developments." Michonne was trying to instill confidence by assuring Forsythia she had backup. This was a fairly intense first experience at spy craft.

"Y-yeah, I will," said Fory who was already staring at the bar.

"Play ditsy and just keep everyone's drinks filled," said Michonne. "We'll be along shortly."

"Well, what the hell is your cover? Why are you coming over here? They're gonna sniff you out like an old shoe! " said Fory as her nerves began to move up her body. "Wait, Wait! Who the hell is *WE*?!"

"Never mind our part. Just do your job tonight with Anna's guests." Michonne knew it was game time. "Go grab rum, Anna won't care as long as you hold it together and look cute for her guests."

"Aye, aye, captain," said Fory who made a bee-line for the Bacardí bottle.

Speedwell Park
Eastern Point, Chatham

Under the cover of darkness, Sasa meandered through the dune grass of the park adjacent to Mobley's property line. The night was still with the exception of the din of noise wafting over from Xanadu. A giant silver moon was just rising on the ocean's horizon.

For this small piece of work, Sasa felt a little overdressed. She donned head-to-toe brown and olive colors in order to provide at least some level of camouflage, but she wouldn't stick out if found walking on the street. She brought along her version of a gig bag that included not only her electronics and navigational tools, but also a ten inch serrated hunting knife and a loaded Glock 17.

With the darkness, came moist air due to a light easterly sea breeze slowing as it crossed over Strong Island. Sasa felt heat rising from the cooling sand as she crouched on the border of the Mobley property. A coyote patrolling the beach took notice of her movements and gazed at her silhouette. Fortunately for him, he was smart to move on to other prey.

She unzipped her pack and pulled out the portable GPS unit. On a handwritten scratch note, she had the coordinates from the locket. She calibrated the unit and compared the numbers. Her target was only a hundred yards away, so she received confirmation almost immediately. She called Michonne.

"I'm here," said Sasa, "and all the numbers match. Friggin' Mobley built her little hacienda right over the spot where Fory's locket says is pay dirt. Smart bitch is gonna use that cottage as an entry way to move out whatever is down there to the dock and then wherever the buyers want. So the guest house is your target; confirmed."

"Okay," said Michonne, "that confirms our suspicion. While you're there, can you get a few photos? That'll help the guys when it comes time for extraction."

Forsythia's Ride

"Yeah, sure," responded Sasa, "I'll grab a few pics and then get the hell outta here. I'm sure Mobley has the place under surveillance."

"Great, thanks," said Michonne. "I'll go speak with Mary and Pratt to see if they have last minute input. I have a feeling I'll be heading over there shortly. Be safe."

"Roger, that." Sasa ended the call and moved another twenty yards closer in order to get a clearer picture. Unfortunately, Sasa's concerns about Mobley's security suddenly came to fruition. Over the noise coming from Mobley's party, she heard steps breaking dried brush.

The move was impressive, as Sasa survived a career with a long record of not being ambushed. Dane's grip was fast and firm. His right hand constricted like a boa around Sasa's neck. His fingers dug into the bottom of her jaw to the point where any more pressure would have ripped into her gullet.

"I see we have a visitor," said Dane flatly. "More precisely, a trespasser. Don't you think it's too late in the day for bird watching?"

Sasa was frozen in shock and physically unable to move except for sporadic shudders.

"I don't see any fishing poles," continued Dane, his tight tone indicating a seething anger or hatred. "Bet you're not here for tossing a line for the night stripers? Too bad—the schoolies are feisty as hell this time of year." Dane relaxed his claw grip just enough so Sasa could speak.

"Fuckin' leave me alone!" hissed Sasa, "I'm just takin' pictures!"

"Right," said Dane. "Unfortunately, I don't see a night lens. Or a camera, for that matter. You see, we have a pretty good idea who you work for, but you don't have enough time for us to confirm that."

"What? I'm just here on my own. You're crazy. Just let me out of here," Sasa said in a semi-pleading voice.

"Don't think so," Dane shot back. "My only regret is I don't have the time or space to squeeze every bit of info out of your little head."

Sasa knelt quietly even though Dane had relaxed his grip. She thought she noticed a weapon in his other hand. She shrugged her shoulders. It was her time. She'd tried to beat the odds on one too many assignments. *At least my brother's debt will be paid tonight.*

"An interrogation would have been fun," continued Dane. "Myself and the boys would have enjoyed your company. Unfortunately our boss has guests and we can't interfere with the affair. I have to hurry, my duties are required elsewhere."

Sasa grunted, "Great... my lucky day."

Dane paused and looked up with a deep inhale of the Cape spring night air. "Not quite."

Dane's arm swung down finishing the pendulum move of the machete. Sasa's head cork-popped and rolled across the sand like a tumbleweed.

The rest of her landed on a dead horseshoe crab and cracked the old crustacean's shell. Another one of Mobley's minions approached to see what the rustling in the grass was all about.

He looked at the head with wide eyes, and then turned toward Dane. "What the hell did you do? Are you crazy?" he hissed. "We have a friggin' houseful of muckety-mucks. Shit, man! What the hell are we gonna *do* with her!? We can't start digging a grave in a fucking construction zone that the boss is giving tours of!"

Dane used the machete to tap sand off his shoes. "Grab Tony and throw her in the bunker for now."

Despite the violent nature of the act, the machete held only a small amount of blood. Dane's cut had arced with precision. He tossed the weapon into thick eel grass and snapped, "Don't forget the head. We might still be able to squeeze out some intel."

Dane exploded with laughter and walked away surrounded by the salty scent of a gentle Chatham easterly breeze.

Chatham Fish Pier

Tommy Reyes held a firm grip on his phone as he stared at the teak boat deck and took in the night's final instructions over his cell.

"Yes, sir. Understood. Of course," he responded to Monarch on the phone. "We'll shove off in five minutes. We're probably about a twenty minute cruise away. I could blast over faster, but I don't want to attract attention, especially at night. I've noticed the folks around here are especially curious about anything out of the ordinary."

Reyes nodded as Monarch responded.

Tommy received his final orders with an eager grin as he put his phone in his pocket.

Reyes loved when Monarch gave risky assignments, it always promised a decent payday upon success.

"Hey, Steamah!" Reyes yelled across the boat deck after hanging up. "Toss the lines!"

"Yeah, yeah, Tom." Steamer sat up after a quick rum induced nap. "No problem, Tommy. Is it go time? Or are we doin' somethin' else?"

"I just talked to Monarch. Sounds like the job's gonna be a little ugly, but hopefully carries a payday if we can pull the shit off. He just told me there's some empty moorings we can snag over in Bassing Harbah. It's close by, so we can tie up and await instructions. I guess all those richies don't put their boats in until after Memorial Day. Must be nice..."

"Hey, Tommy. Speakin' of the richies, ya think the Monarch might cut us in on a little more on this one?" Steamer's mouth was watering at the thought. "I mean, we've been workin' for him for like six years, and we ain't nevah gotten a raise. Know what I'm sayin'?"

Reyes slowly shook his head. "Nah, Steam. I ain't askin' him right now. I can tell he's tense. That question would go over like a séance fart."

"Yeah, Tommy, I guess," muttered Steamer after a sigh. "Don't rock the boat, as they say."

While Steam worked the lines and prepped for shove off, he caught himself gazing over the bay at the rising moon. It had built a white road across the water. He found a rare moment of introspection. "Tommy, ever feel when you look out on the ocean, that it don't really look back?"

"Whaddya mean?" asked Reyes. "Make this quick, we gotta go."

"Ya, ya," responded Steamer. "I know, I know. But, see, I get this dream."

Reyes rolled his eyes knowing Steamer couldn't see. He didn't want to upset his mate. "Yeah?"

"See," continued Steam, "I get this dream that you and I are out there haulin' our pots over in Falmouth, right?" He looked at Reyes who responded with a wave of a hand that meant *yeah, yeah—hurry up.*

"So's you and I are out pullin' the pots and we keep hauling up friggin' empties."

Reyes snickered. "Sounds like more of a true story to me, with the luck we've been having on lobsters."

"No. It's more 'cause in the dream our last pot we bring up contains two dozen keeper lobsters friggin' as fat as Sunday hams."

"Yeah?" asked Reyes who now found himself perturbed, but sadly interested.

"We bring the pot up and toss 'er on the deck," Steamer continued. "You're barkin' orders and I'm checkin' the lengths. But, as I'm measuring them, I realize they're all dead!"

Reyes's square jaw tightened.

"Every lobster wasn't just dead. They was friggin' mutilated. There was one huge guy left who finally died of starvation, after eating all his pals." Steamer knew he had to stop; they needed to shove off. "Think they're might be somethin' to that dream?"

Reyes rubbed his chin and grinned in understanding. "Yeah, you soft-shelled crab, I kinda do," he said as he turned toward the helm while his stoic mind returned to the business at hand. "But tonight, I don't wanna think that way." Reyes paused feeling a cold shudder run up his spine. *Creepy.* "Gather your head. That'll help me find mine."

Fortunately, the usually chilly Chatham springtime air showed a bit of quarter, the winds died down.

"Now, let's fire this lady up!" yelled Reyes from the vessel's helm. "Time to go find us an Easter Egg!" Tommy Reyes turned the key and the old twin CAT diesels immediately woke up with an irritated growl. After ten seconds they laid down like two purring kittens.

"Damn!" yelled Reyes. "What the hell kinda boat is this. Ain't never heard diesels like that. Monarch is sending us in style."

"Tommy, this is a custom Kirkman. It's stem to stern hand-made. Their engineers spend more time on design down to the centimeter than they need to do on actual construction. Kirkman even has a deal with Caterpillar to mold the engine design to the client. Five year wait for delivery of a vessel like this. That's if you're like, Jimmy Buffett," Steamer yelled as he revved up the engine's RPMs. This was his one and only area of expertise and he was totally in love.

Reyes nodded in admiration then said, "She's super quiet, but I can't pin her cause I don't want bullshit from the neighbors for tossing a wake. We're lucky we lost the blow, so we should shoot over there fast and quiet."

"Aye, aye, captain," responded Steamer. "Too bad we ain't heading out for tuna. Imagine being out there at dawn in a vessel like this?"

Reyes melded into the helm station. "Steam, sorry about your dream," he said. "But, at the moment, I got nothin' for you, except next time during an operation, try countin' sheep." He chuckled while catching only a slight scent of diesel despite the calm wind and water.

"Okay, Tommy. You're the captain," said Steam as he undid a hitch knot and tossed the stern line. "Everyone knows, skippah's always right," he said with a half cheek smile. "Just ask Noah." Steamer laughed at his own joke. "Hey, Tommy. You think we'll ever meet him? The Monarch, I mean. We still don't know who he really is."

Matt Fitzpatrick

There wasn't an easy answer for Reyes to tell his partner, but he wanted to try to satisfy Steamer.

"I dunno, Steam... My best guess is we'll find out when the three of us bunk together in Purgatory. Or worse."

Xanadu

Forsythia was frazzled from passing hors d'oeuvres to Mobley's eclectic group of guests and acting as hostess while terrified out of her mind. In the mingle were the owners of Anna's various contracting firms, designers, a couple of nosy town officials, as well as several neighbors who were curious to see what was going on behind those ugly compound walls. The group just returned from a tour of the guest cottage and were gushing about the décor.

Mobley instructed the string quartet to keep the background music at a moderate level so the guests could mingle, chat, and hopefully fawn over her mansion and guest cottage.

Fory worked the room, smiled, and even half-curtsied at some of the people she met. She figured with the power and wealth in the room, maybe she could escape this mini-prison her aunt had constructed. But, deep-down, Fory knew the only prison she was in was of her own doing.

Ding, DONG! was heard again as the front doorbell's two-ring warm tone rang out just above the ambient noise.

Fory turned toward the marble counter and put down her tray. She touched her hair in a quick primp, then went to the entrance.

"Wel—"

She stopped short, and easily could have dropped to the floor. Despite a mild shock, she knew this was part of the plan and she needed to behave. That realization didn't quell her anxiety.

"Hi! We're here with the caterers. Our boss was grateful to have this event and, if do a great job, maybe stay on Ms. Mobley's radar as she continues to entertain," said Michonne in fake tones that still demanded eye contact.

Fory stared at Michonne with alarm, and then quickly pivoted to cooperation. "Y-Y-yes. Please come in," said an upbeat Fory while trying to keep all cylinders firing. "I see you've brought a gift, and also it looks like you might have company behind you?" Fory couldn't make out the person behind Michonne.

"Indeed, I have a gift," said Michonne, "and I also brought along the CEO and owner of our company. He wanted to be here personally to bestow not only this modest token of appreciation, but also he wanted to personally thank Anna for inviting us and our firm into her home. He'd love to discuss with her how all of our catering fare is being received. I trust you'd like to meet him?"

Fory felt awkward. "Ah...yeah, sure. Please, come in."

With a sweeping hand motion, Michonne continued, "Please allow me to introduce Jim Osterberg, the owner of our company."

Fory's cheeks drained to alabaster as Sir William Pratt darkened the doorway. He crossed the threshold while politely tapping his cane. "Hello," said Pratt softly. "I understand your name is Forsythia?"

Fory's eyes suddenly stung. "Y-yes. Yes, sir," said Fory playing along as best as she could. *Fuck, improv is not my thing. They never mentioned I'd have to act so damn much.* "Please come in and meet the host and the other guests."

As Pratt and Michonne passed Fory and walked toward the living room where the guests were congregated, Fory said, "Excuse me, Miss. May I take your gift? I'll leave it on Ms. Mobley's desk."

"Thank you. However, I find that I need to keep it with me for the time being." Michonne's thoughts took a fake pivot. "But, perhaps you can gather up small cordial glasses for all of your guests? Mr. Osterberg has quite a treat for Ms. Mobley this evening. We know she'll love the special gift we brought. Everyone must partake and enjoy."

Fory nodded while beginning to perspire.

"Fory," whispered Michonne, "whatever you do, stick to your rum tonight. Don't drink this stuff."

"O...*Kay.*" Fory was playing along with this charade now suddenly afraid everyone was going to be dead seconds after sipping this stuff. *Accessory to murder, I'll never be rid of these fucking spies.* At this point she was officially along for the ride. No way out. The night's events were officially in play.

She called over to Dane, who appeared to have just come in from the beach. "Mr. Dane. We just received a generous gift. Can you let Ms. Mobley know we have the owners of the catering company here who want to congratulate her on the project?"

Dane gave an apathetic look.

"Please, Dane!" said Fory with more energy. "Ms. Mobley, and more importantly, her guests, will be impressed and I can't do it, I have to get the special glasses from the kitchen."

Dane was skeptical, but acquiesced. "Yeah, yeah, I'll tell her to gather everyone," he said as he slunk off.

"Mr. Osterberg," said Fory as the charade continued, "won't you and your assistant follow Mr. Dane into the living room to present your gift to Ms. Mobley?"

Pratt/Osterberg and Michonne meandered over to the far end of the kitchen where it met the living room. Where they had a quick chat with Anna. Fory was loading up fancy small glasses on a tray. All of the custom chrome accent lights were on full display as Mobley prepared to corral her guests.

"Everyone," Anna called out across the room. "Please gather! My caterer wants to personally bestow upon us a gift that we can all share."

The group gathered around Mobley nodding in interest.

Anna began with histrionic hands. "We have an incredible opportunity this evening to share a true treasure." The guests were quiet and their gazes more fixated.

Mobley continued and moved her body with dramatic effect as she swayed her arms. "Ladies and gentlemen, please let me introduce Jim Osterberg."

The group hoisted their glasses, drank and smiled.

Pratt wanted to exude pomp, but not push it too far. He played the part. "I want to thank Anna Mobley for her vision. Her courage and tenacity saw this cutting-edge project come to fruition."

Pratt's comments were met with polite applause. "My colleague and I came here tonight with a true treasure to share," said Osterberg/Pratt as he pointed toward Michonne, and specifically to the case she was carrying.

"This is an incredible night, not only for Ms. Anna Mobley, but also for all of Chatham. Her project beams us into the future of not only what this neighborhood will be, but also it's a shining beacon for the town!"

The guests' applause grew louder, but not really for what Pratt was saying. They wanted to know what was coming. They smelled something expensive, and even better, free.

"I have here three bottles of the rarest Amontillado sherry every produced," said Pratt as the guests muttered to each other with underlying excitement.

"These three bottles can be enjoyed by all, as a gift of appreciation to Ms. Mobley," said Pratt.

Mobley's smile shined like a moon ray. "Mr. Osterberg, please tell the group more about what we're about to enjoy, *and*, it's significance."

Fory could already taste whatever the hell they were about to pour. She just wanted a shot of something wet and alive. Even though she knew it was doctored with something, her inner monster was still urging her to have a big, deep swallow. She was nearly shaking.

Pratt opened a small notebook. "Ladies and gentlemen, before we enjoy and partake, I'll share some special history, because you will be having a taste of true history in just a few minutes."

The crowd shared nods of interest, but in the end, they just wanted to drain whatever was in Michonne's hands.

Pratt began, "Known in many European wine circles as the finest sherry in the world, the Barbadillo Versos 1891 Amontillado at $25,000 US a bottle, was created for a specific reason." Pratt smiled as that number created an appropriate gasp from the crowd.

"Manuel Barbadillo was gifted the cask by his father as a christening present, pretty unusual present for a new-born, not quite so for this family, and the fact that it has taken on such a great value, just goes to show it was a shrewd decision. The Barbadillo brothers were all given one cask of the Amontillado sherry each and it became known as *las botas de los ninos*. The barrels remained untouched and locked up in the family run sherry bodega in Sanlucar de Barrameda.

"Manuel made his family proud, not only did he work in the family business for over five decades, he was a philanthropist, a poet, and perhaps his dealings in the political arena are what made his family truly proud, for he was the Mayor of Sanlucar. When he passed, and ever since, the family has been brainstorming ideas on how to commemorate this great man. They found the perfect tribute with Versos 1891. In order to keep it exclusive, just 100 bottles of this sherry were produced to honor the memory of Manuel."

Pratt finished with, "And tonight, it's my sincere pleasure to announce that we have *three* of those bottles for your enjoyment. Please get yours and wait for our final toast so we can all share in this exquisite experience together. *Salut!*" Pratt ended with a bowing hand gesture.

The crowd cheered in surprise as Mobley's eyes burst with pyrotechnics. She craved excess of any kind.

As the group took a fancy cordial glass each, Michonne opened the three bottles at the counter, and the lemmings lined up for their pour.

Fortunately, a couple of Mobley's minions decided that they were going to steal Michonne's limelight and pour the drinks. Despite being almost physically shoved aside, she was grateful to slide further into the periphery. *Chivalry is dead with this bunch of morons. Just no more good men like my dad.*

Mobley's guests all held the newly filled cordial glasses and stepped back for their host to lead them. She had even felt so gracious (since the cost wasn't hers) to insist her staff got a glass, after making sure there was enough for the guests, of course.

"Thank you all for being here," started Mobley. Everyone got quiet. "Thank you for being friends, colleagues and neighbors during this project. I'll be forever grateful, and may all our winds be fair," said

Anna as she hoisted her glass. "To all of our happiness and health. And, most importantly, let's send gratitude to Mr. Osterberg and his generous gift of this rare sherry."

Anna and Pratt both nodded toward each other, and she and the guests drank their Amontillado with the eagerness of a baby to its bottle.

The crowd partook of the wine and returned to a conversational din. Mobley looked a little awkward as she attempted to look into a mirror while trying to find the cushy chair since she felt a bit woozy.

With a sly smile, Michonne turned to Pratt. "How long will these folks sleep?"

Pratt grinned. "Oh, the knockout time should be adequate, but like any narcotic it affects different people in different ways, so we still need to work fast. Hopefully, long enough for Mary's guys to grab what we need. None of these people will be harmed, including Mobley. Despite popular belief, we're not murderers," quipped Pratt. They'll just pass out for a couple of hours, and we'll be gone. They'll wake up lethargic and confused, but no harm will be done," he sighed. "It's just that the removal of material of this nature needs to be executed in a secret fashion."

Michonne nodded. "I see. It's not every day I help steal nukes. So, what'd we drug 'em with, and how did you get the stuff into those fancy bottles? I mean, were you lying when you told them that it was real fancy antique wine?"

Pratt fired up a just-packed pipe of Captain Black. "Of course." He lit the tobacco flakes with three starter puffs. "Mary is too cheap with our budget to actually procure three bottles of true Amontillado. If she actually did, I would have stolen one."

Michonne sported a wide grin. She had grown to look up to the old man despite only knowing him for a short time. "So, what did these people drink? They're already yawning."

Pratt laughed. "Yes, they are, which is encouraging. To answer your question, they're drinking from bottles Mary had fashioned in Boston for minimal expense."

Forsythia's Ride

Michonne smiled. *Good lesson, any look can be duplicated.*

"We had these bottles designed and filled with sherry," said Pratt as he tapped his pipe. "They're drinking the sherry equivalent of a dreadful potable you Yanks call *Mad Dog*, along with a generous dose of Rohypnol. I'm told there's enough in those bottles to still a herd of rhinos."

Michonne nodded. "Sir William, not to change the subject, but I can't reach Sasa. She confirmed the coordinates with a visual on the guest house, but since then she's gone dark."

Pratt suddenly assumed a much more sober look than the amusement he was showing as Mobley and her guests stumbled toward couches, chairs and even eased themselves down on stair rungs. "That is not good." Unusually concerned Pratt said, "Excuse me for a moment. I need to call Mary. Go find Fory. Grab her and meet me out at the guest house. Be careful! The guard staff outside didn't drink the stuff."

Pratt turned and scurried down the hallway in search of a better cell signal while Michonne headed toward the butler's pantry to find Fory, hopefully sober.

On the way to the pantry, Michonne almost tripped over one of Mobley's minions who was curled up in a ball on the kitchen floor with his head in a cat box.

She turned the corner into the pantry. The first thing she noticed about her quasi-adopted big sister was the sway of her body. Fory's right hand was holding onto the counter while she rocked back and forth. With her left, she waved to Michonne.

"Hey..." said Fory still swaying. "C'mon in n join the party."

A livid Michonne grabbed Fory's shoulder, one of the two knocked over a bottle of Ketel One Fory found in Anna's storage closet.

"I think I'm gonna move here," said Fory. "Auntie's house is no fun..."

Michonne looked her up and down then into Fory's eyes. While she wasn't totally blitzed, the heavy buzz could be an obstacle.

Matt Fitzpatrick

"Listen to me!" hissed Michonne. "Get your shit together. I've got orders to get you outta here. If one of those goons wakes up and figures out what happened, you're dead! Matter of fact, so am I. So, grab a Red Bull in the fridge, *minus* any vodka! Time to go!"

Xanadu's Guest Cottage

While Michonne was keeping her steady on their trek over the dunes, Fory was gaining composure to an acceptable degree thanks to the sugar and caffeine from the Red Bull.

"Where we goin'?" Fory's voice was still foggy, off focus.

"Hopefully going to where the weapons are," said Michonne. "We're on borrowed time, and we have to start signaling the boat. Mary's guys should be here any minute and waiting just off the beach. I'm gonna start flashing a light as soon as we get our bearings."

They traipsed through soft-sanded dunes until they reached the guest house. The lock on the door was high-tech, but this night the door was propped wide open for the party.

Fory was already beginning to come down from the effects of the alcohol. Her tolerance had grown so strong over the years, that the drug needed to be constantly administered to maintain the desired effect.

"Mobley thinks she's the only one with technology available to her," said Michonne, "your aunt still has friends in interesting places. Okay, you go inside and look around but don't touch anything. They'll know they got drugged so the cops may finger print things tomorrow. I'm gonna start signaling the boat. Mary claims these guys are reliable, but they're not exactly Navy SEALs."

Michonne shook her head and whispered to herself, "Did I just send a drunk into a building full of nukes?" Michonne pulled a high powered flashlight out of her backpack and started signaling. One flash every five seconds meant it was go-time.

"Hmm... Navy SEALs," muttered Fory from inside the cottage with a hiccup, "I bet they're cute..."

Tommy & Steamer
Bassing Harbor

Aunt Mary's hired hands for the night sat on their mooring taking in the speckled light of the Chatham sky.

"Damn..." said Steamer, "I could get used to hanging out here on a hook. Drink some beer. Find a pretty lass..."

"Eye on the prize, Steam," said a stressed Reyes.

The boat barely rocked, the bay was like a hardwood floor. They were lucky to have only the slightest breeze out of the east.

"Hey, Tommy!" Steam yelled over. "Look!"

Reyes followed his partner's pointing finger and saw the signal of one white flash. He waited roughly five seconds and was grateful to see another. He stood up and went to the helm station. "We're green-lit, Steam. Get us off the ball."

Steam untied the knot holding the vessel to the mooring, slid the rope through the eyelet, and stowed the line. They were only a hundred yards from Mobley's beach.

"All set, Tommy. We're live!"

Reyes maintained low RPMs on the boat's engines; he didn't want to attract any attention with the noise.

"Steam, I'm gonna beach her bow-first. It's all sand, so I'm not worried. When we hit ground, grab the anchor and secure it around a tree."

"Aye, skip," responded Steamer.

Xanadu Guest Cottage

"Yes!" whispered an excited Michonne. She loved when a plan came together, and it looked like Mary's guys saw her signal and were heading to shore. Time was ticking as she ran back to the cottage. A buzzed Fory had tripped over a loose board and slammed her whole body into some furniture. Michonne came in just in time to see a table slide, it revealed a hatch in the floor. The dark magic of alcohol kept Fory from feeling any pain. They both looked downward. The rest of the cottage had been built around this rusted ancient hatch. They had found it in less than two minutes.

"Look!" Fory had a grin of satisfaction. "I bet that's it!"

Michonne slowly shook her head and smiled. "Well done! Our newest operative!" Michonne laughed. "Can ya dig for gold while you're at it?"

Fory smiled but was starting to shake. Withdrawal is as punctual as Swiss precision gears.

"Here," said Michonne straddling the cottage doorway, "open it while I get the boat guys situated on the beach. Grab one of those dock lines on the wall and wrap it around the handle as you pull. That old latch will take your knuckles off, so be careful. Gotta go!"

Michonne darted around the corner of the doorway toward the back of the cottage. With her gone, Fory looked down at the door. It looked heavy as well as old.

With Michonne gone, the cottage was dead quiet. Even the usually feisty North Atlantic was taking the night off. Spring Cape winds blow hard and rattle even the largest McMansions. Not this night. All was calm in the moonlight. Fory looked around and found a slice of rope about four feet long. She wrapped a third of it around her left wrist while snaking a slug of line around the eyelet to the door. The rest of the rope would go around her right hand. She pulled with all the steam she had left. She yearned for her special nectar.

Fory grunted as she strained at the hatch which resisted at first, but after a few seconds, it gave way. She stumbled backwards, but kept her footing.

"Okay, okay..." she huffed to herself, "What do we got?"

Fory gazed down into the hatchway.

Since Michonne was out on the beach guiding Reyes's vessel onto the sand, Fory figured she's go exploring. Her nature had not changed one bit from when she was a child. *I might find a 100 year old bottle of something good. Or maybe one of those Navy SEALs.* She smirked.

Fory didn't realize but the reason that the hatch had given way rather easily was that Mobley's crew had oiled the hatch to the old forgotten World War One Navy bunker. The entry door and the bunker were much larger than the one which little Vicki McAree had visited further down the beach just prior to her drowning.

Forsythia walked down newly built wooden stairs. Descending, her senses got confused. While the stairs were new and still smelled of freshly cut maple, after a few steps down, Fory only smelled the dankness of moisture that had called the bunker home for several decades.

Her feet hit concrete. Waving about, she pulled a chain on a single dangling light bulb. It gave just enough light to show two more chains to pull. The old space came to life.

She moved a few steps into the main part of the hidden structure. Fory didn't yet grasp that she was exploring a secret military bunker built in the spring of 1916; a full year before President Wilson decided to toss America's hat into the hellish war to end all wars.

The nitre build-up on the walls looked like the modern art one might see in the gallery windows in lower Manhattan. She always wondered why the rich were so willing to shell out huge money for paintings that reminded Fory of when she would accidentally puke on the wall after a binge.

As Fory walked deeper into the bunker, she noticed the nitre at eye level was thickening, her shoulders felt cold and clammy.

There was what looked like a pile of boxes with a plastic covering against the near wall. She pulled at the plastic to unveil maybe two dozen bins. She popped the lid of the one closest. She feasted her eyes on several white packages wrapped in tape and clear plastic.

Even though Fory's poison came in a bottle, she knew she was staring at a massive stash of either heroin, cocaine or both.

"Shit. Maybe Mobley's starting a bakery?" she laughed to herself.

She pulled the plastic cover back onto the bins and moved deeper into the bunker. As she walked, she fortunately found a pull string that brushed across her cheek at she explored. With a quick tug, more of the way lit up, this time revealing several sets of shelves.

She gazed at the damp, greenish colored wood of the shelving. Its contents were stacked six inches high on each tier.

"Whoa..." she exhaled.

It looked like a display at a local pharmacy. There were bottles of eye drops and eye solution everywhere. Endless boxes of innocuous eye care products.

She gasped, startled by foot falls behind her. She turned and almost screamed until she made out her partner's face in the pale light. Fory exhaled and calmed down. Anxiety had set in, her body was protesting the lack of the poison needed to function. The shakes would soon follow.

"The guys beached the boat and are getting their dune-wheeled dollies. They'll be down here in a few minutes," said Michonne as she looked around. "Did you find the nukes yet? We got to move it. Damn, Fory. What do we got here?" Michonne marveled at how legitimate the boxes looked. "I guess that crazy lady is going retail."

Fory half smiled. "Yeah, she's creative all right. Listen, I found a ton of what I think are drugs and shit back there under the white plastic."

"Not surprised," replied Michonne. "But that's not what we're here for."

"Yeah... But, while we're here, shouldn't we grab all of this other stuff? I mean, damn, look what happened to that little girl? Drowning right next door?"

Michonne nodded. "Yeah. Yeah, I know and I get it. But we're not the Red Cross and we're not the *Catcher in the Rye*. We can't save everyone." She paused thinking. "What we *can* do is keep some serious military technology out of the wrong hands. Trust that when we're done here tonight, this place will be of no use to Mobley ever again, whether the nukes are still here or not. Today was Mobley's last day dealing from the seashore."

"How's that?" asked Fory.

"That's why the guys up on the beach are a bit delayed. You'll see..." smiled Michonne as she looked at her watch. "Speaking of delays, let's see if we can find what we really came for."

The two turned as Michonne flicked on a high-powered flashlight to illuminate the deeper part of the bunker where there didn't appear to be any light switches on the walls or overhead.

"What exactly *are* we looking for?" asked Fory. "I mean, what do nuclear weapons look like?"

Michonne half ignored the question training the beam on different corners and sides of the walls to find any type of clue. "I dunno. We'll know it when we see it."

They continued searching; the bunker seemed to go on forever. The air was damp and heavy, difficult to breathe despite the outside temps being forgiving. Michonne figured this place must criss-cross under the entire beach. She continued walking ahead with the light and peered at the end of the roving beam.

"Oh, shit..." Michonne whispered with a hiss as she settled the light on something in a far corner that didn't look right.

"W-what?" asked Fory. "You forget something? Did you find some bombs?" She wanted to laugh, but held back as she noticed the look on Michonne's face.

"Not exactly," responded the young operative who walked closer to the corner and motioned for Fory to come along. She moved aside a blue tarp, walked further in and shone the light on the wall.

"Those sons of bitches...got Sasa," said Michonne. The light beam revealed the headless body of Sasa hanging on the wall from an anchor hook.

Fory turned toward the beam and gasped. "WHAT! What the fuck!" she wanted to scream, but Michonne anticipated her outburst and motioned for her to keep quiet with what would have been a roundhouse punch if need be.

"T-t-this is insane!" Fory hissed. "What did you freaks get me into?" Fory started to shake from a combination of a natural panic attack and a few deeper steps toward withdrawal. "It looks like Sasa's clothes and her size, but how do you know it's her. Where's her god-damned head?!"

Michonne was quiet for two reasons. One was that she needed to diffuse her partner who was coming apart at the seams, and also she began plotting her revenge for what happened to Sasa. She felt re-sponsible for she not only recruited Sasa for the operation, but did so with a nasty form of persuasion.

"Mobley and her minions play for keeps. I bet it was that Dane sonofabitch! Either he or I die tonight."

Fory shot back with, "We should get outta here. Like now! Let's just go back to Mary's and figure this out."

"Not a chance," said Michonne in her usual focused monotone. "We stay here. Our guys will be down any minute." Michonne studied the cerated cuts around Sasa's headless neck. "This was a violent death. Dammit! Hey Fory!"

"W-what?" asked a confused and panicked Fory.

"You asked what I'm talking about," said Michonne as her tone changed from agent to that of a hunter. "What I mean is that I'm not leaving this place until Mobley and Dane pay for this!" *Nobody who I drag back into this life gets fuckin' decapitated on my watch! Not when I'm running point. Not without just retribution. No. Fucking. One.*

"Great..." muttered Fory.

"Keep moving," instructed Michonne.

"We just leave her here?" asked a confused Fory. "I mean, shouldn't we at least..."

Matt Fitzpatrick

"She ain't going anywhere," Michonne coldly interrupted.

The young woman proceeded to rove the flashlight across the walls as they meandered deeper toward the corners. Up and down each wall, and then into every crevice and corner. Fory followed like a lost dog, but tried her best to keep a brave face and be useful. Michonne was the only one in this power game she even liked, and for some reason Fory didn't want to let her down. *It's silly, but I feel like we are actual friends. I bet we never talk after this, but still, it would be nice to have a stone cold, cool friend. Plus I could teach her about real music and good movies.*

Michonne worked the light until the walls finally stopped.

"We're at the end," she said as she noticed several crates in the last section. "Let's pop a couple of these open to see. Never know." Michonne immediately began opening the old wooden containers as Fory stood still and watched.

Michonne sensed her partner was losing steam on several levels, with certain ones caused by withdrawal. She knew she had to keep Fory's mind on the matter at hand. "Go over and check those crates in that corner. They look old and the latches should be all rotted by this point. Just give 'em a tug or bang at 'em with this," said Michonne as she handed Fory a hammer she had picked up from a shelf.

"Um... okay," said Fory grimacing as she touched the slime-caked old handle. She then walked over to the damp wooden crates and started banging at the latches. Michonne began doing the same on another row of crates.

In the first crate Fory found what looked like costumes from old war movies that her dad liked to watch when she was a little girl. The next crate housed what looked like a bunch of bandages or medical supplies. "There's nothing over here," she grumped to her partner.

"Keep trying," Michonne called back.

Fory tried another two crates only to find similar useless contents, she couldn't get the thought of Sasa's headless body out of her mind. She was going to build *the* biggest rum cocktail once this was over. Better yet, she planned on taking it down straight from the bottle.

Forsythia's Ride

More efficient and fewer calories. This night was going to end with passing out. Oblivion called.

Michonne found a stack of crates that looked interesting. She felt the wood; it was thicker than the other boxes and appeared more sturdy.

She opened the top one on the first pile, and peered inside with a wary eye. She moved a cloth aside to reveal what appeared to be a cache of old school grenades. She shut the lid and popped open the top box on the next pile. She kept to the top boxes because she knew they'd be heavy and probably not a good idea try and move and accidentally drop. Again, she moved a cloth after she opened the lid to reveal what looked like strands of ammunition feeds holding 50 caliber rounds. It was fitting because those were the type of shells beachgoers still found on the Cape shorelines.

"I think we're getting somewhere. Keep looking. I'm finding old military stuff now."

"I'm trying," responded Fory. "Getting chilly down here." *Wonder if these shakes are from withdrawal or the cold.* Fory walked over to the last crate in her line on the right side of the room. This one was much larger than the others. It was old, crusted in mold and dust. She had a feeling...

The rust-caked lock looked plenty worn. Her fingers turned burnt orange as she twisted the metal and opened the lid to peer inside. All she could see was oil cloth wrapped around something that was hard to the touch.

"Michonne..." Fory took a step back. "You gotta see this."

Michonne's gut was optimistic that they finally hit what they were looking for. She rushed over to Fory's side of the room, looked in the crate, and brushed the cloth aside.

"Guys! Guys! Get down here!" Michonne yelled into her walky-talky. "Santa came to town early this year."

Xanadu's Underground Bunker

Fory looked in awe at the contents of the chest and wanted to touch, but Michonne brushed her hand away. "This is serious shit! Don't worry, it's not gonna explode. But, if connected to the right missile delivery system, you could take out a city."

After several seconds, they heard heavy footsteps running upstairs toward the hatch. Fory was startled, but Michonne remained calm figuring it just their own crew. "These guys won't believe this," said Michonne. The footsteps came down the bunker stairs and then stopped. "Fory, go yell to them and tell 'em we're over here."

Fory ran about fifty yards toward the landing and yelled, "Guys, down this way!"

The sound of softer steps approached.

"Whatcha got, Michonne?" asked an out of breath Tommy Reyes.

Steamer caught up and smiled at the group. "Let's find some pay dirt!"

"Okay," said Michonne, "I just need to make sure this is what we're here for."

She pulled out her phone and reviewed several pictures, while peering into the chest with her flashlight every few seconds. "This is it," said Michonne as she looked around at the group. "We actually found the damn things, and there's probably more in those other boxes. Okay, guys, do your thing. Then bring up this box first."

With no response, Reyes and Steamer got to work. They started pulling out various pieces of odd looking equipment and wires from Tommy's large hockey bag. Michonne looked at her watch. "Damn, we're running late. Someone could very well wake up in that house anytime now."

A concerned Fory looked at Michonne her eyes giving her away. "What's going on? What the hell are these guys doing with all that shit they're strapping to the wall? I thought they were supposed to just carry this shit outta here?"

Forsythia's Ride

Michonne's steady response and calm demeanor was on purpose to put Fory at ease. *We found the actual nuclear warheads. Prototypes designed during the Manhattan Project in the 1940s! I gotta stay calm and get this mission green to the end. I need to really calm her and not let the guys know what exactly we are dealing with, loose lips and all that. Damn I don't think I told Fory to keep that a secret from our transpo guys.* "Help me load this cart over here while the guys finish. Don't worry about their part. Let me tell you a little more about your dad. A lot of our initial intelligence that your aunt gathered came from your father. He was involved with a group that had been trying to find this stash for years. Your aunt can tell you the story better and first hand, but I guess your dad was charged with a mission to find these weapons and get them to Ireland to benefit his cause in ways that finally horrified him and he couldn't go through with it."

"That's... that's why he committed suicide?" asked a semi-shocked Fory.

"I can't say for sure on that one, and neither can Mary," said Michonne. "All she knows is that he cracked a code, rumors went around fast that he knew the actual coordinates. When he discovered the bunker location, he decided that he wasn't going to share the intel. He was refusing to come to meetings so he didn't have to outright lie. I hear that some bit IRA muck on the Emerald Island was going to kidnap you. Why he finally killed himself, we'll never know. Mary thinks it's partly because if his IRA pals knew he was withholding that valuable information from the cause, it's most likely he would have been immediately killed if he refused—that's if he was lucky. The more likely alternative would have been interrogation and torture. Probably killing any family and loved ones in front of him. That would have meant you, his precious daughter. So with all those rumors, what I think is, he made his end very public and dirty to protect you. No one knew about the locket but you."

Fory turned pale processing this, her heart cracking open a small bit realizing her dad may have performed that ghastly scene to protect her, not hurt her. The mix of love and hate she had for him was now tipping toward love again, like when she had been little. Before that bloody boat trip.

"Michonne," yelled Reyes. "We're just about done. Let's start wrapping up."

"Okay, Tom. Thanks," replied Michonne who then turned back to Fory. "Your question about why we're not taking this stuff with us is simple. Your aunt had a brilliant idea last minute that we didn't share with you. It wasn't relevant to your part of the mission, and the less you know, the safer you are. We changed Reyes's orders, and he was actually grateful. These boxes are heavy, and we are badly running out of time. Someone's gonna wake up in that house. Now we only have to take one box."

"What is he going to do?" asked Fory.

"You'll see," said Michonne with a smirk. "Your aunt is getting up there in years, but she's still can fire a fastball across anyone's home plate. At this point, you don't have to do anything except get out safely, which is what you and I are gonna do. The guys here will take off on their boat with the small box I just put something in. We need to head down the beach back to Mary's and stay off the road. Once things go down, there's gonna be a police call in Chatham that they haven't seen since the hostage taking years ago downtown."

"Just lead the way," said Fory. "It'll be nice to get the hell out of this dump and away from that house. Looks like the second time this week that I'm escaping to Mary's—"

Fory was interrupted by Reyes shouting, "Okay, Michonne. Steam and I will pack up and meet you ... Wait..."

"Hold it right there!" growled Dane holding a Beretta aimed at Tommy's face. "Nobody's going anywhere. You two, face against the wall with your hands on the concrete," Dane barked at Reyes and Steamer. "Everyone stand and look pretty."

Michonne glowered at Dane. "You killed my friend, you sonovabitch, I know it was you! You killed Sasa, and dammit you're gonna be next."

Forsythia's Ride

"What can you do? Pour punch on my tux at the prom?" Dane looked over at the guys, and then at what they were building on the wall. "A little redecorating, gentlemen? Too bad you won't have a chance to show it to Ms. Mobley. She adores fresh ideas for her walls."

Michonne remained still, waiting. There was a moment when Dane's eyes weren't on her. She gently leaned to feel in the box next to her and sifted through old military junk using her fingers to see if there was anything useful to get them out of this situation, and more importantly before the guests woke up. Her right hand found metal. And it felt like it could cut.

"You," Dane kept the gun focused on the two guys while he yelled to Michonne, "get over here and tie those two up. There's plenty of dock line on the wall." At first, she didn't move which irritated Dane who already was moody at having to kill Sasa before he could rape her. "Move your little ass!" he yelled pointing the Beretta at her.

Michonne stashed the metal in her belt behind her back.

She sidled over sideways toward Reyes and Steam. She picked up some rope from a pile in the corner and began wrapping it around Steamer's legs as he stood still facing the wall.

"If you want these guys tied up, you're gonna have to give me a hand," said Michonne. "I can't negotiate this by myself. Just grab one end of this rope and feed it to me around his legs."

Dane's instincts told him to be wary, but he viewed Michonne as just some kid. He figured there's no way a high school girl could pose a threat or get a jump on him. Especially when he held a gun. "Sure, toots. Maybe we can play with some rope later, just you and I?" said Dane with a toothy grin while glancing at a shaking Fory. *Maybe both of them to make up for my missing out on the first chance.*

Dane walked over toward Michonne and the guys while keeping the gun ready. "Fine, give me that end," he said. Before he got within in earshot, she whispered something to Reyes.

Michonne reached over with the rope with her left hand. "Here, take this and—"

214

Matt Fitzpatrick

In a flash, Michonne grabbed his free hand in a talon grip. Despite being slight, she was stronger than most grown men. Dane swung the Beretta around in Michonne's direction, but before he could complete the turn, Reyes spun and grabbed the gun and Dane's wrist. The gun exploded. Its round benignly lodged into the rotted ceiling. With all his strength from a hard life at sea, Tommy bent Dane's wrist until it cracked like a lobster tail. During that split second, Michonne twisted the hand she had and slapped one half of a pair of old military police handcuffs on his unbroken wrist. With the other cuff, she attached Dane to a metal pipe hanging from the ceiling.

He flailed like crazy happening to kick away his own gun. Dane soon stopped the huge movements, realizing he was trapped. He banged on the pipe and frantically tried to break himself free. The pipe was old, but it was built strong enough to endure more than Dane could dish out.

"I'll kill you! I'll kill all of you and collect your heads like I did with that little slut you sent over here earlier!" Dane seethed as he yelled at Michonne. "You teenage twat!"

"I'm older than you think," Michonne grinned. She then spat in his face while looking him in the eye. "That's for Sasa. While technically I should just take your head right now, I think that would be too quick a death. You deserve worse, and I'm happy to accommodate."

With Dane yelling and flailing violently trying to extricate himself, Michonne gathered the group. "Okay, we need to get out of here and fast! Tommy, is the wall ready to go?"

"All set. I have the detonator on the boat," answered Reyes who turned to his partner. "C'mon Steam, let's make like the wind."

"With pleasure," is all Steamer said. The night was getting a little too hectic even for his fondness for chaos.

As Dane continued to holler and carry on, Fory looked at Michonne. "Going to be a long night for this guy."

Michonne grinned. "Actually... not so much."

Mobley's Beach

With Reyes and Steam already down at the boat with their one box, Fory and Michonne started climbing back up to the main floor of the guest house. Dane's screams were still shrilling and his violent pipe clanking was incessant and turning primal. He yelled even louder as a vein opened up in his wrist from the violent rubbing and tearing against the old, rusted metal cuffs. The ugly sounds were only muffled once Michonne closed the hatch door in the guest cottage.

She and Fory ran around the corner of the building over the dunes and onto the soft sand. Despite the chaos, Fory managed to pause for a moment to look out at the placid bay, which at the moment was a gently rippling onyx mirror.

"Over here!" yelled Reyes signaling Michonne. That snapped Fory out of her nocturnal daydream and they ran over toward the beached boat.

"Well?" asked Michonne.

"We're locked and loaded," said Steamer with a smile.

"Yeah," said Reyes, "We set a timer for detonation. Not CIA grade, but trust it'll work. We're gonna have us early July Fourth fireworks." He checked his stopwatch, and looked at Michonne. "We got just about fifteen minutes. You two should get outta here. Not only are we going to have a big boom, but you're gonna have one helluva shit show of cops. I'd move along."

"Wait!" Fory interrupted. "What's going on here? I thought we were just stealing a box or some shit. What's this about fireworks? Plus! What about all those people in the house? They're friggin' passed out helpless, and you're gonna just friggin' blow them up?"

Michonne touched Fory's shoulder. "Relax. Nobody's getting blown up. Well, maybe *somebody*..."

"No time for discussion," Reyes interrupted. "Our last minute change of plans from Monarch are that we set an explosive to blow up the side of the bunker next to this dune. If you notice, that's why we were delayed a bit when we got here. We had to dig a quick trench so the ocean funnels into that dune."

"W-what?" Fory's mind was spinning. She thought about how a quick knock would settle her down. "What the hell is a monarch? Are you flooding the mansion?"

Reyes reassured Fory. "Lady, nothin's gonna upset the main house except for a few broken windows and one pissed off owner. Only the guest cottage is going to sink a bit and get flooded half-way up the walls." He looked at his stopwatch again. "And maybe we'll be pissing off save-the-plover types!" He laughed at his own joke.

"With all the craziness, did you still manage to get the *one* crate?" asked Michonne.

"All set. It's onboard," said a proud Steamer.

"Okay, ladies," Reyes interjected, "we'd love to stay and chat, but we have an appointment at an after-hours over at Sundancers in Bass River. We're taking off. I suggest you do the same. Please tell Monarch we're grateful for the gig. Let him know that we're always available."

"I'll tell her," replied Michonne with a genuine wave.

Reyes was confused. "*Her*? Whaddya mean, *her*?"

"Oh, sorry," Michonne back-peddled on that fumbled response quickly. "I mean *him*, of course. I'm just tired. Been a long night. You know all the confusion with pronouns these days," she said with an awkward chuckle as she shrugged her shoulders with a forced smile.

"Ah...okay. Thanks," said Reyes as he looked at the water to see how the tide had changed. He hoped for a calm, quick run over to South Yarmouth. "Enjoy your evening. Let's go Steamah!"

With that, the two smugglers grunted as they pushed their vessel's bow off the sand. They hopped on, fired up the engines, and cruised off into the blackness.

"Great," said Fory. "Now what?"

"Now," replied Michonne with a tone of urgency, "we run!"

Forsythia's Ride

Suddenly, an inhuman banshee shriek came from someone running down the sandy path and waving frantic arms.

"Or maybe not," said Michonne. "Dammit!"

The Dark Dunes

With Medusa hair and Exorcist eyes, Anna Mobley ran down the sandy path and stormed the beach like a hurricane. Her heavy footfalls crunched scallop shells as she wielded a machete that reflected specks of moonlight.

"I'll kill you!" Mobley ranted. She stopped running ten yards from Fory and Michonne. "What did you bitches do to me and my guests?! I'm half fucking-stoned!"

Fory was quiet while Michonne tried to diffuse the situation. Time was running short, and she didn't know exactly how long it would be until detonation. Mere minutes by now.

"Mobley. Your friggin' thug killed my friend. Decapitated her, actually." Again the monotone. Fory knew her friend better now, and realized that was a stone-cold delivery that warned violence was the next step.

"Ha!" Mobley laughed out loud. "Oh, that Dane... Always the prankster. That's what happens when you fuck with me. People get these crazy ideas in their heads. Best just to remove their bad intentions right at the neck." Mobley continued to chuckle, still fogged by the drug and not fully grasping the reality of the situation.

"By the way, where is my precious Dane?" asked Mobley as she began swaying back and forth as if possessed. "I think perhaps you three should make better acquaintance." She pointed the machete at her party-crashers.

Michonne wondered if that was the after-effect of the drug, or if she was violating the cardinal rule to not get high on your own supply.

"Oh, we already had a nice chat with him," said Michonne. "He's quite charming, you know."

"He's... what?" Mobley was perplexed and suddenly panicked. "Where is he? Dane! DANE!" Mobley yelled into the night with a shriek.

"Dane drew first blood in killing our friend. There doesn't need to be any more. We're just here to retrieve something that doesn't belong to you. We left him chained to a pipe down in your bunker," said a nonchalant Michonne.

"My bunk...er?" she ran claw-like hands through her frenzied hair. "What the fuck were you doing down there!?"

Michonne's right hand slowly reached around the side of her lower right leg. She usually packed a blade, but tonight she was traveling light in case of a search at Mobley's. She learned how to pack a stealth stiletto from reading about Constance Greene in the Pendergast novel.

Fory wanted to take Mobley down a peg. "Doesn't matter. It's too late, Anna. Why don't you just go back in your house and count your paintings? Have some more of that wine while you're at it. You wear unconsciousness really well."

Fory's remark just made Anna more furious. She gripped the wooden handle of her weapon and began to walk in a hunched over, slow gait toward Fory. "I don't know what you two tramps did with my Dane, and I don't give a damn! And I don't care if you found my little hideout. You'll never get the chance to tell anyone. You'll be too busy rotting and stinking up Hell!"

For someone who appeared unsteady and coming apart, Anna Mobley was fast. She lunged at Fory and grasped a clump of her hair, while pulling her back with her left arm. With her right, she lifted the machete to swipe down at the exposed neck. "There... Now, I'll see about there not being any more blood spilled tonight. I think we were just getting warmed up with your headless hussy," Mobley boasted. "Wanna keep going. Think I'll start with Goldilocks."

As Mobley struggled to keep Fory still in order to slice down with her blade, Michonne used Anna's difficulty to advantage by moving a half-step toward Fory.

"I'm gonna slit her pretty little throat," growled Mobley. "All the boys will be crying in their beer!" she hissed followed by a hyena chuckle.

Michonne's steps continued with stealth.

Fory kept twisting.

Mobley kept ranting.

"I'm gonna kill you both and have one of the boys bury you right here on this beach! Or maybe, I'll take your heads and leave you with your friend. Decisions... Naw, I'll just slit your throat now. Ready?"

"No!" cried Fory.

Michonne crept closer. She still needed to claim another two yards. She was lucky that Mobley was still shaky from the drugs and couldn't get the right hold and angle because Fory was continuously squirming.

Michonne felt for the knife. She could see that Mobley's hand was tightening around the machete's wooden handle. She knew it was now or never.

Mobley smiled, and cemented her grip.

Without a half-second to spare, Michonne crouched and sprang across the sand onto Mobley, while at the same time, grabbing the wrist of her knife hand. In so doing, Michonne lost her hold on her own knife. Mobley bumped Fory to the side as all three were flailing randomly. Anna howled at the night sky like a crazed animal, and bucked like a bull trying to throw Michonne off her back. With all of her strength, Michonne held on.

Mobley quickly changed strategies once realizing that Michonne was stronger than she looked. She flung herself backward. Michonne saw this coming and shifted to the side so they fell apart, Mobley nearly on top. Her plan to crush Michonne failed. She spun around like a snake and pinned Michonne's arms. Mobley held her down with her knees and gripped one hand around Michonne's throat while the other held the machete against her chin.

"This will teach you to come crash my party. Say hello to your headless friend when you arrive in Hell. You'll both will have lot to catch up on. You—"

SMASH!

Forsythia's Ride

Michonne felt Mobley's grip release as her attacker suddenly fell sideways.

Fory smashed the side of Anna's head with a barnacle encrusted stone. While the buildup on the rock provided some nice cuts and scratches on Mobley's face, Fory wasn't able to hit her hard enough to knock her out. Mobley was dazed long enough for Michonne to grab her own knife, hop to her feet and tackle Anna.

The two fell to the ground again, only this time with Michonne on top. She turned the table and thrust her stiletto against Anna's neck.

Michonne firmly held the blade, but not enough to draw blood. "You... s—" Michonne's timbre calmed down as she realized this was work and a professional would not take it personally.

Mobley's sphincter released, soiling her ten thousand dollar Versace dress, unleashing a watery brown river down her leg.

"Oh, Anna," said Michonne. "Your designer would not care for your outfit's newly added aesthetic."

"You little whore!" yelled Mobley. "I'm gonna gut you like a goddamned fish!"

Michonne was quiet for a few seconds while allowing the blade to keep pushing against Anna's gullet.

"For what it's worth," said Michonne, "quite a house. I admire your taste."

Mobley looked up like a clubbed seal.

"Now," said Michonne in her most business-like voice, "your next painting will be featured on your beach, and will have thick splashes of maroon!"

The slice across Anna's jugular was quick and silent.

All that remained was a trail of red that the crabs would eagerly meet at the waterline during the next incoming tide.

"Shit," said Michonne after stepping back and viewing her work. She rubbed her face and felt nothing save for the gentle night breeze shifting by a few compass degrees.

She sat down on the cool sand, exhausted. Being almost incapable of tears, she just stared at the moon. It was so bright that it stung her eyes, and for a few seconds she almost felt rare wetness in her eyes.

Michonne rubbed her face and then massaged her cheeks while dancing with thoughts of remorse, not for killing Anna, but for having to do it in front of Fory. However, there was no time for lamenting. *I just hope this didn't make her horrified of me.* She got up and brushed the sand off her clothes and wiped the hair away from her eyes.

Michonne paused and looked around at the blackness of the bay, and the at sky as the stars poked through. "I don't deserve this!" screamed Michonne over the bay's night sky. "This is ridiculous, what this night is! What are we all accomplishing, dammit!"

She paused and looked down at the body, as her sentiments suddenly changed. "Maybe you didn't deserve that either, Anna, you fool," she said to the corpse.

Michonne looked at the North Star and then back down at Mobley.

"She deserved worse," Fory said quietly to the remains of Anna Mobley but mostly to her new friend.

That statement of solidarity snapped Michonne out of the lament and back to the present danger. "Fory! Help me with her!"

Fory's eyes exploded wide. Out of instinct, she grabbed one of Mobley's ankles and helped drag her to the shoreline.

Once Mobley's body was buoyant a few yards into the current, Michonne pushed Anna off into the tide.

The blood from Mobley's body was leaving a red trail in the dark, yet moonlit water.

With a bleeding carcass, the Chatham white sharks only needed a few minutes to take notice and clean up the mess. Her scent would be greeted eagerly.

The ones who arrive early in the season are especially hungry and aggressive.

Long trip north.

"Let's get outta here!" yelled Michonne. "This way! We'll take the beach all the way back to Mary's. Have to stay off the road once this thing blows. We can't be seen."

Forsythia's Ride

They started running as fast as they could over the deep sand dunes.

"How much time do we have left?" asked a panting Fory trying to keep up with the more physically conditioned Michonne.

"I have no idea. Just keep mov—"

BOOM!!! Then another **BOOM!!!**

The shockwave knocked both of them forward and face first into the sand. Still on the ground, Michonne turned to see seaweed and debris showering down where they had been standing just seconds before.

Spitting out sand, Fory turned to Michonne. "Damn! That was close!"

"Amazing..." uttered Michonne with a dropped jaw. "We need to get inside Mary's before the cops come, but I want to see this!"

Fory yelled, "Are you kidding? Let's go! The cops will rush here any second. Plus all the neighbors!"

"Yeah, yeah," Michonne wasn't deterred, and instead emitted a stoic calmness that can only be learned from experiences. Bad ones... "Chatham PD and the fucking FBI will be canvassing the neighborhood in a little bit. Right now I have my only window of time. Your aunt's a pro. She can play the old damsel in distress with the best of them. We'll head to her place right after I check on something."

She had to confirm their mission was a success, and that all of this carnage was worth it. "Sorry, Fory, I need to see this with my own eyes. "

She hiked over upturned clumps of sand and sea grass. She tried to cross over to where they were standing before, but the path was now blocked by an angry Atlantic Ocean feverishly flooding into the bunker. One blast had exploded up a trench line for the ocean and the other, following a precise second later, blew the guest cottage sky high.

What once was just an innocuous sand dune, had turned into a cave with a tottering destroyed dock on the far side. Michonne shook her head as she watched the gaping hole invite the ocean into the hideaway. The water was pouring in ensuring the ruin of everything that had been sitting idle for over sixty years along with the new improved ways to spread death via eye drops.

Mission accomplished.

Michonne's only regret was that she didn't get to hear Dane's final death moans.

Shoreline, Mid-night
Chathamworld

Lestor D. Hine's sleep was restless. He was fidgety and wanted to see the overnight news. In his own mind, Hines was his firm's cornerstone, even as a retired consultant. He needed news updates around the clock. In a childlike tantrum, he pounded the end table in frustration at not finding the clicker. Suddenly...

"BBLLAASSTTT!!!"

The starlit Chatham sky erupted into blinding yellow and gold beams. Lestor was thrown onto the floor from his couch.

A pound-sized piece of World War II cement smashed through the wall-sized window as it ripped through a counterfeit Monet. Stunned and confused, Lestor figured it must be an invasion by Putin to finally take full control of the globe.

The carefully placed dynamite charge sent most of the scraps of the military seawall back over the bay, but managed to remind the owner that the concept of *ownership* was invented by the most arrogant and naïve throughout history. Now he owned a burned hunk of concrete smoldering on his floor.

The Chatham PD and EMTs arrived, they examined Lestor and found he was shaken up, but nothing more serious than elevated blood pressure. His body was not damaged, unlike his glass and artwork. His bloated ego remained intact.

However, in the weeks that followed, he was forced to schedule multiple appointments with his primary care physician. It seemed that his erectile dysfunction issues had crept back and moved in for good. Lestor's head kept playing the sudden explosion over and over when he tried to concentrate on other things.

Settling Sands & Souls

The exhausted group congregated around Mary's dining room table as sirens of all flavors wailed in the distance.

"Alyce, please give Fory something a little stronger. God knows she's earned it."

Fory's eyes lit up. *Yum.*

"What would you like, Fory?" asked Mary.

Fory could already taste the nectar. "I'll take a nice, stiff..."

She then froze and was silent for enough seconds that everyone took notice. "On second thought," said Fory, "I'll stick with tea for now, but thank you."

Alyce nodded while walking toward the kitchen. Mary sported a half-smile. "Good for you, Fory."

"Nah," said Fory as she brushed away the moment with her hand. "It's just that there's been enough excitement tonight, already. What I need is sleep."

Pratt lit his pipe while asking Mary, "In the end, what happens with those warheads?"

"I'm happy to say that the negotiator you helped arrange seems to be working out great," said Mary. "Looks like we can deliver the crate to the Feds, while still remaining an anonymous donor. Of course, we'll leave the box in a safe house and just give them the address. We don't need any surveillance or interference with pesky couriers."

Fory spoke up out of sudden concern. "Won't they send the FBI or something to track down where that stuff came from? Isn't contacting them right now just after the bombing going to make them come look right here? And help me understand why we took that one crate and left the rest of those things. Why not just leave the damn bomb parts or whatever there with the rest?"

"What's the upside Fory?" Pratt questioned with a pipe tap and a heavy gaze. "Think about it. With the help of your aunt, it's a closed case. You need to understand. Your aunt is not exactly an unknown quantity on this side of the lake. She gets it done efficiently every time. Tonight is no exception. You see, while the Feds would love to know where the weapons came from, they don't dare let it leak out that nukes had been missing for most of an average person's lifetime. In the current political environment, this administration can't afford a scandal of such proportions."

Mary chimed in to explain further. "We're delivering the warheads back to prove to the U.S. government that their sloppy handling of these weapons could have easily gotten into the wrong hands. We're talking World War Three. They need to be shown the errors of their ways," said Mary.

"Plus, Bill and I like to fuck with them when given the opportunity. It has provided quite a bit of sport over the years." Mary looked and Pratt with friendly eyes.

"Language, Mary!" said Fory with a snort of laughter.

"Reason is, Fory," said Pratt smiling, "is we're in the pole position. Uncle Sam quietly and gratefully gets the nukes back; we get a tidy pay day and a promise to keep their Fed noses out of beachfront business. The local cops are already lapping up the idea of a gas pipe-line gone bad. And so thanks to you, the rest of the arms and whatever the hell else was down there, will be ruined. Salt water is even more corrosive than a bad marriage." Pratt chuckled at his own odd sense of humor.

"I see..." was Fory's faint reply, as something else suddenly popped into her mind. "I still can't believe that all of this happened because of my dad's past."

"Life made him choke on that secret," said a stoic Mary. As much as she loved her dead brother, her niece needed to hear it straight. "He was an amazing man and a loving brother. Looking back, I regret he followed me in taking up the cause. However, we all knew back then, as we do now, there are only a few avenues into this life. But, only one road out..."

228

Fory wiped her eyes with her napkin. After a few seconds, she regained composure. "Me too, Mary. I wish he hadn't." She needed to change the subject, lest she started to sob. "Sir William, do you think I might still have a job? In New York I mean, never as a spy."

Mary and Pratt both laughed. Pratt said, "You can have it if you want, but it's not necessary. My guess is you'll recommend us filling your position."

Mary pulled something out of her pocket. "You succeeded! You performed beyond our greatest expectations, and as promised, you are being properly compensated. Here, take this." Mary handed over a business card.

"Next week when you have a chance, go see this woman down at Chatham Co-Op Bank. She's the manager and will be expecting you. Just give it an hour after the Feds pick up their package, and the money will be wired into your account. She'll explain the rest."

Fory's eyes lit up. "Yes! Now we're talking! Ah, is it rude to ask how much?"

"It shows you're green in our world, but a fair query. We figure one million U.S. would be an amount commensurate with all which you've endured on our behalf," said Pratt as he tapped and emptied his pipe. "We've also arranged that your income from this endeavor will not be tax reportable. We have back tracked the records to show it has been there for a decade. It's all yours."

"T-that's insane," said Fory as she got her breath and thought for a few seconds. "Wow! I could maybe do something else? Something that I've always wanted."

"I'm curious what is it you have in mind?" asked Pratt.

"I always wanted my own little shop," said Fory. "Ya know, I'd sell simple things. Quiet things. Scented candles, wind chimes, incense, local art and books. Basically, stuff that nobody really needs but sells great at the seaside tourist traps. But, ya know, just an easier pace of life. Get to flirt with new people all day and just take it easy while making no pressure sales all season long."

"You know, Fory," said Mary, "Chatham is a perfect place for such an idea. The visitors seem to take to such items, and we have plenty of wallets visiting this town every summer. I bet you'd be a hit. I can call Rudy and Opie and inquire about commercial space downtown. You could stay here." Mary then clarified, "Temporarily, of course. But certainly long enough to open your shop and get on your feet."

Mary continued in a more cautious tone, "Of course, there are rules. You understand I'm an old woman. There's to be no partaking of drink, excessive noise or multiple suitor guest under my roof. Are we understood?"

Fory nodded as she almost started to cry. She realized that maybe this was her chance to change her life. A real chance to live and feel like a regular person. Not that she or anyone really knows what that means, but she knew enough that there had to be something more out there than how she'd been living. Her life as an addict at its core was empty and lonely.

Fory just wanted to feel *normal.* If only temporary, the poison allowed her solace. *Maybe Michonne can be a friend to help me through it, and to come visit me between missions. I could use knowing I had a friend to get out from under the rum.* It was not unlike a shark which needs to keep swimming lest it dies. Just to feel clean air through the lungs, and most of all, to stop the noise in her head drove her to drink. It was that constant *noise* that made her crave peace in any way she could find it.

Fory's guilt and shame were tolerable, and paled in comparison to the empty chasm where her every day, sober thoughts resided.

"Yes. Yes, of course," Fory assured Mary. "While I'm here, you're the boss."

"Excellent," said Pratt. "Then it's settled. I will contact my assistant later this morning. I'll have your apartment professionally and meticulously packed up and all your belongings will be brought here. I'll give your landlord two months notice of your leaving and I will take care of all the expenses to wrap up your New York life."

"And you'll have several storage units you can use until you find a place," assured Mary.

"Oh, y-yeah. That'd be great." Fory was still trying to process all the new developments. "I don't have much stuff at all. Nothing of value, for sure. Kinda sad, at my age."

"You have a new start and a new beginning," said Pratt. "Plenty of years ahead to seek your fortune. In the meantime, you earned yourself a little nest egg to get that all rolling."

Fory beamed. "I-I don't know how to thank you. I mean, only a few hours ago, I coulda killed you all!"

Michonne laughed. "You're free to join me again, anytime."

While Fory was ecstatic inside, her normal, worried self changed the topic. "Aren't the cops going to investigate all this? I mean, in the end, there are two dead bodies over there. And one without a head! A gas pipe surely is only a first working theory."

"Two?" asked Pratt. "I thought we had three unfortunate incidents tonight if you include Mobley?"

"Well," Michonne interjected, "I wouldn't be concerned about them finding much of her. She's practicing the dead man's float in shark infested water."

"I see..." said Pratt as he inhaled a haul of Captain Black. "Even in the rather short time that I've known you Michonne, I've taken to admire the level of efficiency you perform at. Perhaps when our Monarch retires you will rise up as a Swallowtail."

Fory turned to Michonne. She hadn't caught the flash in Mary's eyes at that, and still had no clue who her aunt really was. Pratt nearly laughed out loud as the other women's stone faces eased up when Fory plowed ahead with her own concerns.

"I get it you'll be leaving soon?" she said while almost feeling a tear. "You saved my life tonight. Where will you go?"

Michonne smiled. "Don't be sad Fory. You and I had some fun."

"Fun? Right." Fory looked up at the ornate ceiling while slowing shaking her head. "Maybe next time we can just take in a Metallica show?"

"That's too tame," said Michonne with a smile. "Hey, it all worked out. Trust me that this life is not for everyone. For me, it's all I know, and to be honest, I'm afraid to try and learn how to live any other way. Looks boring..."

Fory nodded.

"As far as where I go next," added Michonne, "that's really up to your aunt and my dad."

"I see..." said Fory. "Well, would you come back and visit? I can show you normal fun things. And hey! I got money now!" Fory's excitement suddenly filled the room. "I'm not talkin' nails at the mall.... We're renting out blocks of private spa time at Chatham Dunes. Shit!! We can take tennis lessons! Ya know, get some real hot guy in tight shorts to show us his forehand!" Fory laughed out loud at her own joke. "Think about it! A chance to hang out again?"

Michonne sported a slight smile. No one saw her fists clinch in her lap. *God, please no. Yes. This is exactly what I want; but my father drilled into my head that friends are a weakness.* "Yeah, I dunno, Fory. I'm sure our paths will cross again someday, but most likely not during a pedicure."

Michonne wiped her mouth with fine linen she was not accustomed to, and got up from the table. "If you'll excuse me folks, it's been a long night. Gonna head upstairs and hit the hay. Just gotta make a phone call first. G'night, all."

Before Michonne could leave the room, Fory leapt off her chair and ran over to Michonne giving her a tight embrace.

Michonne hugged her back with as much genuine affection as she could muster. She was more comfortable around danger, weapons and adrenaline. Hugs and spa dates were a dream, they were for those who could actually feel. Still, she wondered what it would be like.

Mary's Guest Room

Michonne sunk into her bed, shut her eyes, and hoped the mattress would swallow her. For someone so tough and experienced, she was still young and often regretted never having a childhood.

While she led a solitary life, often on the road for assignments, she never felt loneliness. Until now, leaving a budding new friendship. She was fortunate to have been blessed with amazing survival skills for someone so young, yet she lacked the ability to share in many human emotions, mostly ones that could be mistaken for vulnerability. Her emotional palate was short a few colors.

Long ago, her heart was once soft like that of normal little girl. Time hardened it, and way too soon.

From growing up with abusive, drug-dealing foster parents, to being trapped by, and then killing a pedophile, she had to scrap and claw for every shred of solid ground. After seeing her new, loving mother almost murdered before her eyes, she realized her identity, her path in life. While it's an unorthodox lifestyle for a young woman, she wouldn't trade it for all the spa massages at The Breakers.

She reached for her phone and dialed Dublin's Westbury Hotel. On the third ring, the front desk picked up. "Westbury Hotel. How can I assist you, this morning?"

Michonne responded, "Please connect me to the room of Justin McGee."

THE

END

Afterward:
Nor'east Bluff Beach
(6 months later)

Chris and Chaunty Trahison loved to visit their grandparents' old Chatham house every summer. They started looking forward to it as early as the end of February when the New England sun gets aggressive and the days grow longer.

They usually stayed about four weeks and were spoiled rotten. There wasn't an ice cream stand they hadn't visited, or a mini-golf course they hadn't played on the eastern half of Cape Cod.

Chris was eleven with his only sister one year his junior; they were at the ages when they were still best friends. Sibling bickering hadn't yet set in, and every fun summer day spent together was a gift they would cherish their whole lives.

Chaunty held the pail, while her big brother searched in knee deep water for crabs and any other interesting creature they could find.

"Look!" cried Chaunty. "There's one!"

Chris thrust his hand into the water and snatched up an unsuspecting crustacean. He tossed it into Chaunty's pail while feeling happy as his sister smiled.

"Oh!" she blurted out again, "There's another!"

Chris looked over toward his sister, and sure enough, a decent size blue-claw scurried across the bottom in a plot to escape his grasp, and ultimately the confines of his sister's pail.

"I got him!" said Chris.

As he thrust his hand into the water to snatch the crab, the creature darted away. While his quarry may have escaped, he noticed something else stuck in the silty bottom. It was white and about two inches long.

Chris picked it up to show his sister. "What's this, ya think?"

Chaunty gazed at the object. "Looks like the drops mom gets at the eye doctor."

"Yeah. Yeah, I guess it does," said Chris. "Hey, that's handy. All this salt air is making my eyes dry and itchy."

The boy peeled off the plastic wrapper. "Weird how they make these things all child-proof," he snickered while twisting off the cap.

Acknowledgements

Expressions of gratitude are tough with any book. The passage and character ideas ebb and flow, but the people behind keeping any writer inspired are the cornerstones.

So grateful to Peter Straub for crafting one of the true, iconic American horror novels with *Ghost Story*. My antagonist is a tip o' the hat to one of greatest to ever attack a blank page.

Also, thanks to Edgar Allen Poe for inspiration from *Cask of Amontillado* and *Annabelle Lee*. Sadly, my version of the latter is a true North Shore, MA, tragedy minus the narcotics.

To my daughters, Kailee and Nicole, "For Those About to Rock... *FIRE*!" I salute you! The world awaits your mark.

To everyone at Van Velzer Press who are the best! Your faith in me is beyond appreciated.

For anyone who gave up on me; trust you're forgiven—you never believed in the first place.

And to my wife, Jennifer... Without your endless love, support and encouragement, Forsythia never would have made it out from under her Manhattan cubicle.

And to all Forsythias out there: "Let us not go gently to the endless winter night..." ~ Neil Peart

"That One Particular" Bassing Harbor, Cape Cod, Summer 2023

About the Author

Matt is a recovering stockbroker.

After 25 years of playing Wall Street, he walked away to pursue his passion as a novelist. He's the proud father of two daughters, a holder of a 100-ton Master U.S. Coast Guard Captain's License, and a passionate rock fan/ frustrated musician.

Matt lives on Cape Cod with his wife, Jennifer.

Also by Matt Fitzpatrick:

Crosshairs

Matriarch Game

Demon Tide

Love Books?

SUPPORT AUTHORS — buy directly from independent publishers. This puts more royalty dollars into the pockets of your favorite author — and gives them time to write their next book.

Visit us for links to our other books as well as many other vibrant publishing companies to find the book for you; join our Launch List to be the first to know about new books:

<u>director@vanvelzerpress.com</u>

Van Velzer Press
Americana with a Twist

These ARE The Books You've Been Looking For.
Vanvelzerpress.com

FORSYTHIA'S RIDE

MATT FITZPATRICK

Made in the USA
Middletown, DE
06 November 2023

41964635R00144